Lasting

A NOVEL

by
Suzanne Love Harris

Ariadne Press
Rockville, Maryland

Library of Congress Cataloging-in-Publication Data
Harris, Suzanne Love, 1942-
    Lasting : a novel / by Suzanne Love Harris.
        p. cm.
    ISBN 0-918056-11-X
    I. TITLE.

PS3558.A6557 L37 2000
813'.54--DC21   99-047901

This publication is supported by a grant from the
Maryland State Arts Council, an agency funded by the State of
Maryland and the National Foundation for the Arts.

Jacket Design: Leslie Murray Rollins
Typesetting: Barbara Shaw
Photograph of author: Susan Jones

Ariadne Press
4817 Tallahassee Ave.
Rockville, Maryland
20853

ACKNOWLEDGMENTS

Grateful acknowledgement is made to the following to reprint previously published materials:

Henry Holt and Company LLC, for "Acquainted with the Night" from *The Poetry of Robert Frost*, edited by Edward Connery Lathem, copyright © 1956 by Robert Frost, copyright © 1928, © 1969 by Henry Holt and Company LLC.

"Moesta et Errabunda," *Les Fleurs du Mal* by Charles Baudelaire. Translated by Suzanne Love Harris © 2000.

"The Back Road" from *Collected Poems*, by Abbie Huston Evans, © 1950, 1952, 1953, 1956, 1960, 1966, 1970. Reprinted by permission of Pittsburgh Press.

The hymn "O Come, O Come, Emmanuel" text, ca. 9th century; ver. Hymnal 1940, alt. © Church Pension Fund, used by permission.

The Book of Common Prayer, 1979, of the Episcopal Church.

Judy Chicago, "Merger Poem," © Judy Chicago 1979, Publisher *Through the Flower*.

"The Man Watching" from *Selected Poems of Rainer Maria Rilke, Edited and Translated by Robert Bly* © 1981 in *The Rag and Bone Shop of the Heart*, ed., Michael Meade, James Hillman, Robert Bly, published by HarperCollins © 1992.

THANKS

I wish to thank my mother, Cynthia Longman Love, for giving me a love of reading and books.

My children, Amy Love Klett, Malcolm Longman Harris, Alexander Sox Harris and Lara Sox Harris for their thoughtful readings, encouragement and suggestions.

My dear friend, Sue Morris, who read this story at every stage, with honest and intelligent criticism, as well as belief in the book.

My writing partner, Karen Bratnick, for her wise counsel and love.

My sister, Louise Love; brother, Andrew Love; cousins, Margot Love Marshall, Betty Love Page, Georgette Love and Neal Love, for their enthusiasm and support.

My teacher, Tim Sandlin, for getting me started, and Maureen Baron, for all she taught me.

Budgie and Carolyn Cunningham for support all the way.

Dick Bernard, for sharing his daily experiences as a double amputee, for his courageous life, and his willingness to teach me.

Elizabeth Linder, for her generosity of spirit and insightful reading.

Warren and Sunny Adler, Scho and Judy Andrews, Chuck Baker, Joanie Brady, Sue Gardner, Susan Jones, Maureen O'Connor, Dave Pinkham, Susan and Ford Schumann, and Karen Terra for reading, expertise and sharing resources.

Especially I thank the love of my life, my husband, George Rogers Harris, for living the story with me, and for allowing the characters to share our lives.

To my husband,
George Rogers Harris

CHAPTER ONE

My cousin Alexandra had her first Greek Easter party in April at the Farm, the family gathering place, and at seventeen I was ripe for blossoming. Alexandra was ten years older than I and an art historian of considerable repute who had spent time in Greece and Italy. She invited a hundred of her friends to the Farm to celebrate Greek Orthodox Easter in the authentic Greek way. They were an interesting crew from archeology, academia and New York cafe society.

Alexandra was tall and ash blond, like me, but she looked more fashionable and sophisticated. Because she knew the best hair stylists and couturiers in New York, even her picnic shorts, denim shirt and leather sandals whiffed of the Riviera and the Hamptons. I saw that my own blue jeans, Lacoste tennis shirt and sneakers labeled me from the suburbs. But at my age I was taking notes and learning fast.

The Farm, in Chester, New York, was two hundred acres of hay fields; a collection of unused barns painted white on the outside, but decaying on the inside; two ponds full of catfish, perch, sunnies, and snapping turtles; a clay tennis court whose baselines had to be chalked daily; an old cement swimming pool whose water we sanitized with Clorox; and a pine forest behind the estately white house on a hill. The smaller, original farm house was occupied all year by our Uncle Hector and his five children who grew up as locals.

Alexandra had brought a whole skinned lamb from the City. She directed our uncles and cousins in building the open fire barbecue pit, where they started turning the meat on a spit about ten in the morning. She set up a loud speaker system to blast Greek folk music everywhere. The weather was perfect. Amazing for April. Sunny, warm, and smelling of a much later spring. The Retzina started to flow well before noon, as the guests arrived in cars from New York City and parked in the fields. Retzina tasted like turpentine to me, but the guests were drinking it anyway. My father and the uncles, I noticed, were sticking to the tried and true gin.

I prayed no-one would ask me about college, and was determined to have a good time. My parents had stunned me a few weeks earlier by telling me that despite my acceptances at Radcliffe and Barnard College, they could not afford to send me to college. How was this possible? So I was looking for a major distraction.

By noon it was warm enough to change into short shorts, and I put my hair in one long braid down my back and pinched my cheeks to give them color. My younger sister Brinny and cousin Wendy went off to play tennis. Julius, another of my eighteen cousins, came down from Cornell University for the party because he hoped to make show business connections. There seemed to be several Europeans, so I looked around to find someone to speak French with me.

I had spent my junior high school year in southern France in a lycee affiliated with the American Field Service. I learned to speak and think in French, became familiar with a European education system, and felt myself become outwardly sophisticated and experienced beyond my American classmates. Now my classmates were all going to college, but I was not. I tried to be detached so I wouldn't be depressed, but it did not seem fair. I was the best student in my school. All of my friends were going away to school, and I was going to get a job as a secretary. I had already submerged a sadness and anger against Rex, my father. I didn't want to bury any more of myself.

The spitted lamb was browning, the Greek music playing, and Alexandra started to teach the guests how to do the Greek line dances out on the big lawn between the house and the hay barn. I joined a line with Aunt Emily, Karl Swensen, the cook, Uncle Max and a lot of guests I did not know. Putting our arms around each other's shoulders, we made lines, then danced sideways, stumbling on each other as we learned the simple steps. We danced and sweated in the sun, laughing, until someone in the line gave up or the music ended so we had to form new lines.

In my third line formation, I noticed a man with startling blue eyes and curly light brown hair. He noticed me too. He obviously knew the dance and smiled across the circle at me when I stepped on the cook's toe. At the end of the music, he walked over to me, and spoke with a romantic European accent when he introduced himself, " I am Antonio Francesco, a friend of Alexandra's from New York. Are you a member of the family?"

"I'm Lili, Alexandra's cousin."

"Lili." He smiled. "You are learning the dance very well. It takes a little practice. Do you want to get a drink with me?"

"Sure, I'm really thirsty. Isn't the dancing fun? I love to dance." I said.

Antonio was not very tall, about my size, small boned, yet well built. He moved in a masculine, sexy way, and he touched the small of my back as we approached the picnic table where Alexandra had set up the bar. I had a lemonade and Antonio had iced tea. He was Italian. A medical doctor. Twenty-nine years old. When I told him I was almost eighteen, he smiled and sparked his blue eyes at me, "So young and fresh," he said.

I was getting a little self-conscious, excited, and nervous, so I began to talk about France. "I've never been to Italy, but I loved France. The food was so good. Do you know how many kinds of cheese they have?"

Antonio answered my breathless questions slowly, as if trying to slow me down, "If you loved French food, you must taste the food of my country sometime. What you call Italian food here in America is Neapolitan and Sicilian. You must come to Roma. I could show you our eternal city."

I blushed with pleasure at the thought, but was trying to act worldly. I sipped my lemonade from a paper cup, as I had seen Audrey Hepburn sip champagne on the screen and imagined my eyelashes looked like Audrey's as I asked, "What do you do in New York? Your English is so good."

The humor in Antonio's expression seeping through his serious answers to my questions reminded me of the Italian movie star Vittorio Gassman, "I have a grant to do research in cardiology in New York—at the Rockefeller University. I learned English in London when I was in medical school. I'm still learning American." Then he smiled flirtatiously at me, "Maybe you could teach me American."

Just as we were getting to know each other a little, Alexandra ran over and grabbed him away. She wanted him to meet another New York friend. Disappointed, I wandered off to the tennis court to see if Brinny and Wendy wanted to dance.

My cousin Julius sat like a Buddha, surrounded by his pals Pules, Gary and a bunch of younger cousins, watching Wendy and Brinny play singles. They were all drinking beer and cream soda.

"Hey, Lili, how do you like the party?" Pules called.

"I like the dancing and music. You guys should come try it," I said.

"Who are all those people?" Gary asked.

"F-friends of Alexandra's, "I said. " I met a real estate guy from Long Island and some art professors and an Italian doctor. I think there are some real Greeks here too. I heard Alexandra speaking Greek."

"It's too bad the pool isn't filled yet," Wendy's little brother, Ricky said. "We could push some people in."

Julius grinned and suggested, "We could call the police and tell them Alexandra is serving alcohol to minors."

"You wouldn't," I said. "Those people are just having fun. Why don't you guys come join a line dance?"

"I don't dance," said Julius. "I direct spectacles."

That was my cue to ask Julius what he was up to, but he and his gang were boring me and I wanted to get back to the interesting people.

"Nice serve, Wendy," I called and hurried back to the lawn party.

The lamb was taking forever to cook, but nobody seemed to mind. Stuffed grape leaf hors d'oeuvres were passed around and special bread and goat cheese. The clips of conversations I overheard were about traveling in Europe and art politics in New York

City. "Didn't I see you in St. Moritz at New Years?" "We're trying St. Tropez this July." Except for the summer with the French family in Toulouse, I had spent every summer of my life right on this farm with my parents, grandparents, uncles, aunts and cousins. I felt ready for a change.

I was looking for Dr. Antonio when I heard the sirens. Two loud fire engines pulled up the hill, their noise drowning out the Greek music. The volunteer firemen, looking at the bacchanalia before them, asked the expected question, "Where's the fire?"

Alexandra ran to the chief and said, "There must be a mistake. There isn't any fire. As you can see, everything is perfectly under control."

"We just got a call that you people had a field fire here. Who called us?" The chief was raising his voice, "If this is some kind of joke, it is not funny. It is a criminal offense to turn in a false alarm. My men have families and lives of their own. You people...." He was getting very red. "Who did this? I'm not going to let you get away with it."

Alexandra kept her cool as she apologized, "I am so, so sorry. I have no idea who did it. I assure you it was none of my guests. I'll try to find out who it was. You can take my phone number, and I'll be back in touch with you. I promise."

The fire department left, but the spell was broken. People began to wonder when the lamb would be carved. Antonio came up to me, took me by the arm away from the crowd. His hand on my skin gently leading me as in a dance was all I could sense or feel, until I heard his sensuous voice again, "Lili, would you like to come back to New York with me. We could go out to dinner and you could stay over at my place. You don't have school tomorrow, do you?"

"I don't have school, but I would have to ask my m-mother," I was a little nervous, but very pleased.

"No, no, sweet girl, you cannot ask your mother. Tell your mother you are going to stay at Alexandra's, if you want to come with me. Do you want to come?" he asked, moving his hand from my bare upper arm down past my elbow to take my hand.

5

I did. I barely knew this man, but I wanted to be with him. I told my mother I was going to New York with Antonio and I'd be home the next day. She seemed to have heard, but did not object. Something else was bothering her, so she did not really pay attention to me. I threw some clothes in a small bag and jumped into Antonio's black Italian sports car. I didn't even say thanks to Alexandra or good-bye to Brinny. We took off.

As we were driving south on the New York thruway, Antonio sang softly with the radio a new Elvis Presley tune, "I can't help falling in love with you." He looked at me, "Lili, I am so happy you wanted to come with me. I have been looking at you all afternoon. You are so beautiful. Your long legs. You have a wonderful nose, no?"

I blushed. I always thought my nose was too big.

"Do you think I am too old for you?" he asked.

"I don't know," I said. "Too old for what?"

He laughed and patted my knee, "I guess we'll see."

We sped through the rolling green April hills back to New York City, talking about Italy and his family and his medical research. He asked me about my family, "How exactly are you related to Alexandra?"

"Alex's father and my father are brothers, but they are very, very different. The only thing they have in common is that they both went to Yale—and they both drink—a lot. Her father played polo at Yale. Mine played football—offense and defense. Her father is the oldest of the seven Long children—he's a bank executive and an art collector. My father is the youngest— he likes the country life— fishing, hunting and animals. Did you meet my father? He's a big, heavy man."

"I think no. I don't remember. What is his name?"

"Rex. My sister Brinny calls him Tyrannosaurus Rex because he is so big and dangerous. He drinks too much, but he's not mean. I've had my problems with him, but I know he loves us."

Antonio pulled up to his apartment on Third Avenue. There was a doorman who looked at me with a smirk as if I were a mistress or something. The apartment was small: three rooms with a kitchenette. Scandinavian modern furniture and interesting paintings on the walls. I liked this. Like two adults. Antonio offered me wine, but I declined. I felt strangely peaceful and happy for the first time since I'd returned from France. I really wanted to kiss him.

"Lili, have you ever been with a man before?" Antonio asked.

"If you mean, am I virgin, yes, I am, but I've had boyfriends. I've never been with a man your age before. I feel...much older with you," I said. I felt about ten years older than I had that morning.

Antonio shook his head and smiled again. He stepped toward me, took me in his arms and kissed me as I had never been kissed before. In the tender way he touched me, I felt not only desire, but the caring for which my body hungered. Like a puppy being rescued from a shelter, my body felt safe next to his body. When he put his hand on my breast, I felt an awakening all up and down my legs and deep inside.

Then he took me by the hand, sat me down and started to walk around the room. "You know, I should take you home right now. I desire you and I wanted to make love to you when I asked you to come here, but... don't you want to save your virginity for your husband, Lili?"

"No," I said, "I don't think like that. I want to live life and have adventures before I get married and then I'll be faithful to my husband." Silence, as I thought about it, and he sat down next to me. "I don't n-necessarily want to lose my virginity right now. I just wanted to run off with you. I don't really know what I want."

Antonio took me home to Riverdale. He said he'd call in a few days, and I prayed with all my youthful hope that he would.

CHAPTER TWO

I telephoned the Farm to tell Mama I was home. She was relieved. When I'd told her I was going to New York City, she was upset about the fire department, and wasn't really paying attention to me. She said, "Your father turned in the false alarm. Alexandra is furious. He ruined her wonderful party."

"How do you know he did it?" I asked.

"All the children knew. Julius and his gang egged him into it. He's just like one of them. He finally had to confess to the police."

"Wh-what's going to happen to him?" I thought he might be safer in jail.

"The police gave him a warning, a lecture about setting a better example for the children, and a fine— $500. I can think of a lot of things I'd rather spend that $500 on, believe me."

I could too: five hundred dollars would have paid for half a semester tuition at college. I couldn't shake my disappointment about college. After my junior year in France, senior year should have been my best yet. After I had already made the college applications, my parents summoned me for a talk in the pine paneled kitchen of our two-story colonial house in Riverdale.

"Lili, we know how smart you are," said Mama, "but...intelligence is for more than academics.... I hate to tell you this...we just don't have the money to send you to college."

"You'll probably get married in a year or two anyway," said Rex. "You should get a job in the city in an office where you'll meet a man with a good income. I can't send all four of you to college on my salary. The boys really need college to support a family."

At first I was incredulous. "B-but I d-don't want to work in an office." I said, "I'd die of boredom. Why didn't you mention this problem before?"

Mama said, "I guess we assumed we would find a way...But we didn't. Your father makes just too much money for financial aid, but not enough to pay for college."

"Some of my friends are b-borrowing the money for college," I offered. "Or how about asking Grandfather? He's paying for Julius to go to Cornell."

"We don't believe in borrowing, Lili. Your grandfather would probably pay for you to go, but your father doesn't want to accept the money."

She made it sound as though there was some moral reason not to accept my college tuition from my own grandfather. "You"ll do fine. Perhaps you can go to night school. You know I never finished college."

I literally did not know how to feel at that time, so I felt mostly blank or numb. Of course, I was disappointed. I had always assumed I would go. All of my teachers and friends assumed I would go. My own parents seemed to be sinking my boat before it was launched. I could not muster a voice big enough to rise up out of my throat and say "No. You can't do this to me," or even to cry.

At least Mama seemed distressed. It was harder to understand Rex. My feelings for my father, Rex Long, had changed dramatically over my eighteen years. When I was a little girl, the playful, romantic side of me thought he was the strongest, handsomest, funniest, man in the world and believed he could throw a truck from New York to Chicago. He stood six feet four inches tall, and in those days was built like a wrestler. When I was five, he gave me a beautiful red Schwinn two-wheeler and taught me to ride it. I put my skinny arms around his big tan neck, kissed him, and touched his coal black hair. He teased me by saying I only loved him because of the bike.

As I grew a little older, the more serious, worried, reverent side of me was mortified by Rex's drunkenness and embarrassed by his use of dirty language. Yet all the cousins wanted to be included in his wild adventures, which were often dangerous, but exciting. Like the time he drove the pick-up truck, full of us screaming cousins into the pond, and sank it. And the time Brinny fell through the ice and almost died in the freezing reservoir.

I never invited a friend from Riverdale to the Farm because Rex and our grandfather swam naked in broad daylight. Well into his eighties grandfather walked from his bedroom on the far side of the house, down the winding staircase, through the living room to the front porch, down the steps, across the lawn to the pool, looking like a pale aborigine, his skin sagging as he removed his glasses, spit out his chewing tobacco and pushed off into a dive that became more and more of a tilt as he aged—all without benefit of a towel.

I don't know how or where I got the idea I was a beautiful woman. Even as a little girl, I walked around in my skinny body with my ears sticking out of my wispy straight hair and my socks falling down on my heels, feeling inside I was really Rita Hayworth or Kim Novac. I guess I had a good imagination.

Hanging in one of the eight wallpapered bedrooms at the Farm was a large photographic portrait of our grandmother, taken in the 1890's when she was eighteen years old, her hour-glass figure cinched in by corsets, and her light brown hair piled up on top of her head. After seven children and fifty years of overeating, Grandma stood a statuesque five feet, nine inches, and weighed almost as much as my father, who claimed 250 pounds of solid muscle. Her hair, turned pure white, was still worn piled on top of her head, except once, when I saw her kneeling beside her bed to say her prayers, when it was hanging long like a waterfall down her back to her feet.

I was named Grace Letitia Long, after our grandmother, but everyone called me Lili.

Brinny, my sister, was my closest friend. Although Brinny was almost two years younger and shorter than me, she was braver and prettier. Her nose was smaller, and her eyes were bluer than mine. We slept in the same room both at home in Riverdale and at the Farm, and shared everything except boyfriends. Our cousin Wendy made us the inseparable threesome at the Farm. Wendy was close to Brinny's age, had short reddish-brown hair and freckles on her small nose. Wendy was the best tennis player of the three of us; Brinny had the best singing voice; and I was the best dancer.

All of us cousins liked to play in cousin Julius's musical productions in the barn. When we got thirsty from singing and dancing, he sold us soda for fifteen cents out of his electric cooler. Wendy, Brinny and I wanted feminine parts, so that we could wear make-up and costumes to emulate our favorite movie stars like Jane Powell and Vivian Leigh. All three of us girls were concerned about bust development, but Wendy didn't like boys.

On a warm August night, when we were fourteen or fifteen, sitting by the dark pool after a cool skinny-dip, listening to night noises, Wendy told Brinny and me, in strict secrecy, that she was in love with Diana Wesley.

"But she's a girl," objected Brinny.

"I **know** she's a girl," said Wendy patiently. "That's how I am. I don't feel attracted to boys."

We had never heard of Lesbians, so it took a while to understand. I said, "I used to pretend n-necking with Isabel, but it was just practicing for boys."

"It's not practice, Lili. I've had an orgasm with Diana. I'm in love with her. It's how I am," said Wendy.

"You know I love you, Wendy," I said, pulling my towel tighter around my chest, "but n-not that way. You're like Brinny to me, a sister."

"I feel the same about you two guys, but it's entirely different with Diana."

"Do your parents know?" I asked.

"My dad knows." Wendy picked up a pebble and skipped it across the black water. "He found me and Diana together and we had a long talk. Lots of crying. But he understands me. He told me about homosexuality and accepts me. He told us it's important not to tell anyone. But I had to tell someone. I figure I can trust you two to keep the secret."

The crickets kept chattering as we three sat quietly in our new reality under the dark starry sky. I wasn't surprised that Wendy's father, Uncle Ed, understood her. We always turned to him to tell us the truth when we thought Rex might be fooling us. Uncle Ed was smart and honest, but he drank just as much as the rest of the adults.

Our family values included the Episcopal Church, good manners (at least for girls), and a high tolerance for alcohol. They thought it was important to sit at the right table at the "21" Club in New York City. They said you shouldn't drink whiskey before noon, but after noon they never stopped. Rex, my father, drank the most because he was the biggest of his four brothers and two sisters.

Mama loved Rex, even though he exasperated her. Between feeding children and organizing the household, she sang soprano arias accompanying herself on the piano. We loved to sing with Mama. I enjoyed, not only the music , but the languages, especially French and Italian. The first words I knew of Italian were the lyrics of Puccini's "Un Bel Di Vedremo" from "Madama Butterfly" and Gluck's "Che Faro Senza Euridice" from " Orfeo ed Euridice."

Brinny and I discussed everything in bed at night before we went to sleep in our twin beds in our matching plaid flannel nightgowns. I complained to her, "Don't you think it's unfair to let the boys watch TV all the time in the den, so I can't play the piano?"

At that time Brinny wore her hair in two thick braids and bangs. She always looked me right in the eye when she spoke. "Sure, but the boys make too much trouble if they're not amused, so Mama lets them watch TV," she shrugged.

"But shouldn't we have to take turns—like shifts. Isn't music more important that some stupid TV show like Superman?"

"Lili, wise up. Do your homework when they're watching TV. You can play the piano when they're asleep. Mama can't manage the house, the cooking, laundry, us and Rex, unless the boys stay out of her hair."

"You're so practical, Brin. I love you." I gave Brinny a big hug, which she resisted.

Brinny wrinkled her forehead and twisted her rosebud mouth into a half-smirk, "You're a little over dramatic sometimes, Lili. Maybe you've seen too many movies."

We did love the movies. We also loved books. At thirteen I read "The Diary of a Young Girl," by Anna Frank, and wondered if we would ever have to suffer like Anna's family. We didn't understand or acknowledge the suffering in our own family. When grandmother died of a stroke, I don't remember grieving. My dreams were filled with frightening uncontrollable fires, which nobody noticed except me. I wished and prayed that Rex wouldn't drink so much.

The children of drinkers learn that prayer is not making wish lists and asking for favors. Prayer is holding on to something strong when you're afraid. Unexplained, on his fortieth birthday Rex went on the wagon. I thought God had finally heard me. Rex was quieter when he was sober, and much more approachable. Mama and Rex didn't raise their voices. Rex didn't tease so much. He didn't do dangerous things or use swear words.

Older cousins, like Julius and his elder brother Charlie, who had enjoyed Rex's drunken antics, were disappointed. Charlie had emulated Rex in size, drunkenness, and pranks. He begged Rex to reconsider his rash decision. Charlie even accused Rex of having a nervous breakdown. Charlie needn't have worried. Rex slipped quietly off his solemn resolves one jigger at a time within two months. No one seemed to care. No one said, "Stop." No one acknowledged a problem. I too was silent. The silence of defeat. My grief for him and what he might have been for me gradually became an unidentified ache. I tried to forget about Rex. I began to look for another god.

Chapter Three

Antonio called two days later and invited me to dinner in New York. Mama let me go, even though it was a school night. I think she was enjoying my adventure vicariously. I met Antonio at an elegant Italian restaurant called Nino's on Madison Avenue: artfully lit, with white tablecloths and fresh primroses in small clay pots. All the feelings I experienced at his apartment returned as he put his hand on my waist to guide me to my seat.

I had a glass of Chianti. We ate little. I felt happy just looking at Antonio, especially when our eyes met. He said, "Lili, there is so much I have to tell you. I am feeling for you something I haven't felt for a long time. In Italian we have a saying 'l'amore annuncia tutto...'" Then he looked down at the back of his hands and said, "I am beginning to be in love with you. That is why I didn't force myself on you Sunday night. Do you understand?"

I nodded quietly. "I can hardly believe this is happening to me." I thought to myself that God was good.

"I want to take care of you," said Antonio, "I had a dream that you were just a little sick, and I came to doctor you." He reached across the table and put his warm hand on my hand and asked, "Do you understand how I feel?"

Antionio's beautiful, almost maternal, voice, accompanied by his masculine sexual energy began to fill an empty hole in my young heart and to light a fire that I didn't know was there. My own words seemed so pitifully inadequate as I said, "I think I understand, but I'm never sick. I don't believe in it."

"That is good. You must never be sick," he said and fell silent. Moving his hand away from me again, he finally said, "Lili, I have to tell you some things about myself, which I want you to discuss with your parents." He thought again, and his voice became more distant, "I was married before—eight years ago in England—to an English woman. We were very unhappy. I hated the climate. So depressing. She was a vegetarian. It just didn't work out. We had a stillborn child, a little girl."

I absorbed Antonio's story, picturing his ex-wife as a dreary, homely drudge. But how could this sparkling man marry an unhappy woman? And the child. How terribly sad to have a dead baby. Especially a girl.

Antonio asked, "Does this shock you, Lili?"

"I'm not easy to shock," I said. "It's so sad about the baby. Did you name her? How did you feel?"

Antonio lowered his head and put his hand over his eyes. All I could see was his soft, wavy hair as he slowly shook his head and continued, "I was miserable. It was a terrible time." He looked up at me, "I hope you never feel like that, Lili. We named the child Teresa, after my mother. We were so young... But that was almost seven years ago. My life has become my work... There have been women, of course, but I didn't think I would be in love again." Silence, then a smile, "What are you doing to me, Lili?" He reached across the table again to take my hand. "I can't make you any promises. You are so young. I am...how do you say...confondere...not confused...maybe bewildered? I don't know what I should do with you."

"I'll graduate in June," I said. "I'll probably get a job in New York City. We could spend time together, so you don't have to figure me out all at once."

"But I desire you," Antonio said, searching my face with his intense blue eyes. "Do you want me to teach you about love? I am a doctor. I know how to prevent accidents. I would love to take you home and teach you everything. Would you like that?"

"I would. But I told my mother I'd be home on the 9:30 train tonight."

Antonio laughed heartily, shaking his head.

"I could come in Saturday and stay all day. As soon as I get a job,

I'll be free all the time."

Antonio kept smiling. "I guess I can wait until Saturday. Come in early and meet me at my place. I'll cook breakfast for you. You can tell me what you and your parents think about my first marriage. If they don't approve of your seeing me, tell them you are going to meet Alexandra. You'll come anyway? You promise?"

This time I smiled, "Yes, no matter what."

Waiting for Saturday to come seemed forever. I didn't tell Brinny or anyone what I was going to do. Antonio was my secret love. When I told my parents about Antonio's former marriage at the same kitchen table where they had told me I couldn't go to college, Mama said, "He is too old for you anyway. You certainly shouldn't be dating a divorced man. No, Lili, you cannot see him any more. I never should have let you go." I decided to blow off my parents, as I felt they had blown me off. If they thought I could manage my life without further education or support, I'd do it my way.

Rex had stopped conspiring with me when I was only thirteen. At first I thought it was my fault. But I remembered, when I was thirteen years old, a boy from my eighth grade class, rang our front door bell in broad daylight. When I opened the door, he came right to the point, "Lili, if you don't kiss me, I'm going to knock your teeth out."

I slammed the door in his face and ran crying to my parents for protection.

My father said, "What did you do to provoke him?"

"N-nothing," I said. "I don't even like him. He just showed up mean."

Rex was uncharacteristically serious, "You'd better be careful how you dress young lady. You're not a baby any more. Keep your skirts down and watch your flirting."

"Wh-what do you mean flirting?" I asked. "I never even talk to that boy. Don't you think you should tell his p-parents or the p-police?"

"I think you know what I mean." Rex sounded sad and angry.

"Why are you m-mad at me? I didn't do anything." I looked at my mother. "Mama, I didn't do anything." I ran crying to my room. How could my own father take his side? I thought my father's attitude was really bizarre. He didn't seem to understand me at all. And Mama always followed Rex.

But that was years before. Saturday finally came. I told Mama I was going to see Alexandra, but I went to Antonio's apartment. When the doorman looked at me suspiciously, I just smiled and stepped in the elevator.

Antonio greeted me dressed in jeans and a turtleneck sweater. He had made strong Italian coffee, fresh fruit, and waffles. The windows were open and the morning air felt like spring. Vases of fresh white tulips stood on the tables in the living room and in his bedroom. After breakfast, he put a Brahms piano concerto on the stereo and took me in his arms.

That morning in May of my eighteenth year, Antonio Francesco taught me about making love. About the slow tenderness of discovery. The feeling of skin on skin. The sweet closeness of shutting out the rest of the world. His wonderful fascinating body. The physical intensity. The gentle small talk, especially the Italian love words he taught me.

"Lili," whispered Antonio, as we were bathing together, "I am a good teacher, no?"

"You are wonderful," I replied like the teenager I was.

We went outside later in the morning to walk all over the East side hand in hand. We looked in the windows of the expensive shops and galleries on Madison Avenue and watched the people walking along Central Park on Fifth Avenue. In front of an avant-garde gallery on 57th Street, Antonio pointed to a small sculpture by Henry Moore in the gallery window and said, " The one thing I value which wealth can provide is beauty—like that piece. It is almost living to me."

I could see how lovely it was and said, "I can enjoy looking at art in museums or galleries—without owning it."

"Of course, but to own an object of beauty like that—to enjoy it every day—gives me a pleasure which is difficult to explain."

"Do you own some sculptures or paintings?" I realized how little I still knew about this man I was so precipitously trusting.

"Yes, a few. My family has more in Italy… Art has the constancy that I have not yet found in myself."

I tripped on the pavement, and Antonio's arm caught me from falling. Anxiety began to flood my veins, "You seem pretty constant to me. I mean you're a doctor, and you're pretty much on time. You don't drink much, do you?"

Antonio gave me his most beautiful smile and put his hand on my cheek, shaking his head, "Carina mia, I don't want to worry you. You look so serious. Sometimes I am too philosophical, no? Let's go to my office."

We walked to Antonio's laboratory where he showed me his desk and the experiments. I felt terribly young and inexperienced, yet he seemed to value my company. When my feet got tired from the pavement, we went back to Third Avenue. The doorman said, "Buona Sera, Dottore…Signorina."

"Wouldn't it be wonderful to go to Italy," I said.

"Someday, yes, we will go to Italy, carina mia," Antonio said.

I took the last train back to Riverdale. When I got home, I didn't want to see anyone because I knew I couldn't hide my happiness. Fortunately, my parents were in bed. Brinny and the boys were watching TV. I turned off the front door light, which was the signal that the last person was home, and went up to my room. Brinny came in when the TV show was over. "How was Alexandra's?" she asked.

I said, "I didn't go there. I went to Antonio's. Don't tell, Brinny. In another month I'm out of here, so I can do what I want."

Brinny sat on the bed, crossed her long legs and considered what I had told her. "You have a secret. Wendy has a secret. When is it my turn?"

"Do you like anyone?" I asked.

"You know I've had a crush on Danny Feldman for years, but he thinks I'm a kid. Anyway he's away at college. The other boys around here are so boring."

"You never know, Brin, dreams do come true."

CHAPTER FOUR

The last month of high school, I felt as though I were an alien on a strange planet. The person I thought I was growing up to be had been exploded. All the other seniors were planning their summer before going to college. Some were choosing college courses. Others got letters from future roommates. I tried to rationalize and be agreeable. I didn't mind defying my parents, but I didn't want to hate them. Surely they wouldn't want to hurt me. Whenever anyone asked me what my plans were, I told them I was going to work, but my heart skipped to Antonio. He was the good thing in my life, but I couldn't talk about him, of course, because I didn't want to get a bad reputation. Saturdays I went to Antonio.

Alexandra invited me to lunch at the Sign of the Dove, a new East side restaurant decorated in red brick arches and hanging green plants. Alex looked even more glamorous in New York, wearing a simple, but beautifully cut, black dress and bold silver jewelry. She always had a great tan. I wasn't tan, and I didn't have gorgeous jewelry, yet I was pleased that my own black skirt and French silk jersey didn't look too suburban. After we ordered salads and iced tea, Alex came right to the point. "You've been telling your parents you're staying over with me, which is fine, but what's going on?"

I felt a little embarrassed, but I had to tell her the truth. "Alex, I met your friend, Antonio, at your party. You know, the doctor. I know he's older than me, but we really...we love each other. I've been seeing him a lot... I'm having an affair with him."

She was shocked: "How can you do that, Lili? You're not that

19

kind of a girl. What will your parents say? How about your religion? You're a good Episcopalian."

I felt myself sitting tall and finding a firmness in my voice, " My parents will get used to it. They seem to think I am old enough to earn my own living. I just turned eighteen, so I am going to make my own decisions. Besides I'm not disobeying any commandments. This is not adultery. Neither of us is betraying a spouse. I still honor my p-parents...s-sort of. They just don't understand a lot. Sometimes, I wonder if they ever did," I said.

Alexandra picked a white iris from the bouquet on the table, sniffed it with obvious pleasure, and said, "I think you should consider a new religion. You know in Greece they used to worship the gods and goddesses. You seem like a child of Aphrodite to me."

"The goddess of love," I smiled, "Isn't it pretty normal in Europe for couples to live together without marriage?"

"Europe is an entirely different place. Believe me, Lili, you would not want to live with Antonio in Europe," said Alexandra, "Most European men are rather difficult. For one thing they are not faithful husbands. I would never marry a Greek or an Italian."

"Well, Antonio is different," I said, "If it weren't for you, I never would have met him. But I'm very curious to know more. How did you know him?"

"Antonio has been in New York for about a year. He has friends in the art world as I do. He has always struck me as an enigma. An attractive enigma," she laughed.

"What do you mean by enigma?" I asked.

"He is a serious scientist, you know. The Rockefeller University is an advanced research facility. But his head seems in the clouds. I never did know what to make of him... Now this infatuation with you. Not that you aren't great, Lili, but he knows some pretty worldly women."

"Maybe that is why he loves me."

Alex threw up her hands and laughed. "I hope your head is not too much in the clouds to pay attention to your studies, young lady. What is this I hear about your being accepted at Radcliffe and Barnard and your parents not sending you to college?"

"Actually, I have a window of hope."

I told my cousin how Mr. Borden, my college guidance counselor, had given us an alternative. "If you are employed by one of the good universities in New York, Columbia or NYU, they will give you two free courses a semester as a benefit. That would enable me to start my college education. In the meantime I'd have established financial independence from my parents and be eligible for financial aid as an independent individual."

I assured Alexandra, "I do plan to start college part-time next fall, but it will take me longer than four years." I put my hand on her arm, "And I really appreciate your covering for me and Antonio. It just saves hassles. They'll probably find out eventually, but I don't want to deal with them yet."

I graduated from high school at the top of my class, and went to the graduation party with a friend, Johnny. But I really wasn't there. I was surfing on a strange new ocean, keeping my balance most of the time, though sometimes in the middle of the night, fearing I'd capsize. Antonio was the joy of my life. My stomach felt normal only when I was with him, but there were repercussions at home. Brinny became angry with me right after graduation, as I was dressing to go into New York. "Lili, you might as well have stayed in France. You never hang out with us any more. You are like... absent."

"I know," I said, attaching my nylons to my garter belt, "Since I found out we couldn't go to c-college, I've felt like a different person. It's as if I don't feel anything except when I am with Antonio. It's so weird, Brinny." I looked at Brinny's worried expression and attempted to be a sister again, " I'm sorry. I know I can trust you. Have you seen Danny since he came home from c-college?"

"As a matter of fact, yes," beamed Brinny, "I sat next to him at the band concert in the park Saturday. He is so funny. And he is so smart. He's the smartest person I ever knew. Smarter than you and smarter than Mama."

Brinny looked like the Cheshire Cat. She continued, "Mama got offended when I said he was smarter than her. She thinks he's a funny pipsqueak, but I think he's cool, don't you, Lili?"

"I haven't seen him in a long time," I said, "but I always liked him. He's so original. You're right about his being smart, but he isn't so good looking."

"To me he is," said Brinny. "He's my type."

According to the plan, I took a job as a secretary at Columbia University's School of Journalism, and commuted from Riverdale at first. With my first pay check, I opened my own bank account. What had Mr. Borden said? An independent individual?

The other secretary in my office was also a night student, Maria Alvarez, whose parents were Puerto Rican people from the Bronx. Maria wanted her degree to teach school, but she had to contribute money to her family. She complained that her parents wanted her to get married, whereas she was in no hurry for more domestic responsibilities.

Whenever possible, I stayed over with Antonio, using Alexandra as my cover. He teased me, as we were squashed together in a chair after love making, "Carina mia, you are a passionate woman—Very surprising in an American."

"It's because of you I am passionate. I wasn't like this before," I said, and gave him another kiss. "I think one of my first two college courses will be Italian."

"Then we will go to Italy together," said Antonio, "and I will have to protect you from all the men who will chase you and say bad things."

"What do you mean 'b-bad things?'" I asked.

Antonio covered my ears with his hands, "Not for your ears to hear, carina mia.

Chapter Five

Antonio brought me to a gallery opening on 57th Street. The gallery was so crowded we could barely see the paintings, which were large, abstract and almost violently colorful. Waiters in black passed long stemmed glasses of champagne. I was tempted to view the jewels on the necks and arms of the glamorous women as the art on exhibit. I'm sure I was the youngest person there, although I looked older wearing black spikes, a short black dress and eye make-up. In my high heels I was a little taller than Antonio, but he didn't seem to mind.

Antonio introduced me to the painter, a fellow Italian, Carlo Cusimano, a short muscular bearded man with bloodshot eyes and liquor on his breath. Trying to fit in and act sophisticated, I said, "I love your paintings. Do you paint here or in Italy?"

Cusimano gave Antonio a questioning look and spoke with a strong Italian accent, "Signorina, I paint here in New York City. Are you an artist? Would you enjoy seeing my studio?"

The expression on his face as he looked up and down my body caused me to suspect the invitation to his studio was a proposition. "N-no." I blushed. "I'm not an artist. I'm a student. I just like painting." I felt shocked that he would make a pass at me right here in front of Antonio, when I had known him only a few seconds.

Looking at Antonio again he said, "Charming, Dottore, you have all the luck with women." Giving me a pat on the fanny he walked away.

I turned to Antonio in embarrassment, "He's so fresh with me. What nerve! Is it because he's an artist?"

Antonio said, "Sorry about him. He's a typical countryman. He thinks there are only two kinds of women."

"What do you mean 'two kinds of women'?"

Antonio put his arm around me as he explained, "He thinks that because you are…here with me and so…openly feminine…that you are also available. That a woman is either a madonna or a …puttana. This is not a polite word in Italian. I think the more proper English word is prostitute." He quickly put up his hands in objection to the idea and said, "But you, cara mia, are different."

"That is exactly what I said about you when Alexandra warned me about Latin men. I said Antonio is different."

"Alexandra is right, carina, in general. You just experienced a prime example. But not all Latin men are like my friend. My father is different, and I think differently." Antonio gave me a tender hug around the waist. "Let me introduce you to a good friend."

We moved through the noisy crowd to a group of people listening to a skinny white-haired man, who was dressed in old corduroy pants, a plaid flannel shirt, and a tweed sports jacket with leather elbow patches. Antonio whispered to me, "This is Professor Penham. He teaches art history at Columbia. He stayed with my family in Rome when he was a post- doctoral student—before the War— when I was a child. He'll come over to us when he finishes talking with these people."

Professor Penham did come to embrace Antonio and then turned to me, "You must be Grace Long, Alexandra's cousin."

"That's my real name," I said, "It was my grandmother's name too, but everyone calls me Lili."

"Did you know we used to call Dr. Francesco 'Tonio' when he was a child? I've known him since he only came up to my knee." Professor Penham's kind voice and expression put me at ease. His shaggy white eyebrows made his eyes dramatically expressive.

"What kind of child was Tonio?" I asked.

"Very curious," said the professor, "always asking questions, which his father loved to encourage. Somewhat impetuous, as I remember." He looked up at the ceiling as if trying to recapture the stories. "There was a time when he drove his parents crazy with his adventures. Antonio's father and mother are lovely people. Elegant

Romans. Very traditional." The eyebrows came together in the middle of his brow, making an emphasis I wasn't sure I understood.

"Does that mean they would disapprove of me?" I dared to ask.

Antonio interrupted, "No, no, Lili, they will love you. I know them. Professor Penham is correct that they are traditional, but they know how unhappy I was. I promise you they will love you."

I looked over at Penham's face, where the eyebrows raised now in the middle expressed a major question about Antonio's parents. I decided this wasn't the right time to pursue it and turned to the professor with a different query, "Do you teach any undergraduate courses? I am starting classes at Columbia in the fall."

"Yes, usually at least one course each semester. Come to my office in September. I'll give you some guidance about your course of study and the best instructors," he said.

"I'd love to," I said. "I'll definitely look you up. Maybe you could tell me more about Tonio too."

When we left the party, it was raining. We walked slowly arm in arm under my big striped umbrella along Madison Avenue, checking the lighted store windows. Back at Antonio's apartment, the doorman had an urgent message from Alexandra to call her immediately. Antonio called Alexandra. She needed to speak to me.

"I have bad news from the Farm," she said. "Uncle Ed is dead. He was killed in a car accident. I'll pick you up in ten minutes. We have to go up there."

I was in shock. "Okay, I'll be waiting downstairs."

Antonio asked, "Do you want me to come with you?"

"I wish you could come," I said, "but it's better for me to go alone. Wendy will need me. I'll call you somehow tomorrow."

Alexandra and I arrived at the Farm in Chester at midnight. Every light in the whole house was on, and everyone was awake. There were empty glasses and dirty dishes everywhere. Cranky children were trying to get attention, but they were too tired to be much trouble. Wendy's mother, Aunt Emily, was in tears, with her three children gathered around her. Even Rex seemed serious and sober for a change. I went to Aunt Emily, Wendy, Cindy and Ricky . We all started to cry.

Mama had red eyes. She said, "They say he was drinking. He crashed into a tree down by the highway. He was dead when they found him. Emily and your Uncle Max had to go to the sheriff to identify him." The whole gathered family spent a long nightmarish wakeful night until morning sent us to an unbelieving sleep.

The funeral was set for the following week in Manhattan. I called Antonio and told him I was staying with the family through the week. Brinny and I stuck close to Wendy and her sister Cindy. They needed to cry and talk. They also needed to play tennis and forget sometimes.

The adults in the family seemed disoriented, sad, confused. They had thought the drinking party would go on forever, I guess. The drinking did not actually stop at all, but became quieter for a while—and more solitary. I now understand that Rex was paralyzing himself. I was losing him as surely as Wendy, Cindy and Ricky had lost Uncle Ed. We were all unconscious in a way—profoundly deaf to the silent screams around us.

CHAPTER SIX

In late September I moved in with Maria and began to share the rent on her two-room apartment just off Riverside Drive, close to Columbia. I called on Professor Penham, who seemed happy to hear from me. He made me feel at home by offering me cookies and tea, which he poured himself amidst the piles of books and papers cluttering his office. He always called me Grace. "Grace, after four semesters you will be eligible to declare financial independence from your parents and apply for a scholarship to study full-time. Do you have any idea what your major will be?"

"I don't know yet. I love French and English, and I also want to take Italian." I looked at the professor, hoping my mention of Italian might open the subject of Antonio and Antonio's family, but he didn't break his professional demeanor.

"Yes, I can see by your college boards and high school record that you have great potential as a student, like your cousin Alexandra. She is becoming an important scholar—world recognized. Her work on Fifth and Sixth Century vases is attracting attention from Munich to London." After a moment's pause, he looked at me over his reading glasses and said, gently but firmly. "Don't set your heart on Antonio Francesco. He is a fine person, but he will go back to Italy when his research is done. There is no place for you there. I know. I lived there. I know his family. You still have some growing up to do, Grace. I'd like to help if I can."

Holding back my tears, I stood to leave before I lost control. "Th-thank you, Professor. I hope you're right about my potential and wrong about Antonio and me. I appreciate your interest." I hurried out of his office and into the nearest ladies room where I let the tears ruin my makeup. There was something both authoritative and kind in Professor Penham's manner that did not allow me to dismiss his warning as I had dismissed my mother's and Alexandra's words.

It was three o'clock in the afternoon. I was meeting Antonio at five thirty at his office in the East Eightys. I pulled myself together, reapplied my mascara, and decided to walk—a good two hours downtown, through Central Park across to the East side. I counted the months since I had met Antonio: April, May, June, July, August, September. Not such a long time. We had never talked about the future except that we would go to Italy together someday. I needed to walk off my worries and focus on our happiness: the present. On how lucky I was. I wanted Antonio's arms around me.

As I walked, I thought about Uncle Ed. How could he be gone? I thought about Grandfather who was sick. I thought about my high school friends away at college starting new lives. The streets of New York are always distracting: kids roller skating in the traffic, mothers pushing babies in strollers, a fat lady walking a fussy little poodle, the windows of grocery stores and shoe stores. I crossed the park in a daze, half-remembering that it was not always safe to walk alone in parts of Central Park, but not really caring.

At Antonio's office, I freshened my lipstick and hair in the powder room. He came out of the lab at five thirty, still wearing his white lab coat and glasses. He looked so serious. The receptionist, Kathleen, who knew me, by then was smiling as she called to him, "Dr. Francesco, there is someone waiting for you."

He removed his eyeglasses and his blue eyes beamed over to me. I threw myself in his arms and started to cry.

"Lili, carina, what is the trouble?" he stroked my back, as if I were a little child. "Why all these tears, my love, my angel?"

I felt foolish and tried to stop crying and making a scene in his office. "I'm sorry," I said. "I didn't mean to do this here. Can we go outside?" Looking at Kathleen I said, "I'm s-sorry, Kathleen, I'm really okay. Just upset. It's my f-family."

We walked out to the East River. The day was turning twilight gray as we watched the barges and tourist boats pass on the water.

A seagull landed on the guard rail and looked right at us curiously. I told Antonio what Professor Penham had said. "Why would he say 'don't set your heart on Antonio?' Where else can my heart be? You know how I feel. I know you love me too. Why did his words upset me so?"

Antonio walked in silence listening to me, holding my hand. When I stopped talking and looked at him, he was facing away from me with tears in his eyes too. He pulled me close and we held each other tight like two frightened children.

Then he exhaled and seemed to regain his adult composure. "Lili, my angel, it will be all right. Professor Penham is trying to protect you from some hard realities of Italian society. He is right to face these realities. I'm afraid I've been avoiding them. I haven't considered the future. I've been simply enjoying you and healing myself."

I kept listening and blowing my nose as Antonio gathered his thoughts. I noticed the seagull take off. Then Antonio took my hands in his. " What I should have explained more clearly to you in the beginning is that I cannot marry again in the Church and in my parents' eyes. So I cannot offer you all you deserve. I have been selfish."

"No, you are not selfish," I interrupted. "How can you say that? You never lied to me. I agreed to everything. I know you love me."

"Lili, my angel, we have two or three years before we have to make any decisions. My work here may go on even longer. Your studies are just beginning." He smiled and teased, "You may get tired of me—I'm getting pretty old. Someday I will go back to Italy. I am not an immigrant. My family has connections in my country and someday I will inherit my family villa and property. I have fantasized that you would come with me. It is beautiful, carina. You will love the sunny skies and the cypress and vineyards. But we would not be married in the eyes of my parents' society. You will have to decide if you want that life for yourself."

I started to speak, but he put his finger on my mouth, "Don't decide now. You don't know what you are deciding yet. First you will study, and I will work, and we will visit Europe together—

maybe next spring. Okay? My angel, let me kiss your tears away. I always want to care for you. I told you that. I want to keep you safe and happy with me, my angel, cara mia."

We went home to Antonio's apartment and forgot the world by greedily losing ourselves in each other's bodies.

CHAPTER SEVEN

My desk in the School of Journalism was situated right off the main entrance hall, where the students passed by on their way to and from classes. I had noticed Phil Cohen before he introduced himself because he often came to class without shoes. Phil was a far cry from Antonio, dressed like a sloppy college kid, with his tee-shirt out of his ill-fitting jeans. He was about my height and still carried some baby fat at twenty-two, but had a lively expression on his face, reddish-brown curly hair that he never combed, and big round eyes which looked at me directly when he talked. Phil was a Harvard graduate. He was not my type at all, but he was amusing and usually cheerful. He hung around my desk and made a pest of himself regularly. "Miss Long, may I call you Grace?" he asked.

"You can call me Lili."

"It sounds French," he said. "Can I take you to dinner?"

"No, you cannot, I'm busy." I playfully pretended to be officious.

"How about tomorrow?"

"No, Phil, I have a boyfriend. A serious boyfriend." I said.

"Are you engaged?" he asked. "If you were my girlfriend, I'd ask you to marry me."

"No, we're not engaged. It's complicated," I said.

"What's complicated?"

"Well, I can't talk about it at work. You run along to class." I tried to joke him away, but I also wanted to talk to someone.

"Okay, Lili, I'll go to class, but we'll have coffee some day soon. Your boyfriend won't mind if we have coffee," said Phil.

Brinny had started wearing her long straight hair parted in the middle, and it kept falling over her eyes, so she developed a habit of flinging it back with a toss of her head. Although our parents considered me a bad influence on the girls, Brinny, Wendy and Diana came to our apartment for lunch on a Saturday when Antonio was delivering a lecture out of town. We ate spaghetti and Italian bread on plates in the living room, drank beer, and listened to Vivaldi. When I asked Brinny about Danny Feldman, she tossed her head to throw the hair behind her ears—trying futilely to look sophisticated and nonchalant, "He's back at Harvard. And we write a lot of long letters, but neither one of us is more than intrigued." She emphasized "intrigued"—apparently a word they had found to describe their tentative relationship.

"What is intrigued?" asked Wendy.

"I wish I knew," said Brinny, "Danny says he is intrigued with me, but he is the most confused boy I ever met. He's majoring in Philosophy." She started to laugh, "Isn't that useless? Sometimes I wonder what I see in him."

Diana, who was hoping to major in voice at Oberlin, asked Brinny, "Are you planning the same route as Lili for college, Brin? I mean working and taking night classes?"

Brinny answered, "I have no choice. I'll follow Lili's wonderful example." She laughed, "that'll thrill the parents. You know, Lili, I hoped I could room with you. Maybe you and Maria and I could find a larger apartment."

"Sure," I said, "and I can fix you up with one of my pesky journalism students like Phil. He's smart and very funny. But his feet get pretty dirty walking around without shoes." We all giggled like children.

I thought Antonio looked very tired when he returned from Italy. Now I realize he was depressed. He said he was worried about his parents who had aged noticeably in the last year. But he didn't want to talk about it. "My life is too complicated, my angel," he said, trying to reassure me by caressing my back. Antonio's darker moods confused and frightened me, but I tried to deny any problems and naively hoped that his work would bring his spirit back to balance.

I was so pleased that Professor Penham seemed to take an interest in me that I visited his office again before registering for spring semester. When he asked me how I was faring, I answered, "Academically, no problems. I just wish I could afford more courses. I plan to take two summer session courses to move more quickly."

"How is your job?" he asked.

"It's fine. Mostly typing and answering the telephone. The dean is easy. Some of the students are amusing."

"Are there any interesting young men in the School?" he asked peering over his glasses, his eyebrows pointing down in the middle like a great horned owl.

"Sometimes they try to flirt with me, but you know I am infatuated with our mutual friend." I tried to speak with a sense of humor about it.

"Yes, that's a good way to think of it," he said. "Try to keep your mind open."

I wanted to keep my mind open, as Professor Penham suggested, but I also started Italian, which came easily to me because of my French and my knowledge of arias, and I took an Art History survey, full of beautiful slides of the Parthenon, Notre Dame de Chartres, and all the artistic glories of Europe.

Alexandra and I planned a big party for Antonio's thirtieth birthday in March to break up the winter. We invited Professor Penham and his wife, Antonio's colleagues from the lab, some of Alexandra's art and academic friends, and we even invited Brinny, Wendy and Diana. Alexandra knew about a barn-like loft with real brick walls to rent in Greenwich Village, and she hired a college band to play. Around a dance floor we set tables covered with red and white checked table cloths and put candles in chianti bottles on each table. Brinny accused us of being corny. There were platters of hot and cold antipasto and lots of red wine for the guests as they arrived.

I was happy to introduce Antonio to Brinny, Wendy and Diana. "Brinny, your sister." He brightened. " I would guess it. Two beautiful sisters."

Brinny blushed and pushed her hair out of her face, "Lili told us you are romantic. I thought you would look older—being a doctor and all. You look younger than thirty," she offered.

"I hope to meet your parents soon and convince them that I am not too old for your sister," Antonio said, putting his arm around my waist.

"What kind of doctor are you?" Brinny asked.

"I am an internist and fellow in cardiology at Rockefeller University. Cardiology means the study of the heart," he said laughing at himself.

"That is funny," said Brinny, "And corny. You **would** be a heart doctor. If you were a liver doctor or a toenail doctor, it wouldn't be so romantic."

Wendy and Diana discovered that Antonio loved grand opera. As I listened to them discuss the bel canto revival, I told Antonio I wanted to learn more about opera, and we decided to get tickets as soon as possible.

After dinner of lasagna and garlic bread from the Italian restaurant next door, Antonio asked me to dance. We had been lovers for ten months, but we had not danced together since the Greek line dance at the Farm. The band was playing the Twist. It was fun to see my serious doctor moving his hips and letting himself play. I thought that we needed to play more. To me his every movement, even walking across the room, was graceful and exciting. Dancing was a new way to love him.

When the music changed to a slow song from the fifties, we were both sweating and smiling. He stepped toward me and put his hand on the middle of my back and pulled me to him. The sweat on our arms and faces mingled. He held me tight against his body as the slow rock beat drummed "Earth angel, earth angel, will you be mine." He led so clearly and firmly that I followed him like a brook follows the riverbed. No separation between his impulse and my reaction. Consummation was the inevitable finale of that duet.

Since it would have been rude to leave the party, we found an adjoining washroom and locked the door. We laughed at our passion.

"I didn't know you could dance like that," I told him, as we lay on the hard cold tile of the washroom.

"Carina, there is a lot you don't know about me. How I love to surprise you."

"Alexandra is going to be looking for us. You are the guest of honor. We'd better go back to the party," I said reluctantly.

"Lili mia, you are my party. You are bringing me to life." He tugged me down again by the hand.

"Get up," I said, "Let's go dance some more."

"I don't think I dare dance with you in public again," laughed Antonio.

A few weeks later Antonio produced two tickets to Puccini's "Madame Butterfly," at the Metropolitan Opera House. I knew the story of Butterfly and 'Un bel di, vedremo,' from my Milton Cross Favorite Operas book. Before the performance I used my elementary Italian to study the libretto, dwelling on the beautiful and sad phrases of the language. "Piccina moglietina olezzo di verbena—Dear little wife, orange blossom," and "Aspetto grand tempo et non mi pesa la lunga attessa —I wait for a long time but the long wait does not weary me," sang Butterfly as she awaited the return of Lt. Frank Pinkerton. The old Metropolitan Opera House seemed luxurious to me as we sat in our dark red velvet seats in a grand tier box, surrounded by Victorian ornate golden carving. As Butterfly sang about her hope that Pinkerton would return to her, tears filled my eyes involuntarily. Antonio put his hand on my hand. Butterfly's story seemed to open a sad and vulnerable place in my soul. In the final scene, when she kills herself, Antonio held my hand tightly as tears ran down his cheeks.

After the performance we walked all the way home to Antonio's place, hanging on each other and talking, "Butterfly was so innocent, trusting, so vulnerable," I said.

"Yes, like you are," said Antonio quietly and slowly. "But the difference is that I will not hurt you or lie to you like Pinkerton."

"Even if you did, I wouldn't kill myself. But I felt the sadness of her hope. I am scared sometimes that I love you too much. Maybe I love you more than I love God. That's what scare me. You are like my father, mother, and my best friend. Professor Penham said something about my needing to grow up. Will you like me as much when I grow up?"

Antonio stopped walking and turned to face me under the glare of a street light which accentuated the shadows on his face. "Lili, I don't know what to say to you.. I have told you everything. I want to enjoy the time we have." He walked out of the cone of light leading me by the hand into the darker street. "We've been together almost a year now. Your innocence has been healing to me. When I feel down, I just remember your smile and I smile. You know I am vulnerable too. I don't ever want to share you with another man. I think I would go crazy if you…well, don't even think about it. You will always be mine if you will stay with me. If that is enough for you."

We sat quietly in the dark on his Swedish sofa, listening to our own breathing. "Butterfly didn't have a clue," I said, afraid that, if I too were that naive, I wouldn't realize it.

"Lili, let's go away somewhere soon. When you finish the semester, I will take a few days off. You can probably take a few days too. We need to celebrate our first year together. I have to convince you that you can trust me. And I need something too….Where do you want to go?"

I was surprised. "I don't know. What are you thinking about?"

"The Mediterranean is too far, but something by the sea, where we can walk on the beach and recollect ourselves," he said.

"I've always wanted to go to Bermuda," I said. "It's not too far but pretty expensive."

"That's perfect," said Antonio, smiling again. "It will be my birthday present to you, carina. There is a heaviness in my heart which needs to hear the sea and hold your hand. I need you to be the heart doctor"; he smiled and began kissing me all over my face. Antonio's touch was like a sweet opiate to me. His kisses and tender voice, his hands on my skin erased my anxieties and helped me forget those who had disappointed me.

Chapter Eight

Bermuda was full of flowers and neat little farms growing bananas, sweet onions and delicious fresh vegetables. We had a pink room overlooking the ocean and a private porch on which Bermudians, speaking with soft island accents, served us breakfast each morning. As we watched, the morning sun turned the ocean into a dazzling display of sparkles. We walked on the soft beach, swam in the clear warm gulf stream, read novels and rode motor bikes on the British side of the road.

At night there was music for dancing with dinner. We had trouble trying to eat dinner and dance at the same time, because we became too aroused. We laughed and decided to dance only after we had finished eating. I remembered what he had said about a heavy heart, but I did not ask him any questions. On our last night Antonio spoke of it again on the beach as the ocean played its continuo, and a full moon littered the waves with light.

"I want you to understand me, Lili. Especially why my marriage to Margaret did not work. I went to England to study medicine when I was twenty years old—soon after the war. I was lonely. She was a lonely person too, so we comforted each other for a while. Although my family objected, we married in the Catholic Church. After we married, Margaret seemed more depressed and lonelier than ever. I was very busy with my studies and she began blaming me for her moods. Then she got pregnant, although we had agreed to wait. That is one reason I now take care of contraception myself. I was angry, and this hurt her feelings more. She had a miserable pregnancy. And then the stillbirth. I was miserable too. We were two sad people who dragged each other down."

I listened and absorbed without comment, feeling the surf on my bare feet. He continued, "But I cannot blame Margaret for all my depression. I have a tendency to melancholia, which you have not seen in this last year because of my pleasure with you. If only we could stay here forever on the beach...I actually think I could be happy."

"I thought you seemed tired when you came back from Italy after Christmas. Maybe you would be happier in America all the time," I said.

"I am happy, carina," he said, but his eyes looked away. "I am happy to unburden myself with you. Although you are young, you have an old soul for some things. Part of your temperament is as old as Aphrodite herself." The thought made him perk up, " You are my own goddess, Lili mia. How can I stay depressed?" The moon didn't flinch, and the surf continued its beat.

When we came back to New York, I was trying to arrange the clutter on my desk, and catch up with the mail and phone messages, when Phil Cohen interrupted me in his cheerful, oblivious way.

"Hey Lili, where'd you get the tan?"

"I was on a honeymoon in Bermuda," I teased him.

"Really? You got married?" He seemed shocked.

I laughed at him. "No, I'm not married. Just teasing you. Are you staying on for summer session?"

"Yeah, I have a job this summer at the New York Daily News, so I'll be around," said Phil. "When can I take you for dinner?"

"Oh, maybe in two or three years, when my friend goes back to Italy," I was surprised to hear myself say it, however facetiously.

Phil looked surprised too. "You mean there's hope for me?"

"N-no," I said, "I don't know why I said that. I should introduce you to my sister, Brinny. She'll be moving in with me next year."

One day during summer session, when I needed a break, I went to the library to look up "melancholia." It is an old-fashioned word for sadness or even depression. The definition reminded me of a book about the English poet Lord Byron, who was young, hand-some, sad, and romantic. Brinny would definitely say he was corny. Lord Byron died of tuberculosis, like Mimi in Puccini's "La Boheme" and Violetta in Verdi's "La Traviata."

As I became more familiar with operas, I was struck by how many heroes and heroines fell in love with people they could not marry, and also how many of those lovers, especially the women, died in the end. Carmen was a gypsy, a free woman, therefore immoral, so she could not marry. Violetta was a courtesan. Lucia di Lamermoor loved a man her brother disapproved. Aida loved an enemy of her father. And they all died. I was glad to be an American woman who did not have to die to make an ending to the story.

One of the operas I enjoyed most was Offenbach's "The Tales of Hoffmann," the story of three ill-fated loves of the writer E.T.A. Hoffmann. His second love was Antonia, a beautiful young singer afflicted with a lung disease. Her doctor told her she must never sing again, but the Devil tempted her to sing with a phantom of her dead mother, who had also died of the lung ailment. Antonio, ever the doctor, was interested in how illness had been romanticized in the nineteenth century.

Drinking coffee in a bar, after seeing a New York City Opera production of "The Tales of Hoffmann," Antonio said, "Antonia's choice is one I would not want to make. To limit myself in order to stay alive goes against my nature. What would you do, Lili, if your doctor told you never to dance again? Would you comply?"

"Of course I would. I love to dance, but life is more than danc-ing. Wouldn't you?"

Antonio was pensive. "You are right. Dancing alone doesn't make life for you, as singing did for Antonia, but what about love, carina? If you had to choose between a life without passion and a risk of death, what would you choose?"

"Antonio, why do you ask such melodramatic questions? We don't have to choose. It isn't dangerous for our health. Maybe if one of us had a h-heart condition, we'd have to choose, but we're young... I love the music of operas and the emotions they evoke, but the stories are ridiculous today."

Antonio shrugged his shoulders. "These questions interest me. I wonder how much risk is the spice of life for me. I wonder if I could live quietly in my own country like my parents."

Holding Antonio's arm as we walked, I considered what he said. I began to have an inkling that his other world, his home, was very foreign to me.

Almost exactly one year after Uncle Ed's death our family made its last pilgrimage to the Farm to collect a few mementos from the house. Julius had taken the grand piano, Aunt Emily took the antique sideboard, Aunt Augusta took the photograph of Grandma as a young woman, which I had coveted. Brinny opened a dusty heavy metal trunk and screamed, "Look, Lili, our costumes from "Carousel." Remember how you danced in the barn and we threw sand on the floor to make it a beach?"

I pulled out the filmy silk dress which was originally a nightgown from mama's trousseau, which I had trimmed in red ribbon for the play. I held it next to my cheek. "Remember, how Julius sang 'If I loved you, words wouldn't come in any easy way'? What a great song! ...And remember how we all sang together at the end, 'When you walk in a storm, keep your head up high'?" I started to sing, and Brinny joined in, "And don't be afraid of the dark. At the end of the storm is a golden sky and the sweet silver song of a lark." We both stood up as I clutched the red ribbon dress to my chest, we faced the audience and earnestly belted, "Walk on, walk on, with hope in your heart, and you'll never walk alone... You'll never walk alone." We looked at each other and burst out laughing.

"There wasn't a dry eye in the barn," said Brinny. "That was the best show we ever did."

"The worst was when Rex blasted the shotgun through the roof in "Annie Get Your Gun," and we almost choked to death from the dust. He really wrecked that day."

We sat there in the cobwebs remembering. I gazed at a shaft of light full of randomly dancing dust motes. I broke the slightly dizzying silence, "Julius was so mad. All that work and practice ruined. The sets were ruined. He vowed never to produce another play at the Farm."

"Weren't you mad, Lili? He shot the gun in the middle of your solo?"

"I suppose I was. I always rationalize the other guy's point of view. I wish I were better at being angry… I have this fear that if I ever give my anger a voice, the whole world will explode." Then I chuckled at the ridiculousness of the idea.

As we drove down the long gravel driveway past Grandma's peonies, past the barn where we had performed in Julius's musicals, past the reservoir of Brinny's narrow escape from the ice, I knew my childhood was over. Grandma was dead. Grandfather was dead. Uncle Ed was dead. I was no longer a virgin. Antonio was everything to me…my hope, my love, my future, my life.

My second academic year I managed to take three courses each semester at night, accumulating enough with summer school by the end of the second year to apply for a scholarship to study full-time. I decided to major in comparative literature and was beginning to explore linguistics. Professor Penham called to tell me the good news. "Grace, you have been awarded a full scholarship for next year."

I felt like a little girl on Christmas, "Thank you. Thank you, Professor. I am so happy." The first person I called with the news was Brinny. "Brinny, it can be done. I got the scholarship. Next year I can take a full load of courses. I can pay the rent with a part-time job. You can do it too."

Brinny was happy for me, but she didn't sound exactly elated, "I know we can do it, Lili, but it is so unfair that our brothers don't have to make it on their own. Mama and Rex are going to give them the money to go to college right after high school. Wendy's going to Mt. Holyoke. I'm very angry. I want to go away to a campus like Wendy and my friends. I want to go to Radcliffe so I can irk Danny Feldman at Harvard."

I knew she was right, but my life felt so exciting that I could avoid my anger. If I had gone to Radcliffe, I wouldn't have Antonio or Columbia or Professor Penham.

After final exams, Antonio and I took ten days off to go to Italy. Sitting next to Antonio flying to Rome in the TWA jet, I felt like a very lucky woman. The stewardess gave us red wine. We toasted our two years together, and my twentieth birthday, which in Europe is a coming-of-age birthday. Antonio said, "Now you are twenty, shall I call you Grace, as Professor Penham has insisted? It is a beautiful name, no?"

I thought a while, testing the suggestion. Mama had called me Grace when she was very serious with me. I could never ask Brinny to call me Grace. I certainly did not intend to call Brinny, Brenda. Yet as I thought of myself graduating from Columbia and going to graduate school, perhaps teaching or writing someday, my true name, Grace, seemed more dignified than Lili. I asked Antonio, pushing my shoulder into his, "Would you love Grace as much as you have loved Lili?"

"More, carina, if possible," and he kissed me quietly on the lips. I put my head on his shoulder and thanked God for all my luck and happiness. The stewardess interrupted us with the dinner trays. When she left, I said, "Yes, I think it's better to introduce me to your family as Grace." I giggled, "It sounds a lot holier." He laughed and said, "A holy heathen to them. Remember you are a Protestant, good as a heathen in Rome."

"But I have received communion in the Catholic Church—when I was in France. My French mother, Mme. Montaigne, took me to the local priest who was amazingly understanding. All I had to do was to go to confession, like any Catholic, and he let me receive."

Antonio said, "The French are more broad-minded than the Italians."

CHAPTER NINE
THE FRANCESCOS

We did not stay with Antonio's family. He thought it was better to enjoy the coast for our vacation and simply have dinner with his parents in Rome on our way back. I thought it was strange to fly all the way to Italy and see his family only one day, but I let him lead. His new red Ferrari 250 SWB called a California Spyder was delivered to us at the airport with the top down—the most gorgeous car I had ever seen. I asked where he kept it.

He laughed. "Cara mia, I love cars. I have quite a few. You'll see them all sometime. I keep them in the country north of Rome. But today we are driving west to the sea. I told you I have surprises for you. All in time."

We set out for the countryside. I was a little frightened by the way Italians drive in the country—too fast for me. But the sun was glorious and the sky as blue as Antonio's eyes.

Speeding along the highway I watched his profile as he drove. Antonio didn't smoke cigarettes in America, but he picked up a pack of Gaulois at the airport. As he drew in the smoke from the sweet-smelling cigarette, he squinted, and the tan skin around his eyes wrinkled slightly; his forehead furrowed too in a worrying way. I was curious to know what other surprises Antonio meant.

Two hours northwest of Rome we found the little inn Antonio had chosen in Porto Ercole. Our room had a big puffy mattress and pillows, and a window facing the sea. There was a calico cat who roamed the premises and kept the birds from begging for crumbs from our breakfast. There were flowers everywhere. We indulged ourselves in sun, sleep and swimming in the blue sea. Antonio found the highest, cool places to sit and sponge up the sunshine. He rubbed suntan lotion over his chest muscles and beamed, "I feel healthy as a fish."

I burst out laughing, "As a fish?"

He laughed too and asked, "What's wrong. You don't say that in English?"

"No, we don't say healthy as a **fish**. We say healthy as a horse. You say fish?"

"Certo. It makes more sense. Horses aren't so healthy you know. Strong, yes, but they have lots of health problems. Whereas, a fish...living in the beautiful sea...yes, I think the Italian concept in this case is superior."

We were having so much fun at the sea, that the change in Antonio when we went to Rome was astonishing. In Rome, he spoke Italian with his friends and family, so I could understand only about one third of what was going on. His face seemed to close up. He was nervous. He looked older. I was frustrated that I couldn't figure out what was happening. I knew something was wrong, but there was no opportunity to ask him about it.

We met five members of his family for a Sunday dinner at a restaurant in the via Pinciana near the Villa Borghese garden. His father looked like an older Antonio: the same curly hair, but gray, and a mustache. His mother was delicately built and elegantly dressed in a designer suit . Her dark hair was streaked with natural gray and pulled tightly back in a chignon. Next to Signora Francesco I felt like an American giraffe.

Antonio introduced me as his friend. The chill I felt from his mother almost made me sneeze. Aunt Caterina, Signora Francesco's sister, seemed warmer, and her son, Gian Carlo and daughter-in-law, Marissa, seemed more friendly and approachable to me. Signor Francesco kept a curious, but not entirely cold, distance from me.

Signora asked Antonio to sit at her right and Gian Carlo on her left. Signor Francesco was at the other end of the table with Aunt Caterina on his left, next to Antonio, and Marissa on his right. I was grateful to be sitting between Gian Carlo and Marissa. Signora Francesco asked me politely if I spoke Italian. "Not very well, just a little," I answered in Italian. "I speak French better. I went to school in France."

"Perfect," she said in French, "then we will speak French so you can better understand us."

The dinner was beginning to feel like a meeting rather than a social occasion. Clearly she wanted me to get a message. The food and wines had all been ordered in advance and were served to us impeccably as the meeting proceeded. As we ate the cold langoustine salad, Signor Francesco asked Antonio when his research project would be finished. Speaking French to his father, Antonio seemed tightly restrained. His normally sparkling blue eyes looked weary and sad. He was evasive in his answer and valiantly tried to change the tone of the conversation to something lighter or more social.

"Papa, how are the horses?" he asked.

"The horses miss you, Tonio, as we all do. Your sister is sorry she could not be here today. You understand, of course," Signor said.

Antonio grew red : "No, father, I do not understand why my sister cannot be here on the one day I am in Rome this year. If you and Mama have some nineteenth century, puritanical reason why she may not meet me with my dearest friend Grace, my sister is the loser. Please tell her I am most unhappy."

I really wanted to get up and leave, but that was unthinkable. The coldness to me seemed unfair, but what really upset me was Antonio's misery. I had never seen him like that. I tried to make small talk with Marissa, but her French was as limited as my Italian.

After the longest dinner of my life we stood up from the table, and Signor Francesco suggested a "passeggiata," a Sunday afternoon walk. As we left the restaurant, Signora Francesco took Antonio's arm and walked ahead, followed by Signor Francesco, Gian Carlo and Marissa. Aunt Caterina took me in hand and surprised me by her excellent English. Aunt Caterina told me that Professor Penham had written to her about me — asking that she take good care of me. "Professor Penham told me that you are a decent and gifted person. I am sorry if our ways are strange to you."

"What do you mean exactly?" I asked.

"We cannot accept your relationship with Antonio, of course. It is not personal, you understand. Really it is very sad for him. He made a terrible mistake in marrying Margaret, but there you are. It is done."

"Must he pay forever for his mistake?" I asked.

"He seems to be living his life as he wishes," replied Aunt Caterina, "but how about you? Don't you want to be married and have children?"

"I am just twenty years old," I replied. "I have a lot of time."

"At twenty, my dear, you are at the peak of your beauty and desirability. Why waste it on a man who is not free? If you were to give him up, it would be better for everyone concerned eventually. He would get over you. I sense you are stronger than he is. You would snap right back."

I didn't respond but walked on pensively. Why was the world attacking us? Why didn't they just leave us alone? The family parting was painfully polite. Antonio stiffly kissed his mother, father and aunt. I shook hands with them, and we walked away into the park. Antonio's whole being was transformed. His body moved less fluidly. His eyes struggled as if desperately trying not to drown in rough waters. Even his color looked gray. He asked me in a low voice, "Lili, what did they tell Caterina to tell you?"

"She told me I should give you up, and then everybody would be happy," I said.

Antonio turned and grabbed me so tightly with both arms around my body that I was almost afraid. He was terribly angry and visibly pained. "I will never subject you to this rudeness again. My family is living in another century." After calming his breathing somewhat, he let go of his hold on me and put one hand over his face and said, "I don't know what to do. As ridiculous as they may be, they are important to me. Perhaps in time…." He didn't finish his sentence. He took me by the hand and headed back to the Ferrari. " Let's go for a drive."

The way Antonio sped out of Rome that day was frightening, but I didn't complain. I just prayed and hoped the speed might help him shake his anger and gloom. He pulled up on a hilltop about an hour outside the city to the northwest, and we walked around a field until the sun began to go down. "I am completely stuck," he said. "Do you believe in heaven, Lili?"

I was really puzzled now. "Heaven? Of course, I do. I don't know what it will be like, but I believe that we will be safe after death."

"Maybe the only place we can be together is in heaven," said Antonio.

"Antonio, p-please don't talk like that. You sound like an Italian opera. There are always options. We can live in America. Let's not have a melodrama. We could even be married and have a normal life."

"Lili mia, you don't understand, and it is my fault," he said.

"Look, it's okay," I tried to be soothing. "You need to get back to work and away from Italy. Your family is not good for your state of mind. I understand that. My family is not good for me either right now. Let's just take life day by day, year by year. We can't know the future."

He took my lead. I kissed him and brought my body close to his, which always distracted Antonio. Luckily, we had one sure way to forget the world.

CHAPTER TEN

"Now you see for yourself why I have discouraged your relationship with Antonio." said Professor Penham from behind his paper laden desk. "I know the family. Theirs is a different world. You can only be hurt, Grace. You'll do better to concentrate on your studies. How is your schedule this semester? Who are your professors?"

I didn't want to argue with Professor Penham about the Francescos; I was still stunned by the experience. His academic questions were easier to address. "I'm taking the math requirement, Peterson's survey of American literature, Dante with Venezia, and Intro to Psych. Next semester I can begin to choose more in my field."

"That is what counts. Just stay on track. This other situation will resolve somehow," said the good professor.

On three separate occasions, I told Brinny, Maria, and Phil about my disastrous Roman holiday. Brinny said, "Lili, how did you ever find such a corny man? It sounds like a bad Italian movie." I had one sympathetic ear—Maria. She was dating a foreign student from Mexico, whose family was pretty old-fashioned too. But her boyfriend, Riccardo, planned to stay in the U.S. Phil, of course, was elated. "This is perfect. He is not free, but now you are. You can begin to cast around for other possibilities. I'd like to meet this guy so I could see what attracts you. I promise to wear a suit, you know, and shoes and comb my hair. I'll bet you didn't know I speak Italian."

I didn't know that Phil had an ear for languages. He was still hiding his light under the bushel of his careless appearance.

Brinny landed a bookkeeping job at the Registrar's Office, so we could have lunch together whenever we wanted. On a sunny September day on the wide stone steps that face Low Library, I introduced her to Phil, as we ate tuna sandwiches and grapes and drank coffee from insulated paper cups from Chock Full o' Nuts. "Lili told me a lot about you," Brinny said to Phil, as she peeled her grape with her teeth, "How come you don't wear shoes?"

"It gets me a lot of attention, I guess," Phil admitted, "How come you are so blunt?"

"Life's easier that way," said Brinny, "I don't have to remember what I'm not supposed to say." She tossed a grape in the air and caught it agilely in her open mouth.

Brinny and Phil immediately took to arguing about everything, especially American involvement in Vietnam. Phil felt that the West had to draw a line against Communism. Brinny challenged him, "Would you want to go over there and die in a foreign jungle, when the issues are so muddy?"

Phil answered, "I wouldn't mind going as a journalist. It might even help my career. And I'd see what the issues are for myself."

"You'd still be supporting the war. I wouldn't even pay taxes for killing people whom I don't even know." Brinny was already a strict pacifist. "I believe in loving our enemies and to returning evil with good."

"You gotta be kidding. Love Hitler? Love Mao? You want those pathological killers to rule us?" returned Phil.

I could understand both sides of the argument. I had been hoping Brinny and Phil would like each other, and they actually seemed to enjoy their confrontational talks. But it didn't seem very romantic to me. Shortly after Brinny and Phil had met, I asked Phil, who was hanging around my desk with his morning coffee and donut, as usual, "So how do you like my sister?"

Phil said, "I like her very much. She's a great person— bright and fun to talk to." He held his donut to his eye and focused on me through the hole. "But it's you I'm in love with, Lili. Don't you get it?"

I couldn't believe my ears. He never seemed serious before, just a teaser. I didn't know what to say. I fumbled, "Oh, you don't mean it," but I knew he did.

"Lili," said Phil, "I don't know how that Italian smooches you, but I'm a nice American Jewish boy. They say we make great husbands. And I know what I want. I've wanted you since I first saw you, and I won't give up just because you haven't taken me seriously yet. I am very persistent."

"I've noticed that," I said, stunned. "Don't you think Brinny is pretty?"

"Lili, you're so naive. I don't want you because you are pretty. Lots of women are prettier. It's...a special vitality. Something in the air around you attracts me."

I smiled at Phil. "Something in the air around you makes me laugh. I think it's that hair sticking up—and the sugar on your nose."

Walking up Broadway past Juilliard School of Music with Brinny after work in good weather when the windows were open, we often heard Juilliard students practicing their instruments. Someone playing a piano transcription of Mozart's "Voi Que Sapate," "You who know what love is," prompted me to asked Brinny if she was interested in any boys. She answered, " I'm not like you, Lili. But I'm not like Wendy either. Boys are mostly friends to me. I don't know if I ever want to get involved. In fact, if you can keep a secret, I'll tell you my real hope."

"Cross my heart, Brin, you know I can keep a secret."

Brinny stopped and seemed to be listening to the innocent Mozart before she said very quietly and hesitantly, "I think what I would really love is to become a nun...only for God, forever."

I looked at my little sister in amazement. We were both pretty religious, but to enter a convent forever was a tremendous step.

She continued, "That's what makes me happy. To think about working for God all my life in a black habit and a new name like Sister Mary. I don't want to get married and have to deal with a husband. Human beings are so difficult. God suits me better."

"Brinny, I'm in shock," I said, "I used to talk about being a nun, but not seriously. I would be the worst nun in the world. But you are really serious, aren't you?"

"I want my love for God to show to all the world every minute of the day." She started to walk again up the street, away from the Mozart and into earshot of a string quartet practicing Brahms. "Remember how we used to play we were nuns?"

When we were children, we fantasized at night in bed that we were nuns with special powers like angels or Greek goddesses to change the lives of our friends and family. We could stop arguments. We changed wine into water—the reverse of the Biblical miracle. I wondered if Brinny had thoroughly considered that the reality of monastic life was nothing like our childhood playing.

She said, "It would be a dream come true for me."

"You sound as though you're in love," I said, identifying with her starry-eyed enthusiasm.

"That's right, I am in love," said my sister. "A love that can't disappoint me."

"We're both passionate women," I said, listening to the Brahms fading behind us.

"Yeah, we're both corny," laughed Brinny. "With Wendy we make a real weird threesome. You'll have to have all the grandchildren."

"Not likely with Antonio," I answered, "and I don't love Phil that way. Phil told me he is in love with me. Can you believe that?"

"It's as plain as the nose on his face. And you don't see him at all. You're blinded by your romantic heart doctor, who probably won't work out anyway. Phil has a lot of qualities. If I were you, I'd marry Phil," said Brinny.

"I see Phil's qualities. I wish he were my big brother, not that I need more brothers. He's just not my type."

"You're hopeless, sister."

Antonio, Brinny, and I went to the opera to see Bizet's "Carmen." The Habanera—"Love is a gypsy child who has never known laws. If you do not love me, I love you; and if I love you, watch out for yourself."—reminded me of the craziness of our lives.

I told Antonio about Phil, and I was dying to tell him about Brinny, but I remembered my promise to her. Antonio didn't seem too worried about Phil. He smiled, "So I have a rival. I'm not surprised. Is he younger than me?"

"Well, he is younger, but if you saw him, you would know he is not a rival. He is like a puppy dog."

"Puppy dogs can grow up," Antonio mused.

CHAPTER ELEVEN

During the next year Antonio did not visit either his parents or Italy. We worked, studied, enjoyed the opera and art galleries, denying the future. Some days he suffered dark moods. I waited them out. Antonio encouraged me in my studies, gave me insights into European history and helped me practice Italian. When his fingers brushed my cheek or my arm, my whole body changed. This language between us felt deeper and stronger each year, a bond beyond words or covenants. An agreement between us at the cellular level that was healing to both of us.

Brinny didn't talk much about her secret. She went to church almost every day at the Cathedral of St. John the Divine on Amsterdam Avenue, where she met the Reverend Timothy Thompson, one of the curates who ran the group for young singles. Antonio and I met Tim one Sunday when we accompanied Brinny to church. Greeting us at the door of the church, the young priest, who wore a Roman collar, said: "So happy to meet Brenda's sister. You sisters are lucky to be able to live together while you attend school. Doctor, happy to meet you."

"Brinny told you about her family, and you still let her come to church?" I said, shaking his hand.

Tim blushed. He was pretty cute actually, and I could see he liked Brinny.

Brinny saved him, "Tim has been telling me about the various religious orders in the Episcopal Church. He belongs to the Order of the Holy Cross, as well as being a priest."

"What is the Order of the Holy Cross?" I asked.

"We have a monastery up the Hudson where the brothers live a traditional monastic life, but anyone can join as an associate and go there for prayer and retreats. I've invited Brenda to come for one of the parish retreats this spring to see what we are about. You are welcome too. Both of you."

Antonio and I looked at each other and smiled. We weren't ready for a monastery, at least not together.

Phil often joined Brinny, Antonio, and me for a gallery opening, a movie, or even the opera. Antonio and Phil liked each other. Phil asked Antonio to help him choose a pair of good Italian shoes and some silk ties. Phil only occasionally looked pained when he witnessed the physics between Antonio and me.

We had just come out of the Beekman theater, where we had seen the latest Italian movie, Antonioni's "L'Avventura," which none of us liked, when Antonio asked Phil what he planned to do after graduation in the spring.

"I'm interviewing at several TV networks here in New York. I'd like to write for the news programs. There's a lot of power in deciding what gets aired as news and how the stories are shown."

Antonio was interested, "In Europe television is just beginning —an open field of opportunity. It could be an interesting future."

My parents finally met Antonio at one of Alexandra's birthday bashes in Greenwich Village. There were hoards of people tightly packed—very noisy with an amplified rock band and singers. Holding Antonio's arm tightly, as I brought my treasure before my parents, I didn't know if I was protecting him or he was protecting me. "Mama, D-dad, this is Antonio."

Antonio extended his hand to shake and spoke loudly over the din, "Mr. and Mrs. Long, I am happy to meet you. I hope you may learn to approve of me."

Shaking his hand, Mama spoke loudly, but we could hardly hear her, "We don't disapprove of you, Doctor. We were concerned only about the age difference, but now Lili is twenty-one, she is an adult. I was married at her age."

I didn't want to get into that discussion, so I said, "It's so hard to h-hear anything, we'll catch up with y-you later." I didn't want to catch up with them that night. I was deathly afraid Rex would say something to embarrass me, or even worse, to embarrass Antonio. I persuaded Antonio to leave the party. We went back to his place, played Mozart, and talked about the evening. "Cara mia, you seem so agitated around your parents. I have never seen you so...how should I say...high strung? Like a violin string that is over tightened. Now you seem like yourself again."

"That is your effect on me. I've always been a sort of nervous, worried person. You say that I am healing to you. You see how you are healing to me." I put my fingers in Antonio's curls, my other hand on his chest and comforted myself like a cat.

He said, "Yes, I see now. What was so frightening to you, carina mia?"

"Everything. They say I was afraid of everything when I was little: dogs, snakes, water, grass, even crossing the street. But I still had fun. I don't have many fears now. I feel normal. I'm still afraid of excessive drinking. I'm glad you don't drink too much."

Antonio looked sad. "It's complicated to be human."

Antonio and I had been together three years when his research project was completed and the grant money ran out, as well as his visa. He was offered several good positions at hospitals in Milan, London and Houston, Texas, and decided to go to Milan for a year. I had only two semesters left to complete my B.A.; by the end of the academic year, I would know where I would continue my graduate studies: in the U. S. or Europe. My first reaction to Antonio's leaving was shameless: I begged, "Why don't you just stay here and marry me. Forget your old world scruples."

"Lili," he said, "I wish I could do that. I wish it were that simple. We'll both learn something in the year. We'll write letters and visit. I'll come back for your graduation, and we'll know more."

I was obedient. We closed his apartment in August. He gave me his furniture, which we needed, and a beautiful painting by Carlo

Cusimano. He also gave me $3000 to put in the bank for emergencies. I let him get on the plane and go to the University Hospital, Milano, Italia, a place I had never seen. My head said good-bye, arrividerci, adieu, but the cells of my body were bereft. I wrote to Antonio the night he left.

My dearest Antonio,

How did I let you go? How can I spend nine months before seeing you again? You are breakfast, lunch and dinner to me. Must I be hungry for so long a time? Why are we doing this?

Yes, I know why. I can be reasonable, but I have to figure out how to survive these nine long months. Please write immediately. I am starving already. I know I love you too much.

Your only angel.

In part to fill a lonely weekend in October, I joined Brinny and Tim at a Holy Cross retreat. The retreat house was an old stone mansion in the woods north of New York City near the Hudson River. The sleeping rooms were plain, but welcoming in a simple way. We each had a small room, single bed, one window and desk. There was a crucifix on the wall and a Bible on the desk.

The first evening, after soup, bread and butter in the cavernous refectory, our group of twelve from the Cathedral met with Brother Gregory, the retreat leader. The meeting room, like the dining room, was stony and austere, but a warming blaze in the wide fireplace helped set a mood of positive expectancy. In his long hooded white tunic, cinched by a white rope, Brother Gregory introduced himself, "I've been the abbot of this house for twenty-three years and am happy to welcome you to our home for some quiet instruction and reflection. We will spend most of these forty-five hours together in silent prayer or sleep, but I will give you guidance too and pray that the Holy Spirit will give each of you what you need. Let us introduce ourselves and explain what brings each of you here this evening."

Tim took the lead: "I am the Reverend Tim Thompson, an associate of the Holy Cross and a curate at the Cathedral. I'm here to practice contemplative prayer and to encourage these people of my parish in their own spiritual growth." Tim looked to Brinny, sitting next to him, who spoke next:

"I am Brenda Long, an undergraduate at Columbia University. I've been a Christian all my life and am struggling with my vocation." She turned a smile to Tim, "Tim has been helpful to me. He thought this retreat might be enlightening."

It was my turn to speak, "I am Brenda's sister, Grace Long. I came to reflect on my life… I'm quite lonely since the man I love, Dr. Antonio Francesco, went away for a year. I've often wondered if I love him too much. Does God place limits on how much we should love a human being? Is God really jealous as the Bible says? The church has always been a comfort to me, so I hoped this might help."

Three of the other retreatants were Columbia undergraduates; two were older women, widows; there were two married couples. After introductions Brother Gregory led us in a guided meditation on suffering and healing. He emphasized the importance of silence to grieve our suffering and silence to heal so that new life can take root. I cried for myself and for Antonio. I remembered my year in France, when I was separated from my country and family, but found friends in the Montaigne family and a church home in the Catholic Church. I prayed for Brinny and Wendy, Maria and Riccardo, Phil Cohen, my parents, my aunts and uncles and cousins. I prayed for Uncle Ed, Professor Penham. I asked God how I should spend nine months so far from a relationship that had so filled my heart and soul for three critical years.

When I had a session with Brother Gregory in private, he responded to some of my questions: "We don't believe that God is jealous. God is not a selfish ego like we are. We believe that God doesn't want to punish us for our weakness and shortcomings."

"But can a relationship be an addiction? How can I tell?"

"Only you, Miss Long, can judge if your relationship is addictive. A good question to ask yourself is whether the person you love encourages you in your own growth and sanctification, and do you encourage him in his. You said that he thought the time you are experiencing apart is actually good for you both. He may be exactly right."

The quiet music in the chapel was beautiful and peaceful. My breathing slowed down. I looked at the light coming through the stained glass windows and wept. Yet I felt anchored. Perhaps more anchored than ever before. I walked around the grounds, enjoying the cool autumn sunshine and yellow maple leaves, looking for signs.

Saturday morning, I noticed Brinny and Tim Thompson in deep conversation outside in the garden, when we were supposed to be keeping silent. He took her hand and held it in both of his. She was looking at him in a way that did not remind me of a nun.

Cara mia,
Milano is cold. I am trying to work hard to make the days go by. Your picture on my table when I come back in the evening is the light of my day. I don't think we should wait nine months. We need a visit sooner. Will you come here for Christmas, my angel. I need you, vita mia. Antonio.

Dearest Antonio: Yes, I'm coming for Christmas. I made my reservation already. How I miss you. I arrive December 21, 8 a.m. Your Lili.

Chapter Twelve

As I was packing my one small suitcase to go to Milan for Christmas, Brinny told me another secret: "Lili, I want to tell you something before I tell the parents." I looked up from folding my nylons and underwear. She seemed hesitant to say it, turned a little pink and looked down, "Tim and I are going to get married. I'm going to Vermont to meet his parents the day after Christmas. And I want you to be the maid of honor."

I was shocked and yet not at all surprised: envious and happy. I started to cry. "Brinny, you are so lucky. I am so happy for you. But you are so young." I put my arms around her and cried while laughing at myself.

She protested, "I'm twenty years old, almost twenty-one. Mama got married when she was nineteen. Tim is almost thirty. You know how I thought I could never love or trust a man, but Tim is kind and moral and trustworthy...We believe God gave us to each other."

Brinny looked happier than I had ever known her...and more mature...and softer.

I asked, "When?"

"June 22, a week after your graduation. Will you be the maid of honor?"

"Of course, I will," I started to cry again, "I always figured you would be m-my m-maid of honor." So I went to Milan.

When I saw Antonio waiting for me in the airport, I just stared at him for a second or two before he saw me: admiring his curly head, beautiful suit and Latin composure. Then my feet started to run, and he saw me coming. His eyes lit up as he ran toward me too. We collided and laughed and kissed and looked at each other like a mother looking at her lost child. It was a selfish, wonderful Christmas. Just the two of us and a few long distance telephone calls.

Milano was dark and cold. We walked in the streets under one umbrella humming our favorite Christmas songs and opera tunes. Our favorite was the Barcarole from "Tales of Hoffmann," which we sang in harmony until we messed it up—always at the same place, where the parts separated. We were warming ourselves with brandy in a little cozy bar when I told him what was on my heart:

"I have wonderful news, but it makes me so emotional. I'm going to cry…. Just don't mind me…" I was trying to control my tears as Antonio looked at me in anticipation and concern. "Brinny and Tim are getting m-married next June." Tears came.

"Carina mia, come let me hold you," responded Antonio. He pulled me closer to him and put his arm around me. "You want to be married, no?"

"Yes, of course, but let's not ruin our week together by discussing the impossible. Can you stay in June for the wedding? Brinny and I really want you to be there."

"Sure, I will be there, angelina. They are so young. Very innocent. Very lucky."

Preparation for Brinny's wedding brought our family together more often. Brinny and Tim planned a full church wedding with Holy Communion at the Cathedral in a side chapel, officiated by the Dean. Brinny fit beautifully into our mother's wedding dress, and she cut her long hair into a short bob which gave her a more elegant look. The reception was to be held at the church reception room, and the whole Long family was invited, along with two hundred other guests.

As I was helping Brin and Mama write the invitations at the kitchen table in Riverdale, Mama started to choke up.

"What's the matter, Mama?" asked Brinny.

"It is a very confusing time. I feel happy that you found such a suitable, lovely husband, whom you love—and sad you are growing up so fast." Mama tried not to look at me, but I knew she was feeling worried about me too. She said, "I'm so proud of you both. Lili graduating so soon and doing so well. Maybe you'll be a professor. And Brinny marrying a priest."

Brinny chimed in, "I'm going to graduate too. I'm not quitting school just because I'll be married. But Lili will have to get a new roommate."

"I'll be going away to graduate school, so Maria will have to get two roommates. Maybe she'll get married too."

Mama couldn't resist asking, "Any chance of your getting married, Lili?"

I answered, "Miracles do happen," and said no more.

Professor Penham had been guiding me through the process of applying for graduate fellowships. He was optimistic about Columbia and an international fellowship at the University of Paris. A Fulbright was always a long-shot, but I applied to study comparative Romance languages in Rome, although Penham wanted me to go to Madrid or Paris. The Fulbright would allow me not to work, which was a luxury I had not yet experienced.

When the Fulbright came through, Professor Penham was more excited than I had ever seen him. "You see. What an honor. You are fulfilling all the hopes I have had for you. This clinches your career. Do you realize what this means?"

"I can't believe it," I said. "How my fortune has changed from no college money to a Fulbright.... Rome." My memories of Rome were not very happy. "But I'll have to leave you and Brinny and Tim and my family. It could be a big adjustment."

I telegrammed Antonio and he telegrammed back: FANTASTICO. IMMEDIATELY STARTING TO LOOK FOR WORK IN ROME. BENVENUTA A ROMA.

News articles ran in the local home newspaper about my fellowship. My parents were very proud and bragged to their friends and family about me and Brinny. I also learned that I would graduate magna cum laude and that my honor's thesis was being considered for publication in the *Modern Language Association Journal*.

I think even Alexandra was impressed and perhaps a little envious. "Aren't you the Cinderella. One day a struggling night student, now a Fulbright scholar. What happened to our doctor friend?"

I told her that our relationship was still very much alive. She said, "I warned you about him. Better that you go to England."

Antonio did come for graduation, but it was not the best time for us. I was distracted with University and departmental ceremonies and preparations for the Fulbright experience, not to mention preparations for Brinny's wedding. He seemed to understand and tried to be supportive in the background. Still, I was frustrated not to be able to give him my usual full attention.

I couldn't even sit with Antonio at Brinny's wedding since I was the maid of honor. He sat with Phil, as a friend of the family. I managed to walk down the aisle ahead of my sister and father in a composed manner, but when I turned and saw her walking towards us in her white wedding dress, beautiful as a cloud in the sky, beaming like a planet, the tears fell down my cheeks. I looked at Tim— wearing a tuxedo instead of clericals— a blushing groom, smiling ear to ear. I nodded to Mama and Rex, Aunt Emily and Wendy. I think all of us in the family were wondering how little Brinny grew up so fast.

Then my eyes caught Antonio's. He had my full attention for the first time in a week. He was looking at me, not the bride and groom. His longing eyes told me that he understood that I wanted to be married too. We sealed an intimate unspoken agreement across the ladies hats, bouquets of flowers and church candles. When our gaze ended, the music had stopped. I heard the dean's voice saying:

> **Brenda, will you have this man to be your husband; to live together in the covenant of marriage? Will you love him, comfort him, honor and keep him, in sickness and in health; and, forsaking all others, be faithful to him as long as you both shall live?**

At the reception I could finally join Antonio. We floated to the edge of the room, and kissed each other like thirsty birds finding water. He acknowledged our wordless engagement, "So my Lili, you will be my wife?"

"Is it true?"

He said, "I have never wanted anything more."

We couldn't say any more words because the cells of our bodies were going mad. We slipped out of the reception hall to a small chapel used for clerical private prayers, shut the door and he put his lips between my breasts. "How can I not be your husband? We belong together. I want what you want."

I couldn't speak. I just kept crying and kissing.

We didn't tell anyone our plans right away. In fact we didn't have a plan. After the reception, we stayed up late talking in Antonio's hotel room.

"My only fear, carina mia, is that I will not be as good a husband as a lover. I have been a good lover, no? When two people are lovers, the differences between them can be intensifiers— rather exciting. But for married people those differences can be problems. As you know, I am more old-world than you are. And of course, there is my family. It will be difficult to avoid them as much as I have, when we are in Rome. I am so angry with them. I am truly a man divided in too many pieces."

"We will both have our work. We will have each other. I don't ask for more."

CHAPTER THIRTEEN

The weeks following Brinny and Tim's wedding were as hollow as the ring Antonio did not give me before he went back to Italy for business in Rome.

Alexandra threw a going-away party for me at her brownstone in the Village. There seemed to be a conspiracy of silence about Antonio. No one asked me about him. I had not told anyone about our plans, not even Brinny. I think people were hoping the whole affair would blow over. My parents, brothers, Aunt Emily and the whole extended family showed up. Wendy's sister, Cindy, now a glamourous New Yorker working at a 57th Street Gallery, came with Phil, who looked like a man of the world in a dark grey Brooks Brothers suit and a good haircut. Wendy came from Connecticut with her new love, Jessica.

Alexandra gave me telephone numbers of her many friends in Rome at wonderful sounding addresses. In his farewell toast, Professor Penham emphasized the distinction of the fellowship and hopes for my academic career. My fellowship was for only two years, but Penham assured me that Columbia would pick up where Fulbright left off. Phil made a toast after having four glasses of wine: "To Lili. May she see so many Italian men that she becomes inoculated —better yet revolted— and comes back to the United States searching for an American."

Brinny gave me a good-bye hug, whispering, "Take care of yourself, sister. Come back soon. You can always stay with us until you find a new place."

I felt very lonely. I didn't know if it was because I was leaving so many loved ones, or because I missed Antonio, or because no one shared my anticipation of joining Antonio in Rome. We knew we could not get married in Italy, and so had talked of eventually eloping to England, Switzerland or France.

By the time I arrived in Rome in mid-August, Antonio had already rented a flat, twice as large as his New York apartment, the whole upper story of a lovely house in the newer part of Trastevere, the oldest neighborhood in Rome, on the Via Filippo Casini. We had our own entrance; a front room, as yet unfurnished except for a large Turkish rug; a dining room, where Antonio had put an antique dining table and four chairs; European style kitchen; two bedrooms and a balcony, which I eventually filled with red geraniums. Around the corner from the house was a lovely wide staircase leading up the hill to the park adjoining the Villa Sciarra.

I didn't have much time to work on nesting in the apartment. It was hot. No air-conditioning. My classes and meetings began soon after I arrived. We did make a few purchases together—with his money, of course: a set of new heavy linen sheets for our bed, a goose down quilt for winter and pillows, and a life size porcelain cat that had flowers painted on her head. She was our pet. I named her Kate after the heroine in Douglas Moore's opera "On the Wings of a Dove."

I plunged into my studies, figuring Antonio and I would live as we had in New York: working all day and enjoying each other in free time. But the pace of Rome was different. I remembered how I puzzled over Antonio when we visited Italy two years earlier. He was different here— not free to include me in as many of his activities in his country, as he had been in New York. Sometimes I didn't mind having the day or a few days to myself, because I needed the time to work. Other times I resented his involvement with friends I did not know and his family who clearly didn't want me. I was not invited to their home, yet Antonio made obligatory visits.

I sensed that the friends I did meet were not the best ones. He did not introduce me any Italian women of his class, only single men. We had dinner one balmy night in Trastevere with his old friend Marco, who worked for the Banca di Roma and his nineteen year old German girlfriend, Katya. My Italian was getting fluent. I began to be annoyed at the two men's discussion of Italian women. Marco said, "I have no taste for Italian women. They can be beautiful at fifteen, but at thirty- five they look old. Miss Lili, what is your national background?"

"I'm a mixture of English, Scottish, Irish and French. I think I even have some small bit of Italian way back. Do you think I'll be a hag in ten years?"

"That depends on how many babies you have and if you get fat," he answered smugly.

"Antonio?" I asked, "Would you love me if I were fat?"

He laughed at my pique, "Would you love me if I lost my hair?"

I laughed too but continued my questioning, "Seriously, do you agree with Marco about Italian women?"

"What I don't like about Italian women is their lack of freedom. They have the same mentality as Italian men, which I explained to you: two kinds of women. I don't like to think in that pattern, but most of my countrymen and women do. You would say in America, we are a stone-age society. Lili, are you happy here and now?"

Antonio had never asked me that question before. I guess he could see I was not so happy.

> Dear Brinny: I don't like Rome. Even though my studies are okay, and the city is magnificent, Antonio is different here. You know how he always seems serious but pretty relaxed. In Rome he looks miserable, even irritable at times—not even as handsome somehow. I am worried about him, but I can't seem to figure out how to communicate with him.
>
> How is married life? You are so lucky to be married to the man you love. What is it like to be the priest's wife? Please write. Say Hi to Tim. I miss you.
>
> Love, Lili.

Dear Lili: Married life with Tim is beautiful. He understands me better than I understand myself. He has some interesting observations about our family, especially Dad, which I will discuss with you when you get back. He thinks Dad is an alcoholic. I always thought alcoholics were falling down drunks on the street. We talked to Mom about it, but she says we are overreacting. Tim's own father had a serious drinking problem, but he is recovering in AA. It is interesting to learn more about psychology.

I am becoming a pretty good cook, at least Tim thinks so. He is even gaining a little weight. He was too skinny anyway. I like being called Mrs. Thompson.

I am sorry to hear about your problems with Antonio, because I know you are in love with him. It would sure be easier if you were in love with an American. Is he planning on coming back when you come back? By the way, Phil said to tell you he's waiting for you. I miss you too. It would be so much fun to be married couples together. Tim and I are meeting some really nice couples from the church. Some of them have babies. We are going to wait a year or two—until I finish my degree, but it is great to think about having a family. Maybe then Tim will get his own church in the country. I would love to raise my children in the country.

Lili, I am praying for you and so is Tim. We think you should live in America. Are we too bourgeois for you sophisticated people? I love you.

Brinny.

Brinny's letter made me homesick. I didn't want to complain to Antonio about the change in him. But I was not satisfied. He lacked zest. He didn't touch me as often in the course of the day. He lost his enthusiasm for little things like walking in the streets. I felt as though he was moving away, although we had just moved in together.

After several weeks I chose a quiet rainy Sunday afternoon to speak to him. We were listening to a recording of Mozart's Requiem.

The beauty of the music helped me be hopeful enough to raise the question. "Antonio mio, is there something worrying you? You are changed since I came to Rome. I miss my old Antonio."

He looked at me like a scolded dog, which almost made me regret having raised the subject. He said, "Rome changes me, carina. I don't want to stay here. I see my father and mother. I don't please them, and they don't understand me. My sister is a stranger. Some of my old friends are so provincial. It is beginning to strangle me. I have started to see a doctor of psychiatry for my depression."

"A psychiatrist?" I felt suddenly sad. I associated psychiatrists with serious mental problems or with troubled personalities like my maternal grandmother who was hospitalized for being addicted to amphetamines. I didn't want Antonio to need a psychiatrist.

"I met him on Wednesday. He thinks talking can help me. It is worth a try. You don't realize how divided I feel. I sometimes feel there is no way out."

I grabbed his hand and kissed it. "H-how can I help?" I asked.

"You do help, carina, but Rome is hard on me...coupled with my temperament. Mostly I don't want to hurt you," he said.

"What do you mean hurt me? How could you hurt me?" I asked, suddenly afraid. "You don't have another w-woman, do you?"

"No, no, angelina. That is the last thing I need." He cracked a smile.

After a deliberate silence, in which he seemed to be weighing his words, Antonio looked at me and said slowly and softly, "If I hurt myself, carina, you would suffer and grieve. What is keeping me going is that I want to protect you."

"H-hurt yourself?" I began to cry. "Why don't we just go b-back to America? I hate this melodramatic European mentality. I don't understand it. Please let's get back to normal somehow?" I was struggling to stop my tears. I tried to stop myself from begging.

"Carina, the clouds in my mind have always been a problem. My hope is that this doctor will help. Please don't put pressure on me. You have always been so accepting and calm. Just be patient a little longer. It is better for me to sort it out if I can. If I can get through this bad time with more insight, then I may be free to act on my own as a man, not only to please my parents or to please you, carina."

I wanted to seduce him away from his unhappy thoughts. Maybe I wanted to seduce myself away from unhappy thoughts. "Who is the psychiatrist? Can I talk to him?" I asked.

"He is Dottor Belsanti, an Italian Swiss. For the moment I need to talk to him alone. Maybe later you can meet him." He smiled, "Next to finding you, my angel, I think it is the best thing I have done. I believe he can help."

I immersed myself in my work. My goal was to study the influence of Chretien de Troyes, a French poet of the late 12th Century on Spanish and Italian literature of the following two centuries. Chretien wrote stories about the conflict in Medieval aristocracy between romantic love and adventure. His style was elegant and humorous. He told delightful tales, but it was hard to care about 'amour courtois' when my own living love was so pained.

My academic advisor in Rome was an Italian Professor, Paulo Passacantando, whom we addressed as Professore. He met with his four graduate advisees every Thursday for dinner at noon at his large, airy old house. Two of the other students were Italian men, Salvatore and Stefano, both Latin scholars, both Jesuit priests. The third student was an auburn-haired English woman about my age, Anne Lawrence, who specialized in medieval Church Latin.

Anne and I became frequent companions for meals and walks and studying. It was a relief to speak English some of the time. Anne had been in Rome three years and knew her way around the city and the Italians. Like my cousin Alexandra, Anne advised against relationships with Italian men. She was living with a Dutch journalist. I tried to explain to Anne about Antonio, "He is different from what you have experienced, but I am worried. In the United States we agreed to get married, but since we moved here, he is changed. Even our sex life is different. He used to be like electricity— charged up and ready at all times. Now sometimes he has low voltage. Or none. His warmth is fading. I don't think he loves me less, but he is distracted. It is lonely for me. I miss my sister, cousins and friends."

About this time I received a note at the University from Antonio's sister, Annamaria, whom I had never met.

To Miss Grace Long:
Please join me for tea Wednesday at four in the afternoon at the Cafe Roma at the Piazza Navona. I hope it is not necessary for you to tell my brother about our meeting. He is under great stress. I hope you can come.
Annamaria Francesco

My first thought was, "More melodrama. I've had enough of this family." But I went to the Cafe at four . She was sitting at a back table drinking tea. I recognized her immediately from photographs and the shocking resemblance she had to Antonio: The light brown curls, the blue eyes, but especially the confident way she held herself and moved to extend her hand. It was difficult to approach her dispassionately. I was very uncomfortable as she rose to shake hands with me.

"Signorina Long, thank you for coming."

I said in Italian, "I am pleased to meet you. You boycotted me two years ago when we were in Rome."

"I was rude. It is part of the Byzantine nature of our family. It must be hard for an American to understand us," she said.

"Some Americans have strange families too," I offered.

She motioned gracefully to the chair opposite her, "Please, make yourself comfortable. I wanted to meet you because I am very worried about my brother. Two years ago we hoped his infatuation with you would pass, like other hopeless relationships he has chosen. His marriage to Margaret was very unfortunate. He was too young and headstrong. I suppose he has told you about that."

"He has told me some of it," I said, "I don't push him to reveal more than he wants. I have been concerned about him too. He says he is depressed."

"It is not the first time, nor will it be the last." said Annamaria.

"How did he come out of it before?" I asked.

"It just passed. Once he had a car accident which frightened him and shocked him out of it. He totally wrecked the car and suffered a concussion and some minor scars."

I didn't speak to Annamaria about the psychiatrist or about getting married because I didn't know what Antonio wanted his family to know. I summoned the courage to say, " Perhaps Antonio would be happier if your family supported him in his life decisions instead of opposing him."

"He makes his own life difficult. Don't you think there are many suitable women who would have married him. Or he could live as he likes abroad. Why should he come here and flaunt his relationship with you in my parents home ground?"

"That is entirely my fault. I applied for the Fulbright in Rome. Honestly I never thought I would get it. If I had known how painful this is for you all, I certainly would have gone elsewhere. You are Byzantine to me." I ordered a glass of wine.

The afternoon air was very pleasant as the sun disappeared behind the church. I knew Annamaria was twenty-seven years old. She dressed like her mother in expensive high fashion; her wavy light brown hair fell loosely around her face. "What do you do?" I asked.

"I am a teacher in a Catholic School. Of course I don't need the money. I teach very young children," she replied.

"A teacher and a doctor. Both noble professions—at least in the United States they are." Suddenly on impulse I asked, " Why don't you come to the country on Saturday with Antonio and me. You might get used to us together. You seem to be intelligent and reasonable. It is really not so awful."

"Did you tell him I wrote to you?" she looked worried.

"I really don't understand you," I said, "I haven't told him that you wrote, but I see no point in keeping it a secret. What are you afraid of?"

She looked at the clouds clamoring across the gray sky and said, "I would like to see him smile. I'd really like to come, but my parents mustn't know."

I shook my head, "Suit yourself. We are leaving around nine in the morning. I think it would be good to break some of this ice."

Anna smiled, "Maybe so. Miss Grace, you'll lead us both astray."

"I don't get it," I said.

Chapter Fourteen

Part of the Fulbright experience was supposed to be "cross-cultural interaction...on a person-to-person basis in an atmosphere of openness, academic integrity, and intellectual freedom." At our Thursday noon dinners in Professor Passacantando's eighteenth century house, he sat at one end of his ten-foot long dining table, and his friendly, round wife Ursula sat at the other. Their cook, Rosa, made us a five- course dinner, complete with good wines which were supposed to facilitate our conversations.

The good Professore began choosing the weekly topic for each meeting; it had no particular relevance to our researches. The first topic was ecumenical relations of the Roman Church since Vatican II; then contemporary Italian poetry. Anne Lawrence was interested in discussing the iconography of Romanesque church facades. I asked for a discussion of psychoanalysis. Salvatore wanted to discuss sex.

"What aspect of sex do you want to talk about, my son?" the Professore asked.

Salvatore was twenty-seven years old and not unattractive. He was thin and pale from being indoors too much, but he had long eyelashes and an earnest forehead. Stefano, by contrast, was thirty years old, short, chubby and buck- toothed. Anne Lawrence and I looked at each other, barely suppressing our laughter. These two celibate priests, this lovely old Italian couple, and we two foreign women, who were living in sin—it could make a hilarious discussion.

Salvatore answered the Professore's question, "Any aspect of sex. It is a gap in our education. And how are we to learn anything?"

The poor Professore did not know how to start. "Do you mean you want to know the facts of life?"

Salvatore turned red, but more animated, talking faster and using his hands as pointers, "No, of course not, I know the facts of life. I want to know how women and men differ in sexual attitudes and pleasure. Poetry is filled with sexual imagery. Why can't we have a rational discussion? We should not be inhibited because of mixed company."

Professore Passacantando looked befuddled. "My son, why don"t you initiate the conversation."

Salvatore was ready. "I want to ask Signorina Grace and Signorina Anne to tell us men the women's point of view on birth control— one of our church's basic moral teachings."

Anne pushed her chair back from the table and took the high road in her answer, "I think the Roman Church makes an error in this teaching based on the account in Genesis of the sin of Onan. You all surely member how Onan spilled his seed on the ground to prevent his dead brother's widow Tamar from conceiving a descendent. The sin was the crime against his brother, not the mere spilling of seed. Secondly, the Old Testament valued procreation highly because of the need of the tribe of Israel to become more numerous, to survive and defeat enemies. That is a demographic condition that no longer applies today in light of global overpopulation."

We all looked at Salvatore, who had regained his cool and said, "That is a very interesting scholar's point of view, but I am more interested in your view as a woman. As a woman, under what circumstances do you feel birth control is desirable and why is the rhythm method not sufficient?"

Silence. Then he reiterated, "From the woman's point of view."

I took his bait, although I suspected he was trying to titillate himself. "I use birth control because I am not married and the rhythm method is too risky. I had a friend in high school who got in trouble using the rhythm method. Even for married couples, the rhythm method is crude." Silence again. I added, "For very passionate people, we can't wait on the calendar."

I realized I was teasing Salvatore, figuring that is what he wanted to hear. He blushed again, "I didn't mean to embarrass you, Signora Grace. You don't have to tell about your private life," he said.

I was amused. "I am not embarrassed or apologetic about my private life. I am a monogamous Christian. I just don't want to conceive a child yet. My sister is married to an Episcopal— Anglican— priest in New York. They don't want to start a family until she completes her college degree, so they use birth control. There is nothing against it in the Bible."

Stefano said, "You Protestants always cite the Bible, as if God has revealed nothing to the Church since the canon was established. What kind of God would stop revelations to humanity in the Fourth Century?"

Anne quickly countered, "What assurance do we have that God's continued revelation to us came through the Roman Church?"

Professore Passacantando said, "We seem to have a division of opinion between Catholic and Protestant, men and women, Latins and Anglo-Saxons. I have noticed that Anglo-Saxons have more difficulty in general with authority than do Latin people. Latins may not obey authorities, but we don't like to pull the whole system down. We prefer a delicate sort of hypocrisy." The Professore's comment was interesting to me as I continued to try to understand Antonio and his family's attitude toward our relationship.

When I told Antonio that Annamaria had contacted me and that I had invited her to join us Saturday, he brightened a little. "You are a miracle worker, carina. Let's take her to the beach with a picnic."

I packed sandwiches, fruit, wine and mineral water. Annamaria came to our house at nine on a fresh October morning, bringing some sweet biscuits for our feast. I knew her coming was a big concession to Antonio in the battle of the Francesco family. She smiled at him. He greeted her warmly, gratefully. They were beautiful together, like twins. All three of us packed into the two-seated sports car and speeded out to the coast. We didn't talk about anything serious or painful all day. Neither brother nor sister mentioned the parents. We played frisbee on the beach and gathered shells like children.

By the end of the day Annamaria called me Lili, and I called her

Anna. Antonio seemed more pleased than I had seen him for many weeks. As we drove home, he said to his sister: "Anna, I am seeing a doctor of psychiatry twice a week for my difficulty. I am hopeful that this talking cure can end it once and for all."

Anna said, "I pray for it every day."

I looked up at the stars and said a silent prayer too, "Dear God, heal this man." I believed in short prayers to the point. I felt more hope than I had dared feel since coming to Rome.

That day was a small beam of light in a gathering tornado. Antonio tried not to show me, but he was getting worse, not better. Sometimes he didn't sleep well at night. I tried not to pressure him, but it was terrible to sit by and watch a person sink into the dark.

Antonio came home from the clinic one evening, looking tired but peaceful. He took me by the hand and said, "Carina mia, I brought you something that is long overdue." He gave me a blue velvet box. When I opened the box, tears fell from my eyes. It was not an engagement ring, but a wedding band of gold and diamonds. Engraved inside the ring were the words "My Love, My Wife." The ring was gorgeous. He put it on my finger and took me in his arms. I began to breath easier, but I wondered what motivated the change. Then he frightened me by saying, "There is something else important I have to tell you. Just in case something happens to me, I have opened a bank account in Geneva in our joint names. You only need to call Arturo Ricci at the Credito Italiano and give him this identification card." He pulled a card out of his vest pocket. What was going on? Why was he getting so organized? As if he were leaving?

"Oh, n-n-no, Antonio, you're getting ready to go. You can't leave me. What does Dr. Belsanti say?" I tried not to cry, but I was terrified.

He remained calm and said gently, "You cannot know, carina. You see me here and hear me and touch me, but I am not here. I am already separated from you by a wall you cannot see. Dr. Belsanti has suggested electric shock treatment, but I know the risks. I have enough life force to want to continue to be a whole man. I have decided to try hospitalization and intensive psychoanalysis. Belsanti has a sanatorium in the Swiss mountains. I'll be away for a few weeks.

After two weeks you can visit...Coraggio, carina...coraggio."

That night, wearing my new ring, I didn't sleep. In the morning I called Dr. Belsanti, who asked me to come to his office in the afternoon with Antonio's parents and Annamaria. Antonio packed a suitcase for his journey.

CHAPTER FIFTEEN

I looked like hell when I entered Dr. Belsanti's office. My eyes were puffy red. My hair was not properly combed, and I wore no makeup. Antonio's parents looked as elegant as I had remembered them. Annamaria was composed and serious.

The office conference room was furnished like a small living room with comfortable chairs and prints of flowers and herbs on the walls. I was the last to arrive, and I guess I was barely civil to Signor and Signora Francesco. I embraced Annamaria, who looked embarrassed. I shook hands with Dr. Belsanti. He addressed us as a group:

"Signore, Signora, Signorine, as you know now, Dr. Francesco, has been my patient for eight weeks. He has given me permission to speak to you four about his condition. In the beginning I thought his depression might be relieved by talking and insight. I have come to believe that, while the life force is still fighting to live, his subconscious urge to die is dangerous to him. His 1953 automobile accident may have been a failed suicide attempt. I don't want anything like that to occur again. His healthy side recognizes the danger. That is good. He has voluntarily committed himself to my clinic in Switzerland for four weeks. There he will be safe, protected from his destructive urges and removed from the complications of his life, in which each of you play an important part. I called you here today to impress on you the seriousness of his mental distress, which is difficult for a well person to understand."

He hesitated a minute and said very deliberately: "We could lose Dr. Francesco. Your cooperation is vital."

I was in shock. My stomach contracted to a pit. I couldn't look at the Francescos' faces. I kept staring at the Doctor. He said, "What I want each of you to do is to feel free to write him as regularly as you wish. But do not telephone or visit until he initiates that personal connection. In the meantime he will be in the care of my associate Dr. Reinhardt in daily psychoanalysis."

Silence in the room. I could scarcely breath, much less speak. Dr. Belsanti continued: "As you all know, the division in his loyalties is a major cause of distress for Dr. Francesco. I cannot tell you or him how to resolve that problem. I can only become the ally of the force for living in him. I would think those of you who love him would want to do the same. Do you have any questions?"

Signor Francesco asked, "What happens at the end of four weeks?"

"That we do not know. My associate Dr. Reinhardt and I, in consultation with Dr. Francesco, will have to evaluate. I want to impress on you that Dr. Francesco is in no way incapacitated mentally—except for his dangerous urges. It is possible he may elect to stay longer than four weeks, or he may find a way to reconcile himself sooner.

Signora Francesco asked, "What should we tell his friends and family? Does he want the hospitalization to be kept a secret?"

"I think he would prefer you all to be discreet. I think he hopes you will not blame each other, which could only exacerbate his agony. He doesn't want to have to choose between you. He wants to continue a relationship with each of you."

As we stood to leave, Dr. Belsanti came to me and said, "Signorina Long, may I speak with you privately before you leave?"

I felt as though I had been beaten up. Every inch of my body hurt. The doctor signaled me to follow him into his inner office. I sat in the patient's chair facing the doctor across his desk. He said, "There are facts you don't know which Dr. Francesco has authorized me to tell you. He doesn't want you to be hurt, but I have convinced him that you need to know all the truth. He is too mentally exhausted for any upset right now.

"He spoke to his parents about his intention to marry you. He realized you would have to go to another country and that the Roman Church would not recognize the union, but as he said, 'There are other churches.' His parents think you want to marry Dr. Francesco for his fortune. They insist that you sign a pre-nuptual agreement, relinquishing any claim on their or his estate. Dr. Francesco was so incensed by their suspicion that he slammed the door in their faces and hasn't spoken to them since. I thought you should know."

I said, "Antonio always has nice clothes and cars and gives nice gifts. But I haven't thought much about it, because he is a doctor. I don't know anything about his parents' estate, nor do I care. I just want him to be well again."

"That is what Dr. Francesco told me," said Dr. Belsanti.

I called Annamaria when I got home and asked her to come for tea. The empty house was too depressing. When she knocked at the door, I was writing a letter to Antonio. "Thanks so much for coming, Anna. I am a mess. How are you?" I asked.

She looked a lot more composed than I was. "Lili, dear, we have been through this before—maybe not as serious, but similar—mood difficulties and hints of suicide. We prayed he would outgrow it. And sometimes he seemed so well. His studies never suffered. He has always had many friends, men and women."

"Has he been in therapy before or hospitalized?" I asked.

"No, we never believed in psychiatrists. This is his new idea, probably he was exposed to it in America," said Annamaria.

Suddenly I was curious about Annamaria. "Anna, you are twenty-seven years old and a beautiful woman. How is it that you are not married?" I asked.

"I've had boyfriends, but never a sexual liaison like yours and Antonio's. You know in Italy there are only two kinds of woman."

"Yeah, I've heard that somewhere before. But why haven't you married?" I persisted.

Anna wasn't exactly defensive, but became a little reserved when she answered, "Our parents have very high standards. I just haven't found the right person."

I showed Anna my ring. "Antonio gave me this the night before he left." Then I started to cry again, "Why is this happening to him? He was never depressed in America."

Anna came over to me and put her arm around me. "You are discovering it is costly to love a Francesco."

I kept trying to write to Antonio, but I didn't know what I should say:

"This was the worst day of my life"?

"I have filled every glass, cup and sink in the house with tears"?

That would only make him worse. Yet I didn't want to condescend or treat him as an invalid. Dr. Belsanti said he is perfectly mentally competent. I finally just put words on paper.

> Antonio Mio, I am wearing my ring, which I love. It doesn't fill the void you have left in my heart, but it is something to hold onto—like my "speranza" locket. Dr. Belsanti spoke to me with Annamaria and your parents about your depression. He spoke to me privately to tell me about your parents' fears that I am after your money. You know how far from truth that is. In fact I would be happy to sign any agreement they wanted me to, if it would allay those concerns.
>
> The china cat and I are sad without you, but we are happy you are safe and, we hope, healing. You used to say I was healing to you. Please let me come with my potions and poultices to be your nurse. Then you can take care of me, my love, my husband, my brother, my friend. Your Lili.

I wrote a short letter every day. Then I drowned myself in my research, trying not to hurt so much inside. In our weekly dinners at Professore Passacantando's house I told my colleagues in confidence that my fiance was hospitalized for depression. Of all people, Salvatore had had some experiences as the priest in a sanatorium. He told me he had seen many depressed patients, some much worse than Antonio. He was a good listener. It helped me to talk about my fears, loneliness, and sadness. Over coffee in a cafe I told Salvatore how I wished my sister could be with me. He asked, "Why don't you visit your sister at the end of the semester?"

"If Antonio comes home in four weeks, I want to be here, but if he stays, I might go to New York for Christmas." I said.

"How are you praying for him?" asked Salvatore.

The question touched me and I wept again. "I pray he will come back and live—the way we used to live: dancing, laughing, listening to music. I want to get married, but that is not the most important now. I want him to live and be healthy."

Salvatore said, "He is a lucky man. I hope I can meet him."

"When he gets well, we'll have a party and invite you all to celebrate with us. Thank you for your kindness, Salvatore."

"That's my job," he said and smiled. "Also talking to you teaches me about love and sexuality."

"If you're so interested in sex, why did you become a priest?" I asked.

"Celibate people are not people uninterested in sex. We are people who have sacrificed one aspect of sex in order to simplify our lives. If there is no sexuality, there is no sacrifice. I am sexual, but not in a genital way like you and Antonio. Still I am interested."

Chapter Sixteen

At the end of two weeks Antonio telephoned me at home. His voice sounded good—lighter than when he left. Was I hoping too much? "Lili, remember me?"

"Antonio, how are you? Did you get my letters? Can I see you? Oh, I'm not supposed to ask that. I miss you terribly. Let me hear your voice."

"Lili, I am doing well. Yes, I want you to take the train and come here for the weekend, if you can. They have facilities for visitors. I made a reservation for you. I miss you too."

"What do you do there?" I asked.

"I'll tell you about my experience when you come, angelina. I am sorry to have inflicted these worries on you."

"You can inflict all the worries you want. I just want to see you." My voice began to shake.

"Okay, carina, its going to be okay. Come soon and bring me those potions and poultices you wrote about, whatever they are. I want you too."

Before leaving I called Dr. Belsanti to tell him I was going and asked if I could act normal. I was so scared. The words, "We could lose Dr. Francesco," had burned a raw place in my gut like acid. Dr. Belsanti said, "Yes, you can be normal. Don't patronize or pity. He needs your love and respect. And don't expect a miracle. He is not out of the woods."

"How will you know when he is out of the woods?" I asked.

"He will know better than I. We have to trust him," said the doctor.

I bought a new pair of soft Italian leather boots and a Norwegian sweater for the mountains. I fantasized that if I could be beautiful enough, Antonio would get well.

I took an overnight train to Milan and Geneva, arriving late Saturday morning. The clinic had a driver waiting for me at the station. Snow already covered the tops of the Alps. I had never seen such mountains. Their cold white peaks against the sunny blue sky caught me by surprise and gave me hope. My aching heart and upset stomach seemed to quiet down. I remembered one of my favorite novels by Thomas Mann, *The Magic Mountain*, where the hero went to visit a cousin at a tuberculosis sanatorium in the Alps and stayed there for seven years.

As we drove up the road, the snow on the roadsides got deeper. Yet the bright sun was warming the crisp, crystalline air. I was excited, maybe still a little scared, but the mountains had a good effect. Antonio was waiting outside the front door, wearing sunglasses for the snow glare, a two-weeks growth of beard, a black Austrian sweater and tight jeans. I had never seen him with a beard before. He looked incredibly sexy.

When he saw me and his serious face brightened, I rushed to put my arms around him and bury my face in his shoulder. He held me so long and so quietly, the driver was embarrassed. Antonio took my bag from the driver and led me to my room in the visitor's quarters. The room reminded me of my simple room in the retreat house on the Hudson River: a single bed, a cross on the wall, a little window with country curtains.

I touched Antonio's face to feel the new growth. It was both scratchy and soft. I wanted to feel it with my hands, my cheek and my neck. I wanted to feel it on the soft skin inside my thighs. I felt his passion was a healthy sign. Mine was the deepest I had ever known. My desire rose from every corner of my body, caressing his body, telling his body to be well, reaffirming our physical bond.

As we lay quietly on the small Swiss bed after our love making, I suppressed a giggle, "Is this allowed here?" I asked. Antonio barely smiled.

"I like your beard, Dr. Francesco."

There were tears in Antonio's eyes. He shook his head and closed his eyes. "Lili, mia," he kissed me quietly.

I didn't know what to say or how to help. Finally I said, " Tell me if you don't want to talk about it." I still hesitated. " I have been so confused. Can you tell me why there are tears in your eyes, Antonio mio?"

"Lili, I am sad that I am such a fool, or such an ingrate—I have so much. And you are so good to me and so beautiful, yet I cannot control my mind..." He hesitated this time. "I don't want to upset you more."

"But I want to understand," I said. "If possible tell me. I'm not a child any more, Antonio."

He sat up on the edge of the bed and looked out the window. "Lili, I have told the doctors that thoughts and ideas come to my mind about how to get out of this world. I could so easily inject myself with an overdose, or drive my car into a wall. These ideas frighten me. The doctors say they also attract me. I have had something like them since I was a young boy. When I spoke of them, people got very upset, so I stopped speaking about them. They have been my personal secret vice. Now with Dr. Belsanti and Dr. Reinhardt I am speaking these thoughts again. I am beginning to believe that my very attraction to medicine had something to do with my attraction to death. Does it sound terribly morbid to you, carina?"

"Yes, it is morbid, but I want to know everything about you."

"When I met you," Antonio continued, "your humor and vitality lightened my dark thoughts. I hoped maybe the curse was broken. So I pulled you into my life. Now I am trying to unravel many knots in my head. It is complicated."

I was sad but relieved to hear Antonio talk of his suicidal wishes. Even these terrible thoughts were bearable as I sat near his warm breathing body.

At dinner I met the other seventeen patients and some of their guests. Most of the patients looked as normal as the guests to me. I figured, since I grew up in a crazy family, I was not much of a judge. Antonio introduced me as his fiancee. It was hard to fathom that we were in a mental hospital. It seemed more like a slightly antiseptic country inn. Dr. Reinhardt didn't eat with us but came in at the end of dinner. To my surprise Dr. Reinhardt was a middle-aged woman. Antonio introduced us. She asked if I would meet with her Sunday afternoon before leaving. I looked toward Antonio for his approval. He nodded and smiled. I wasn't sure how one acted in a mental hospital. We had to sleep in our separate rooms.

In the morning Antonio and I took a walk along the snowy roads toward the village. I had a million questions, but the high altitude morning was too perfect to interrupt our silence. We walked into the old country town and bought hot chocolate and croissants at a cafe. On the way back it started snowing. I was holding Antonio's arm and said, "I am thinking about getting snowed in here for seven years."

He patted my hand, "It is tempting, isn't it.... I expect I'll spend the winter here. The psychoanalysis is taking me back to examine my relationships with my parents. It is a slow process. I have dropped out of the research world for the moment, but obviously the work I am doing here is more important now."

"What do you think Dr. Reinhardt wants to see me for?" I asked.

"I don't know, but she is a smart lady. Don't worry about it. She is on our side, carina."

At three in the afternoon I knocked on Dr. Reinhardt's door. She ushered me into her consultation room and asked me to sit in a chair facing her desk. I noticed the patient's couch on one side of the room and asked, "Does Antonio lie down there to talk to you?"

"Yes, Miss Long, of course. How does that feel to you?"

"I'm sad that he needs a psychiatrist," I answered, "When we first met I was only eighteen years old, and he was a doctor and, sort of, man of the world. I'm not used to feeling stronger than Antonio."

Dr. Reinhardt said, "We all fluctuate between being stronger and more vulnerable. Actually Dr. Francesco is a very strong human being. He has an excellent chance of overcoming or at least vastly diminishing his destructive ideas. He has an ability to look at his own mind and is, of course, highly intelligent."

"I am happy to hear that," I said.

"I have asked you here to tell you one thing that might help you in the unhappy event Dr. Francesco should ever succeed in suicide, which we are doing everything possible to prevent. You must know that neither you nor anyone in his family is to blame. His urges come from his unconscious mind. They may even be in his genes. We hope to help him back into the balance he felt in New York when you met him, but these shadows may persist all his life."

"That is not very good news," I mumbled.

"You need to know all the possibilities." she said.

"May I call you or Antonio if I have more questions? It is all overwhelming now."

"Why don't you write me your questions. Our procedure is not to allow incoming calls to patients. It is for their protection," said the doctor.

"How often may I visit?" I asked.

"That is up to Dr. Francesco," she said.

Antonio was waiting in my room. I had to leave by four thirty to get the night train back to Rome, so we didn't have much time. I was depressed. Antonio seemed warm and calm. His eyes were smiling, and his touch lifted my spirit. He took a bank check from his vest pocket and said, "You will need this to pay the bills, carina, and the train fare to come here. I'll telephone you every week so we can make plans. I don't want your work to suffer."

I said, "It is December 12. What are we going to do for Christmas?"

Antonio began to chuckle and put both hands around my lower back, his nose almost touching my nose, "All I can offer you is Christmas in a mental hospital. Please come, Lili."

"Okay," I said, "This will be a first. What do you want for Christmas?"

"What I really need is my razor." he said fingering his new growth. "They won't let me have a razor."

"Oh, no, you look so sexy with a beard. I won't give you a razor," I teased.

Only later did the thought occur to me that he was capable of using the razor self-destructively. The tightness came back to my gut. I prayed that the psychoanalysis would help.

CHAPTER SEVENTEEN

The strong, dark space of Santa Maria di Trastevere was built on the site of a pre-Christian miracle of a spring of oil, and was decorated in mosaics of Jesus, Mary, and sheep. I bought a candle and put it on a chapel altar and knelt to pray and cry. "Dear God, stay with me. I am lonely and afraid. I know I love Antonio too much. If it is a sin, please forgive me. Make him well, and I will try to be more balanced. But I don't want to love him less. Please preserve him, Dear God. Please preserve me."

Next to Mary in one mosaic, is a pot of flowers, maybe lilies. Contemplating the lilies and the sheep soothed my mind. I began stopping at the church every day, not for the mass, but just to pray quietly and look at the soft, friendly sheep which calmed me. I bought a rosary of jade beads and said the Hail Mary over and over like a chant.

> Hail Mary, full of grace, The Lord is with thee.
> Blessed art thou among women
> And blessed is the fruit of thy womb, Jesus.
> Holy Mary, mother of God
> Pray for us sinners
> Now and at the hour of our death. Amen.

"Us sinners," meant Antonio and me in my prayers.

Annamaria and I consoled each other on Sundays at my place. Antonio had not yet invited any of his family to see him. When Anna asked me how Antonio looked, she blushed at the look in my eyes. "Your brother looks in the peak of health. But don't forget he is completely protected. I almost wish he could stay there."

Anna was shocked, "How can you say that, Lili? He has his medical studies and so much life to live. Sometimes you talk like a gypsy."

"Do you remember what Dottore Belsanti told us—that we could lose him. That is what terrifies me," I said. Lose him? I was afraid to think what would be left of me without Antonio. I didn't want to be like Butterfly, or Romeo and Juliet, or Tristan and Isolde. I knew better. But my heart lagged behind my head.

Just before I was to leave for Switzerland for Christmas, Signor and Signora Francesco wrote me a note in Italian:

> Dear Signorina Long:
> Our daughter has told us that you have seen Antonio. Since our mutual meeting with Dottore Belsanti, our extreme worry about our son's condition has tempered our fears about your relationship with him. I ask your indulgence. Please do us the favor of coming for dinner Sunday with Annamaria. We would be most grateful.
> Sincerely, Teresa Francesco

I so wanted to call Antonio to tell him. I decided to forgive them for their behavior towards me, reserving judgment on whatever Antonio's psychoanalysis might reveal about their treatment of their son. Anna and I met after church Sunday. She drove me to their home in the Via Aurelia Antica. Through an arched gate we entered a cobblestone courtyard, which was surrounded on four sides by the three-story mansion. A maid in a black uniform with a starched organdy apron opened the door to a beautiful entrance hall with antique paintings of what I assumed were ancestors on horses, posed like princes and princesses. Signor and Signora greeted me in the formal salone in Italian this time. "Thank you for coming, Signorina. Please sit down. Would you like an aperitivo?" I sat on an emerald silk chair which matched the heavy brocade drapes, and gestured 'no grazie' to the drink.

"We have been suffering for more than a month since Antonio went to Switzerland. What can you tell us? How is he? We have letters, but you have seen him, no?" said Signora.

I felt sorry for them. These people who seemed to hold all the power were now vulnerable. I tried to be honest and kind, "Your son is physically very well. He is resting and exercising outside in the mountain air. He seems sure of what he is doing. He believes Dr. Reinhardt will be able to help him come back to balance." I smiled, "I think he is doing better than the rest of us, frankly."

"He wrote to us that you will be with him for Christmas," said Signor Francesco. "We realize we have been too hasty in our judgment of your relationship. You see we have a prejudice about English and American women. You know the story of his marriage?"

"Yes, I know he made a mistake. I don't hold that against him," I said.

Signor continued, "We thought that our apologies to you might help Antonio forgive us. We are too old to be estranged from our son."

I said, "Thank you Signore and Signora." I looked at Annamaria, who was grinning. I said, "You might even get used to me too."

Dinner was served in an opulent dining room. The table was set so beautifully with four crystal wine glasses at each place and myriad eating utensils, that I almost forgot the sad reason for our meeting. I had difficulty imagining that Antonio had grown up in this atmosphere, that he belonged here, that he might even want to live like this. I began to worry that his parents might have been right to oppose our love. I could never be bothered by so many things. After fruit and coffee, Signor asked me, "Signorina Long, are you Catholic?"

"I am an Anglican, but I have been going to Santa Maria di Travestere every day since Antonio left. When I was in school in France, the Catholic priest let me confess and take communion, so I have always considered the whole church to be Jesus' church, not just denominations."

Signor continued, "But divorce is permissible in the Anglican Church, no? You could legally marry a divorced person?"

"Yes," I answered, "one would need a bishop's special dispensation, but it is permissible under the right circumstances."

Signor persisted, "Signorina, forgive me for being so bold to say it, but we think it would be more honorable for Antonio to marry you than to live with you without any legal status or church's bless ing."

I laughed, "I couldn't agree more. Let's pray he gets well enough."

They gave me Christmas gifts and cookies to bring to Antonio and asked me to call when I returned to give them a report. We parted friends, at least, if not family.

Annamaria came back to the house with me expressing her amazement: "You have no idea what a miracle just took place. I can't believe my father said Antonio should marry you… That it would be **more honorable** to marry you."

"After all, it is reasonable. And I told Antonio I would sign any prenuptial contract they wanted. And I guess they are as scared as I am. I am their only living link with him right now." I looked squarely at Annamaria, "I had no idea how you lived. I mean, how wealthy you are. Antonio really never gave me the picture."

"Antonio has very mixed feelings about our position and the family. Believe me, the family are not exactly flexible people."

I smiled and remembered that Antonio had told me that he liked to surprise me. But the question remained: how could we bring our two worlds together after the secrets were known.

At Christmas when I told Antonio about my visit with his family, he seemed unsurprised, "I thought they would come around eventually. That conflict was difficult for me, but only part of the true issue. Dr. Reinhardt is convincing me that I have to claim my own life, rather than living out their ideal expectation. Even more importantly, I have to claim my own destructive thoughts."

"I don't understand what you mean," I said.

"The self- destructive thoughts arise from me. So in theory, I can give them air time and power or cancel them—as long as they are conscious."

"Do you mean that it's important to express those feelings?"

"I don't have to talk about them, but I do have to notice them, and acknowledge that I cause them and can stop them. And I will always have to guard against depression."

"How?"

Antonio laughed and pulled me to his lap, "By keeping you close by, carina mia. You are my best medicine."

After Christmas our Thursday group became like a little family gathering. We came to know about the Passacantando's children and grandchildren; Anne Lawrence's publications in four languages; Salvatore's struggles with his manhood and his priesthood; Stefano's ecclesiastical ambitions, and my increasing interest in psychology and psychoanalysis.

By March Antonio was feeling confined in the clinic. He planned to discharge himself after Easter, but remain in the village at the inn to continue his analysis with Dr. Reinhardt. On a sunny spring day we walked outside the village on a lane wet and muddy with melting snow. By then Antonio had a full beard which he kept in short trim at the barber shop. The beard highlighted his eyes, which were squinting in the sun. "Carina." He stopped, faced me and smiled, "This has truly been a crazy time. I am not an ideal suitor. First we agreed to marry; then I gave you our wedding ring, and now I feel I should propose again. Are you still willing to marry me?"

I put my arms around his neck, kissed him on the mouth and whispered, "I have never wanted anything more."

"I have a plan," he said, "I have talked to my lawyer in Rome and to a minister here in the village. We can be married here, carina, before I leave. We can invite our families to come if they please. If you want, Tim could assist at the Protestant ceremony. We could have the wedding banquet here at Streuli's Inn. There is even a local band. We haven't danced in a long time, carina."

Antonio's enthusiasm was like the sound of a spring mountain creek to me. I said. "Are you sure you are ready to come back to Rome?"

"Rome was never my problem. My problem is myself. I can manage Rome. I want to introduce you to all my friends and take you on my arm to all the snooty parties. You will finish your doctorate. Then we can decide what kind of life we will lead as Dottore and

Dottoressa Francesco." He sounded strong, back in charge of his life. I was happy yet cautious in my enthusiasm.

I found a moment to speak to Dr. Reinhardt. Of course, she knew Antonio's plan. She sensed my concern. "Miss Long, nothing in life is ever perfectly sure. Where there is no risking, there is no gain."

CHAPTER EIGHTEEN
THE WEDDING

What do I remember of our wedding day, May 21, 1965.

I remember the wildflowers in my bouquet and in Brinny's hair.

I remember the church bell sounding throughout the green valley.

The spring clouds moving through the mountains at eye level playing children's games with bright blue skies.

I remember Tim Thompson pronouncing God's blessing on us:

"Defend them from every enemy.
Lead them into all peace.
Let their love for each other be a seal upon their hearts,
a mantle about their shoulders,
and a crown upon their foreheads."

I remember Antonio's parents crying.

My parents did not come. Rex wouldn't travel. I decided to think of him as paralyzed.

I remember Professor Penham meeting Professor Passacantando and arranging further grant money for me so I could study in Rome at least another year.

I remember Alexandra and Annamaria, both dressed in beautiful designer dresses, in animated conversation. Two birds of paradise without mates.

I remember Salvatore taking notes and Phil Cohen making a move on Anne Lawrence.

I remember the patients of the sanatorium mixing with the other guests, Drs. Belsanti and Reinhardt observing from the sidelines.

Most of all I will never forget my husband, so handsome in his beard and tyrolean jacket, the joy in his face, the sparkling blue eyes full of life, the warmth in his two hands around my waist as he claimed me to dance the first song, "The Mattinata" of Leoncavalo:

"Ove non sei, la luce manca,
Ove tu sei, nasce l'amor."

I remember how we waltzed high in the mountains like two eagles mating, Antonio graceful and vital. Both of us full of what Albert Camus called "La Bete Espoir Humaine." The innocent hope that life can stay still. That once achieved, love is enough.

During the celebration at Streuli's Inn Antonio introduced himself to Salvatore, "Father Salvatore, my wife speaks so fondly of you. I want to thank you for your companionship to her during my recovery. It was important to both of us."

Salvatore blushed as usual, "Dottore, it was my pleasure to be a friend to Signora, your wife. I am so happy to say that she is now Signora. I have told her that I think you are a lucky man."

"Perhaps when we return to Rome, you and I could meet for a drink," said Antonio, "I want my wife's friends to be my friends also."

Professor Penham gave us his personal blessing, " I must say you two surprised me." We looked at each other, all smiling. I said, "Thanks to you, Professor. For everything—your help with the Fulbright. Your good words to the Francescos. Your belief in me."

Penham looked a little embarrassed by my affectionate gratitude. He feigned gruffness, "You haven't finished your degree yet, Grace. How goes Chretien de Troyes?" he asked.

"You know he is wonderful, but he doesn't change much. I wish I had chosen a broader field like philosophy or psychology, where there is more new thinking today."

"New thinking is your job, Grace. There are always new layers of meaning in great literature. Then you can come teach for me at Columbia."

"First I intend to become a mother."

We stayed in Switzerland for a week after the wedding, as my husband closed his case at the clinic. He planned to continue to see Dr. Belsanti in Rome while he made the transition back to what is commonly called normal life. Everyone seemed optimistic. I asked Dr. Reinhardt if I could speak to her in private. She saw me in her office: "Signora, it is good to see Dr. Francesco so happy. You know he was very low when he came here."

I said, "Dottore, my husband's sister told me that he has always had these periods of depression and thoughts of death. Is he cured? Or is this improvement temporary?"

"I must be honest with you. Only time will answer your question, Signora. The attraction to death is a long- established pattern. In the past, he kept these thoughts in secret, which made them more powerful. He now knows much more about himself. I think there is good reason to hope— cautiously," she answered.

I had to hope. We sent our belongings to Rome and flew to the United States to see my family. I was happy to see my mother, who clearly had wanted to come to the wedding. We showed my family the wedding pictures and tried to explain who all the people were, which was slightly awkward since half the guests were patients and doctors from the clinic. Mama wrote a letter to Antonio's parents. She was gratified to see the ring on my finger and was cordial to Antonio.

Antonio was always a gentleman, but he observed my family as a cultural curiosity as well as a clinical question. Rex was peculiarly shy with both Antonio and Tim. He didn't tease them, as he used to tease us all. He even cleaned up his language. Perhaps he was intimidated by Tim's collar and Antonio's elegance. He was non-communicative with me. I felt a widening gulf had formed in the past five years between me and my parents. They knew little of Rome or Romance languages, of operas or Jesuits, of sanatoriums or psychoanalysis. It was hard to share a whole world by letter. Their world, which had been my world, seemed to me shrunken.

Brinny and Tim invited us to their apartment on Amsterdam Avenue for chicken casserole and an evening of newsy conversation. They told us Wendy had suffered a depression during the winter and had found a helpful counselor at college. Julius was managing an off-Broadway theater and planning to produce a new musical. Maria and Riccardo were engaged. Tim turned to Antonio: "Lili told us you too were depressed and asked us to pray for you. You looked so happy at the wedding. How are you feeling now?"

Antonio said, "I was depressed, but more exactly suicidal. It is a demon I have fought all my life until now. This talking cure has relieved me of such thoughts at last. Some psychiatrists think we all have a life-wish and a death-wish. I had to bring my life force into control again. The clinic was good for me. I have never felt better in my life than now." He beamed at me and took my hand. "I am a lucky man, no?"

Tim answered, "You are lucky to marry Lili, and to have found such competent doctors to help you. Unlucky to have suffered demons all your life."

My husband said, "Everyone suffers something, eh? I have money in the bank, a good profession, a good family behind me and the most beautiful wife in the world." He laughed looking at me and Brinny, "I should say 'one of the two most beautiful wives in the world.' You are a lucky man too, Tim."

Brinny said, "We are all lucky now. I just wish we all lived in the same place—at least the same country."

Antonio said, "When Lili has completed her doctorate, who knows? I am not as attached to fulfilling my parents' dream of taking over their properties as I once was. I can practice medicine almost anywhere I choose. I hope to go back into research. I am interested in how this whole psychoanalytic enterprise might connect to physical health, especially the cardiovascular system."

When we returned to Rome, Antonio resumed his professional position and his research. We took walks in the cool of the evenings—passeggiate—in the Villa Sciarra gardens. Sundays we had dinner with Antonio's parents and Annamaria. Antonio regained his warmth, humor and hope. We talked about buying a house and hiring a cook so that we could entertain his friends. We met with his lawyer and signed papers to protect my interest in his estate. Although our marriage wasn't legal in Italy, our marriage and bank accounts were in Switzerland.

One hot summer afternoon in an outdoor cafe in the shade of a linden tree Salvatore and I drank lemonades and sipped espressos at the same time. Salvatore's education in the ways of women was continuing, although the conversations at Professore Passacantando's home were suspended for the summer. "Now that you are married, and the Dottore is well again," he posed, "I wonder if you will become more...how shall I say it...ambitious in your career—like Signorina Lawrence."

"You know, Salvatore," I responded, "the opposite is happening to me. Honestly I am losing interest in my thesis. I am embarrassed to say I am more interested in learning to cook than in the subtleties of Chretien de Troyes. The study of literature at this level is too specialized to hold my passion. I expect to finish my thesis, but also I expect it will be ordinary. I'd rather be researching psychology right now."

"That is because of the Dottore's problem, of course," said Salvatore. "You and Signorina Lawrence are so different. For her, love affairs are only a secondary concern, almost a physical necessity. Her strongest interest is in her medieval studies. But for you," he grinned and pointed to me with both hands and said, "Love is first."

"Salvatore, you are a philosopher," I teased him, but then I asked, "Seriously, Salvatore, I've often wondered if it's morally okay to put love first. Aren't we supposed to put God first?"

Salvatore's whole posture softened as he motioned with his hands to the creatures around us—the trees, birds, and sky: "There are many ways of finding God, Lili—as many ways as creations on the earth... The sparrows, the linden tree, the sun, moon, you and me. God is experienced, at least partially, in all real love. Remember what it says in John's Epistle, 'God is love.' That doesn't mean possessive love or extensions of our egos, but caring for someone or something outside ourselves."

Salvatore appeared to me to be without hostility or guile,

"Salvatore, I experience God in our friendship too."

He was pleased. "Friendship is love, too, Lili."

"Did you know Anne Lawrence is considering a teaching position in the States because of her flirtation with my friend Phil Cohen at our wedding?"

"No, no, no," said Salvatore, "She does not move to the States because of a man. I know her better. It is the prestige of the offer and the pay. Your friend is only a diversion to Signorina Anne."

"Well, I guess you are the expert."

Antonio and I walked into the Santa Maria in Trastevere one Sunday evening after our family dinner at the Francescos. The church was getting even darker than usual. I led Antonio to the little altar where I used to light the candles and pray. " My mother prays too," he said, "I am not adept at prayer. I think my religion is the love of beauty, perhaps the goddess Aphrodite— in art and music. I think Guiseppe Verdi must be a saint." Antonio fingered my hair, "There is also something of the divine in love, carina. I think you are a child of Aphrodite too, no?"

"Alexandra once accused me of it, but Salvatore says God is love too."

As a late afternoon light angled across the altar making a long shadow in front of the ancient cross, I knelt at the rail quietly, where Antonio knelt close beside me. As I looked at the mosaics— the little flowers and birds— the tears welled up from deep within me. I began to shake. Antonio put his arms around me and whispered, "What is it, carina mia? It is okay now. It is all over. I am here."

I turned to him and put both arms around his neck and held him tight crying. "I was so scared."

CHAPTER NINETEEN

I didn't really care if small-minded people gossiped about us or thought I was the wrong kind of woman. I knew who I was, as did Antonio. When Antonio went to Milano for medical meetings during the opera season, I often accompanied him to attend La Scala. The great tragic operas seemed to put Antonio in touch with his own tragic attractions. I was not alarmed. I thought, "Better in the operas than in real life."

Antonio's favorite opera was not Italian, but Wagner's "Tristan und Isolde." The legend of these lovers came from my period of literature. In fact, Chretien de Troyes was believed to have written his own version, which was lost. The story is known in fragments from versions in French, English, Italian, Scandinavian and German. But the Wagner was not my taste. In the silence after listening to a recording of Joan Sutherland singing the Liebestod, I commented, "It's gorgeous, but I prefer the Italians."

Antonio speculated, "Lili, you are too modern, maybe too Christian, for this legend."

"It's not the story. I've read the French versions—Beroul and Thomas d'Angleterre, which I loved. I like the idea of the magic potion, which made them love each other. What I don't like is the emotional linking of love and death, discarding the gift of life because one person is gone."

"You don't like Romeo and Juliet?" he asked.

"Of course, not. Someone should have saved those children."

Antonio laughed, "Carina, you are a pragmatic American. I wonder how you keep me so crazy for you."

I smiled, "Animal magnetism— maybe we drank a magic potion."

On weekends we went to the Francesco's villa in the hills of Sabinia. The flocks of sheep grazing peacefully in the fields reminded me of the mosaic sheep in Sta. Maria. I was happier in the country house than in their opulent Roman house. The terra cotta tiled floors, wood beamed ceilings and stone fireplaces gave the house a comfortable, yet elegant feeling. The Francescos seemed finally to have accepted me as part of the family.

Antonio was an excellent horseman. He often rode alone, but sometimes I followed him high on the back of the gentle black Arabian, all over their estate, up steep rocky trails, through neat groves of olive trees and forests of pine trees, through streams and ponds. I had learned to ride as a young teenager on the Farm—that is, I learned to stay on a horse. I didn't ride with the style of Antonio— or the speed. Antonio was a daring rider, as he was a daring driver.

Signor and Signora Francesco kept hinting that a grandchild would enjoy the beauties of the villa. I figured I needed at least two more years to complete my academic work— more likely three. I was still only twenty-three years old. Antonio was thirty-four and seemed in no hurry for parental responsibilities.

In June we went to my parents' home in Riverdale for Brinny's graduation party. The usual old crowd from Aunt Emily to Julius was in attendance. Brinny was very tired and stressed between graduation, preparing to move to Virginia, where Tim had been called as Rector of his own church, and being four months pregnant. She was just beginning to show her rounded condition, and I was jealous. I told myself at least I'm married now. And I'm still young—only two or three more years. The party was fueled by the usual alcoholic consumption. I saw Wendy for the first time since I had moved to Italy. She had grown up too, wearing a tailored suit and shirt, and eyeglasses which hung around her neck on a chain when they were not balanced on Wendy's little freckled nose. We hugged each other like long lost sisters. "Ciao Wendy. It's so great to see you. You just graduated too, n'est-ce pas?"

"How many languages do you use in one sentence, Lili? Yeah I graduated, and I see you are married," said Wendy, moving her glasses to her eyes the better to scrutinize me.

"Antonio's over there with Alexandra," I said, "See my ring?"

Wendy kept looking at me evaluating, "You look happy…. How is your work going?"

"Honestly, I wish I were studying psych right now. I'm kind of burned out on Romance languages," I said.

"Really? I majored in psych. I got interested when I recovered from my depression. I've learned a lot about myself—and the family. I'm applying to graduate school in psych," Wendy said.

"Do you know what caused your depression?" I asked.

"They say depression is 'overdetermined.' That means there are lots of reasons. For starters, it is not easy to be gay in this society." I nodded in agreement. She said, " Then my parents taught me not to feel much. I am trying to learn to allow myself feelings," said Wendy.

"What feelings?" I asked.

"All of them: anger, fear, sadness, happiness, love, sex, envy—you name it."

"But you were in love, Wendy—even before I was," I said.

"Yeah, that was the good part of my life. You met Jessica, didn't you, two years ago at your farewell party? She's my soul mate. She got me into therapy when I was down. She's the redhead over there talking to Phil Cohen. He flirts with everybody, doesn't he?"

"Phil's a great guy, but he hasn't figured out women yet. What happened between him and Cindy?"

"She said Phil was preoccupied with his career. You know he and Julius are cooking something up."

"Phil is very creative… I understand your interest in psychology—people are so complicated to understand. Speaking of psychology, could I ask you a very personal question, Wendy?"

"We're still cousins. Sure, ask away."

I wasn't sure I should ask even my cousin this delicate question, but I continued to worry about Antonio at times. I lowered by voice,

"When you were depressed, did you ever consider suicide?"

Wendy removed her glasses and thought a minute. "I wanted to die in a way, but I wanted it to happen to me. I never actually considered killing myself. I don't think I'm brave enough—or violent enough... Why do you ask?"

"I worry because Antonio had a problem with depression too. I'm just trying to learn as much as I can."

Six months later, just before Christmas we received the news that Brinny and Tim were the parents of a healthy daughter, Louisa Grace. I longed to see and hold the child and to kiss my sister. They asked me and Wendy to be the godmothers and postponed the Baptism until our next visit the following spring.

During the next two years Rome became home to me. The fat butcher around the corner; the flower vendor in her widow's black dress, black stockings and shoes; the street smelling of baking bread and garlic in oil; the stunning fashionable women in a hurry to their rendezvous; the incessant whistles and calls of men in appreciation of feminine allure.

Professore Passacantando's house was a hospitable oasis. After Anne Lawrence left, he took a new graduate student in medieval studies, a stuffy English cleric named James Worthington. He and Stefano got on famously. They always wanted to talk about the Papacy, or the Albigensean Heresy. Salvatore and I favored topics like Jungian Archetypes and the symbolism in Fellini movies. The good professor was a fair moderator and drew generalizations from our different viewpoints. He kept me on track when it would have been easy for me to quit.

Antonio and I stopped using birth control in the spring. I submitted my thesis in March, 1968, and took the oral examinations in April. The Spanish examiner was a kindly encouraging old scholar. The Italian inquisitor was Jesuit from the house where Salvatore and Stefano lived. He was exacting but reasonable. The French woman examiner was a bitch, the kind of woman who gives academia a bad reputation She was interested in all the minutia and none of the important things. I think what finally made her decide to pass me was that I knew by heart so much old French poetry— from Chretien de Troyes to Francois Villon—and could recite verses to her, which she enjoyed.

When my thesis was accepted in May, Antonio and I drove to Porto Ercole to the inn where we had stayed on our first trip to Italy. We ate dinner on the patio outside by the sea listening to the waves and to the combo playing American music inside the inn. Antonio was proud and pleased—he toasted my success with a glass of champagne and said, "Doctoressa Grace Francesco, let's dance." We smiled the intimate look, which we both understood. He put both arms around me on the dark patio, where the air was like sweet peppers mixed with seasalt, his hands flat against my back pressing our bodies together as we swayed hardly moving, in the starlight sparkling on the surface of the sea. Our cheeks lightly touching each other creating a warmer space from which to sense the other's movement. I was grateful and blissfully happy. Now we were free to build our life together—our family. I wanted to keep that moonlit hour forever.

But reality was brutal. Less than a week later, less than three years after we were married, I received the terrible call and phoned Salvatore to drive me to the hospital. I was taken to a room, where my husband's body—bruised but not bloody— appeared to be sleeping. He had been driving alone from a medical conference on a rainy night. I don't know what shadows followed his car around the curves on the autostrada. I'll never know what his thoughts were. Was his mind preoccupied by medical affairs? Was he humming an aria? Was he thinking of me? Two hours outside of Rome a truck slammed into his Ferrari. He was killed instantly.

I took his head in my hands. Incredulous, I touched his limp curls, and kissed his eyes, his beard and his neck. I examined his body like a new mother examines her infant child, checking the hands and feet, his ears, his beloved forehead. I wanted to lie down next to him and hold him—to keep him warm. I wanted to wake him up. I spoke to him quietly, "Antonio mio, your bad dream is over. Please wake up." His skin was beginning to feel cool. "No,

God. Please. No." I couldn't believe it. I couldn't walk away. Salvatore had to hold me up physically because I kept collapsing as we tried to go back to the car.

At that time I did not really know how I could live at all, except hour by hour. My parents and Brinny wanted me to come back to the United States, but I could not leave our home. I begged Mama to come to Rome for me, but she could not leave Rex and the boys.

With my husband's bereft parents and sister, I buried his body at the family cemetery at their country villa. Officially, the funeral mass should not have been said in the Catholic Church because of our marriage, but the Francescos used their influence. Alexandra and Phil came to represent our family. The service is a blur in my mind. Whole months are a blur. The earth had been removed from under my feet. I was twenty-five. Antonio had been thirty -seven. I found that I could not bear to say his name.

I started wearing a black wool dress from that day forward because it helped me express the emptiness. Every day I put on the same long-sleeved, high neck dress. I didn't care if I was hot or cold—whether I ate or drank. I lost fifteen pounds. I was no longer the same person. I was no longer Carina or Angelina. I didn't even feel like Lili. I felt as if I had been run over by a truck. Complicating my grief was the thought, the fear, the suspicion, that this accident was intentional. Did he leave me willingly? I searched the three years of our married life for clues. When I could manage to talk coherently, after about five months, I washed my face, pulled a comb through my hair and went to Dr. Belsanti with my questions. He greeted me, "Signora, I am deeply sorry for your loss—a terrible loss to us all."

"Grazie, Dottore," I said. "I have come to you with two specific questions. I don't know whether or not you can answer them. My first question is: Do you think my husband could have run into the truck intentionally?"

"Signora, how I would like to help you. No one knows the answer to your question. We know about his problem. Yet accidents do happen—especially auto accidents on our roads. They are very treacherous," said the doctor, "I can tell you that your anger at him is normal, whether he left by accident or on purpose."

I began crying, "You have no idea how young I was when I met him. He became almost everything to me. I'm afraid I can't live any more. I used to say I had three emotional safety valves: dancing, music and God. Without Antonio dancing is out of the question. Music makes me sadder. And I am pissed as hell at God."

"This is an excruciating time, Signora. I would be pleased to extend a professional courtesy to the widow of Dr. Francesco, if you want to come talk to me each week. It could help you with your question," said Belsanti.

I managed to stop crying, "I would like that, Dottore. My other question is, why am I unable to say my husband's name? I cannot choke it out."

"Signora, you need to talk. I have an opening Thursday mornings. You can start this week."

And so I began to visit Dr. Belsanti once a week. I looked forward to this hour. I imagined my husband sitting where I sat. I dreamed at night that we were still together and awoke to my pain over and over again. I went to church with my husband's parents almost every day. Their grief seemed to be as raw as mine. It was a bond between us.

When I visited Santa Maria in Trastevere in those days, I went to the third chapel on the right, Our Lady of the Sorrows, who kept me company in my grief. Many months would pass before I could speak to God. Salvatore was a gentle friend, calling daily to check on me, joining me for coffee, listening, encouraging me to go outside for sunlight and fresh air. If Dr. Belsanti played the role of my ideal father, Salvatore was my mother.

As I told my story to Dr. Belsanti, he encouraged me to write, bringing my husband back to life in my imagination, reliving all the moments, especially his touch and his presence next to me. Writing our story was a way to grieve. Dr. Belsanti suggested that I needed to grieve also over the loss of my ideal of my father. Since my father was still living, I had never dreamed of mourning for him. Yet my first love, the father of my young childhood, was gone, as surely as my husband was gone. My many childhood expectations of my father, which were not realized, needed to be acknowledged and released. I was surprised that I felt so much sadness and anger about my father and realized that my attachment to Antonio had drawn intensity from powerful disappointments.

The wise doctor thought that I must also grieve for the loss of my future with Antonio: the rest of our story that will never be—and his children. I imagined our unborn children and even named them—two boys and two girls. Over and over again I explored the same problem:

"What continues to depress me is I don't know how to move on. I'm only twenty-five years old, and I may have to be a widow the rest of my life."

"Have you considered that eventually, even the happiest matches become accustomed to each other and may discover areas of dissonance and dissatisfaction. You might have grown in different ways."

"I know, he might have lost his hair, or become more depressed. I just wish we had the chance to experience all that—even if the passion eventually diminished."

After two years of visiting with Dr. Belsanti, and writing my stories, both the real one and my preferred ending, I was preparing to end my therapy. I had gone over everything dozens of times. I still had one important question unanswered which I posed to Belsanti, "Why can I write my husband's name in this fantasy of our future, but I cannot say his name in normal conversation—even after two years and five months."

"Signora, I have another writing exercise for you. Perhaps if you write a letter to your husband…and don't censor your feelings. Perhaps you will find his name again. Write a letter to Dr. Francesco."

I went home and sat down to my assignment. To my utter surprise I wrote:

Antonio, you bastard. How much pain have I suffered.

You left me childless—homeless —sometimes godless because I couldn't even pray. I am not like Isolde who died to be with Tristan. I do not take my own life. I am crushed, broken, but I live and I will live.

But I miss you, my love, my husband, my angel. I am happy only in my imagination when I remember our time together. I have written it all down. I read it over and over.

People are saying I will recover and even remarry. They are wrong. No, Antonio, I will never marry again like this. I hope I will recover. There will never be another Antonio in my life.

I don't believe you left me on purpose.

I don't know where you are.

I don't have a sense of your presence—you were so physical to me.

You are gone, except for my story.

I shall always love you.

Your wife, Grace Long Francesco.

I brought my letter to Dr. Belsanti the following week. He read it, "Good, Signora, good," he said, "You are going to get through it now."

A poem by Victor Hugo helped me begin to pray again: "A Villequiers" was written in 1847 after the drowning death of Hugo's sixteen-year old daughter. The poet addressed God as he "came out of the grief that had darkened his soul, and he sensed the peace of nature enter his heart..."

"Fields, forest, rocks, valleys, silver rivers
Seeing my smallness and seeing your miracles.
I come to you Lord, father in whom one must believe
I bring you, pacified, the pieces of this heart all full of
     your glory,
Which you have broken..."

Hugo's tone was both sincerely humble and bitterly hurt. Every time I read the many verses, they helped me cry. I needed no help in crying for Antonio, but I needed help to cry the tears of reconciliation with God.

I asked Salvatore to read the poem. He said, "It is a great protest to God—a form of prayer."

"God has been distant to me, Salvatore, but you have been right here with me. You may have saved my life."

CHAPTER TWENTY

RONDEAU DE LA MORT

Deux etions et n'avions qu'un seul coeur;
S'il est mort, force est devie
Voire, ou que je vive sans vie
Comme les images, par coeur,
Mort?

We were two who had only one heart;
If he is dead, strength is gone with him
You see, how I live without life
By the pictures, by heart,
Dead?

XVeme Siecle, Francois Villon

With Antonio's death, my first life was over, but I survived like the vacated cocoon of a moth who flew away. I stayed in our house in Trastevere, near the steps to the park. In spite of myself, I kept looking for him in every crowd. When I'd see a man his height and build, my heart beat wildly, although my mind knew it was not Antonio. I wondered if I would ever stop searching.

I visited the United States twice to see my family and enjoyed seeing my niece and god-daughter, Louisa Grace, grow from an infant into a lovely little girl. I began to recover my sense of humor. I didn't go to the opera. It pissed me off. I didn't even listen to beautiful music because it broke my heart to think Antonio was missing it. I did go to church.

During those years when I was in deepest mourning, Wendy became a full-fledged psychologist and set up a practice in Boston. Professor Penham became the dean of the faculty at Columbia. He offered me a teaching post, which I was seriously considering. Phil moved from TV to Broadway, producing plays with cousin Julius. He widened his business interests to include media such as radio stations, newspapers and even advertising. Phil was becoming a rich man. Alexandra visited me several times in Rome, as she was doing research at the Vatican Museum and the Museo Nationale in Naples. Every time she saw me, she must have told my parents that I looked terrible, because following her visits, they always tried to get me to come back to the States. Professore Passacantando retired. Salvatore, who was teaching Latin at the University, became my closet companion.

Annamaria remained an enigma to me. Her reserved manner outside the family circle caused people to think she was arrogant. In the family she was warm, yet somehow unreal to me. She could never have been Brinny or Wendy to me. I think she was most comfortable with her brother, at least when they were not in a battle. He teased her and joked with her. Perhaps she was more lonely than anyone else.

Brinny, Tim and little Louisa visited me to help me pass the fourth anniversary of Antonio's death. Louisa resembled Tim's side of the family more than ours. She had his pale complexion, beautiful dark eyes with thick eyelashes. I enjoyed showing them my city: the parks and fountains, the ancient ruins, the churches and cafes. I took them to the Francescos' villa in the county where Louisa rode a pony. The Francescos spoiled her with tears in their eyes. It was hard to be with Antonio's parents because their grief was so raw. Yet I couldn't abandon them. They still needed me as the link.

Brinny didn't say much to me. She hugged me and let me be, which was best. When we were at the villa, Tim asked if he could pay respects at Antonio's grave, so I took them out among the pine trees to the stone. Tim knelt down to pray, and I asked him to pray for me. As we rested there in the bright Italian sun, our knees scratched by the tough grasses, I reached out for Brinny's hand, and little Louisa took my other hand. Tim said the prayer for those who mourn,

"…not sorrowing as those without hope but in thankful remembrance of your great goodness."

Grateful tears fell from my eyes. Little Louisa said, "Aunt Lili, why are you crying?"

"I have been sad, Louisa, for a long time, because your Uncle Antonio died. But I am crying now because I am happy you and your Mommy and Daddy are here. And I have made a decision. How would you and your Mommy like to go shopping with me? I am getting tired of wearing a black dress. I think I need some new dresses. Maybe one with stars on it. Do you want to go?"

Brinny embraced me. We walked slowly off the hill back to the villa for tea.

INTERLUDE

Comme vous etes loin, paradis parfume,
Ou sous un clair azur tout n'est qu'amour et joie,
Ou tout ce que l'on aime est digne d'etre aime,
Ou dans la volupte pure le coeur se noie!
Comme vous etes loin, paradis parfume!

Mais le vert paradis des amours enfantines,
Les courses, les chansons, les baisers, les bouquets,
Les violons vibrant derriere les collines,
Avec les brocs de vin, le soir, dans les bosquets,
     Mais le vert paradis des amours enfantines,

L'innocent paradis plein de plaisirs furtifs,
Est'il deja plus loin que l'Inde et que la Chine
Peut-on le rappeler avec des cris plaintifs,
Et l'animer encor d'une voix argentine,
L'innocent paradis plain de plaisirs furtifs?

        Charles Baudelaire
        "Moesta et errabunda"
        from *Les Fleurs du Mal*

LASTING

How distant you are, fragrant paradise
Where under sky blue all is love and joy
Where all we love is worthy of love
Where the heart drowns in pure sensuality.
How distant you are, fragrant paradise!

But the green paradise of childlike loves,
The chase, the songs, the kisses, the bouquets,
Violins vibrating behind the hills
With casks of wine, in the evening, in the woods.
But the green paradise of childlike loves,

Innocent paradise, full of secret joys.
Is it already more distant than India or China?
Can we remember with begging cries,
And animate again with a silver voice
The innocent paradise, full of secret joys?

Translation by Suzanne Love Harris

CHAPTER TWENTY-ONE
MAY, 1972

I decided to accept Professor Penham's offer to teach a survey course in French Literature at Columbia, not because I wanted to teach or to leave Italy but because something had to change. It had been four years since I'd lost Antonio. I was only alive, not living. Everyone, including our psychiatrists, encouraged me to take a job and start meeting new people. Once I had been a person of energy, but I couldn't seem to ignite myself without Antonio. I began to talk to my husband in heaven. I imagined his voice telling me, "It's okay, carina mia. I am in a different world now. You must live, my angel. We can't touch each other any more, so you must touch someone else. It's okay, Lili mia."

Saying good-bye to my Roman friends and to Antonio's family was difficult, but they seemed relieved to see me reaching out. They didn't know how little heart I had for it. I asked Annamaria to help me buy some elegant suits and dresses, like the ones she and her mother wore, so I could start my new life in a style and dignity that would honor Antonio. I was still Signora Antonio Francesco. I had a doctorate I had never used. I felt like a wounded bird.

Salvatore and I took a walk in the Villa Sciarra Gardens on a hot August morning the week before I left. We walked very slowly seeking the shady places as the inevitable sun mounted higher and hotter above us. Only young children moved quickly around the garden. Some humming insect was buzzing in the trees. Salvatore was clutching a book to his chest and seemed to be hiding behind his sunglasses. I said, "I'm going to miss talking to you. You've been my best friend, as well as pastor through a nightmare."

"And I will miss you, Lili. I'm sure you will be all right. I wish I

could go with you, but you have to meet new people. I'll be await-
ing your return." Salvatore delivered his pep talk as if he were re-
minding himself what was reasonable. He looked up into the cloud-
less blue sky, "I wonder what God is doing in your life now."

"I wish I knew. I'd like to see a beam of light or some sign that
I'm doing the right thing."

Salvatore pointed to a flickering grey dove eating crumbs around
a park bench, "That pigeon over there can be a sign. Anything you
take as one is a sign."

"Do **you** think I am doing the right thing?" I asked.

Salvatore stopped and looked at me, "Yes, Lili, though...
personally, I don't want you to go...Yes, I do think it is right."

Salvatore was always a proper priest with me, so I asked his permission, "May I kiss you good-bye?"

He blushed easily. "Yes, of course."

I was sad, so maybe I hugged him a little too long as I kissed
him on the cheek. I said, "You have my address. Please write."

Phil and Alexandra met me at JFK International Airport. I had
asked Phil to find me an apartment on the East side of Manhattan,
in the neighborhood where Antonio lived before we moved to Europe. I wanted it to be cheerful with plenty of light, and with a new
kitchen and at least two guest rooms for my sister and her family.
Antonio left me a generous income, so I didn't worry about the expense. Phil made a great choice. It was a corner apartment on the
tenth floor with four bedrooms, a living room with fireplace, dining
room and library/office. The sunshine filled the kitchen and living
room windows in the morning. The doorman was Italian, like
Antonio's doorman on Third Avenue. When he learned I was teaching at Columbia, he called me Dottoressa, which pleased me.

Phil, Alexandra, and I went out to dinner that first night at a
Lexington Avenue bistro and looked back on the past. Alexandra's
hair was going grey, but she looked more elegant than ever, wearing
chunky gold earrings and a heavy gold bracelet. She asked, "How
does it feel to be back in New York?"

"It reminds me of happier days," I said. "I think I'll be fine.

There's an energy and freshness here. Thanks, both of you, for all your help in getting the apartment and the basics."

Alexandra said, "I'm living on East 57th Street now, so we are practically neighbors, but you know I am never home. We'll have to plan a 'coming out' party for you, Signora."

"I wonder what I'm coming out of," I said.

"You are coming out of mourning, I hope. It's been a very long time," Alexandra said. "We've been worried about you. You know, in Italy some women never take off those black dresses."

"I'll never get over it," I said. "I just have to learn to move on anyway."

Phil had grown up a lot since the days when he greeted the world like a puppy with its tongue hanging out. He said, "Take it slowly, Lili. You're still hurting."

"Thanks, Phil," I felt a catch in my throat. "You've been so good. I love the apartment. I'm lucky to have such wonderful friends."

Alexandra had a plan. "I think we should have a big party after Thanksgiving at the Tavern. Julius and Phil know an interesting theater crowd. I'll invite art and academia—and of course, the family."

"That sounds like good timing," I said. "I need a few months to get settled in my new job."

Professor Penham sat behind his wide desk in his dean's office surrounded by bookshelves and big windows overlooking the Columbia Campus. I hadn't seen him in person since Antonio's crash, although he had written to me and to Antonio's parents. He got up from behind the desk to embrace me, "Grace, I'm so glad you've come. Please sit down. How are you?"

"I'm okay, Professor. It's hard to see people I haven't seen since my loss. But I know I have to go to work."

"You are scheduled for two sections of French 201. Andre Beaulieu is head of the French department now. If you want to teach other courses eventually, you can arrange it with him. We may need an instructor in Intermediate Italian spring semester. Do you know Beaulieu?"

"No, can you believe it's been eight years since I was here? There are probably a lot of people I don't know," I said.

"There's a faculty reception Wednesday at the President's house. Do you want us to accompany you?"

"I'll meet you there. I have to get used to being an independent woman."

I invited my parents and youngest brother, Peter, to my place for dinner. I hoped they would like the apartment, which was turning out to be quite comfortable and chic. I planned a soft silk wallpaper in the living room and shopped for antique tables and mirrors. I kept flowers on my table—next to the photograph of Antonio smiling in the sunshine of the Alps. I barely knew my little brother and he barely knew me. Peter was ten years old when I moved out. I enjoyed cooking for the family, treating them to some of the good Italian dishes I had learned to prepare, but they never stayed very long. My father felt uncomfortable everywhere except his own home, so they left after an hour and a half. Whereas Rex had once been a giant in my life, he had become a shadow.

Walking in the park that October, watching the gold and red leaves gather on the wet grass, breathing the familiar humid air of the North American oak forest, my sad feelings connected to the season. I saw that the leaves, soon to decay, were part of the familiar cycle. I was glad winter would be the next season, the cold, darker, quieter season. Autumn, Advent, winter suited me.

Phil invited me to dinner every week. He had let his hair grow longer and bought his suits at Brooks Brothers. At thirty-five he was enjoying fantastic success as a producer in TV, radio and the Broadway theater. He was recognized all over New York and had developed an authoritative sense of himself. Incredibly, my old friend Phil was a presence. The maitre d'hotel of the fashionable east side restaurant made a fuss over us. It was fun to share Phil's success, but more important to me was to be with an old friend to whom I didn't have to explain my life. He seemed much more solicitous of my needs than I remembered, "I thought we'd just have a quiet dinner tonight. Anytime you feel like it, Lili, we can go to the theater or the opera."

"I haven't been to the opera in four years. It's too emotional. Dinner is just great, Phil. Tell me about your life."

As we drank a dry Chateau Neuf du Pape in the quilted private booth of the lowly lit restaurant, Phil told me about himself. "I'm enjoying my life. Julius and I have a partnership that works. He is the creative genius, and I work the contracts, raise the money and oversee the details. When I was in TV, right after graduate school, I saw how they managed this business. I said to myself, 'I can do that,' and I can. I'm doing well financially, Lili. You'll have to see my apartment. Can you believe I've got a penthouse?"

Phil's surprise at his success was endearing. "You sound satisfied. I imagine it's an exciting world," I said.

"It's okay. It keeps my juices running. I have to watch my ego. A lot of guys in my business get arrogant."

"I don't think you have to worry about that. Anyway, Julius has enough ego for two. How about your love life, Phil? I'm surprised you're still single."

He teased me, "You know I loved only you, Lili. And you have been more than occupied. But I do have a friend, Alicia. She is a singer who works for us sometimes. I have a hard time sorting out who is real and who is trying to get something out of me. But I think she's a good kid... You remember your English friend, Anne Lawrence?" I nodded yes. "She wanted to use me. She's an ambitious bitch. My parents are always bugging me to settle down and get married. My brother, Howard, got married four years ago. He has two children already. But I hate to settle. I have too many options. Maybe I'm not the marrying kind."

"So you are an uncle?" I smiled inside and said aloud, "Uncle Phil and Aunt Lili. Do you think we'll ever be parents?"

"You make it sound as though we could do that together." Phil looked at me with question marks in his eyes.

I blushed and shook my head. "Phil, I'm no way ready to talk like that."

"Sorry. I don't mean to crowd you... Forgive me?"

"It's okay, Phil. I'm still sort of fragile. I don't know if I'll ever change."

For the faculty reception at the President's house I wore one of my new Italian designer suits: a thin black and white silk stripe with a pink silk blouse. I had cut my long hair into a short Twiggy style and wore gold hoop earrings. We were given name tags at the door: "Dr. Grace Long Francesco, Instructor, Romance Languages." The President of the University, making his obligatory greeting to the faculty members as we arrived, looked at my name tag, "Grace Long Francesco, aren't you related to Alexandra Long?"

"She's my cousin," I answered.

"I see a resemblance," he looked me up and down. "I remember now, Dean Penham has been courting you for several years. You've been in Europe?"

"Yes, I've been living in Rome until recently. Dean Penham has been my mentor since undergraduate years." I heard the words coming out of my mouth, but there was some dissonance or alienation between my words and my heart. I didn't feel real. I felt an irritable mood rising in me. I was not ready for chit-chat. I couldn't explain myself so facilely.

I began to float around the reception, looking for a non-alcoholic drink, and was happy to see Professor Penham and his wife across the room. I traced my way over to them and saw they were talking to a tall, professional person, whom he introduced to me immediately. "Grace I want you to meet Andre, your department chair—he just arrived from Paris."

Andre Beaulieu looked about forty years old. Graying hair, bookish with typical European wire-rimmed glasses, and very French pointed shoes. He preferred to speak French, which for some reason annoyed me. I was on edge. He said, "Enchante, Mademoiselle."

I corrected him lifting my wedding ring, "Madame."

"I beg your pardon, Madame. But you look so young. Is Monsieur here?" he looked around.

Having to explain my tragedy to strangers is just what I dreaded.

I began to feel tears of confusion and anger fill my eyes when Professor Penham took the responsibility and changed the conversation back to English, "Andre, Grace's husband passed away four years ago. I thought I had told you about her. Grace arrived from Rome just ten days ago."

"Oh yes, excuse me, signora, I remember now. Of course. I am sorry. I guess life goes on, n'est-ce pas?"

I wanted to kill him. His glib manner infuriated me. What could he know about life going on? What could he know about me? How dare he talk to me about anything? For Professor Penham's sake, I remained barely polite. "I hope teaching will help me build a new life."

Beaulieu said, "If you need any help acclimatizing yourself to New York, I'd be pleased to help. I know the French restaurants and quiet corners."

I was undoubtedly rude, but I couldn't bear his presumption of intimacy with me. "I was born in New York, so I am quite acclimatized. I only want to work. Excuse me, please." As I walked away, heading for the front door, I almost crashed into Alexandra. "Lili, what's your hurry?"

"I'm sorry. I practically ran you down." I lowered my voice, "I'm escaping from my department head—Beaulieu."

"Oh, he's harmless," said Alexandra. "A little pompous, but you'll get used to him."

"I'm not sure of that. I usually like everyone, but I took an instant dislike to him. Is he married or single?"

"He's been married several times. I think he's not at the moment," said Alexandra.

"What are you doing here, anyway?" I asked my cousin.

"I'm invited as a graduate who published this past year. I really don't have time to teach any more. I've been touring all the museums with my book speaking about their vases. Last month I covered the Archeologico in Florence, the Vatican, the Louvre, and the Antikensammlung. But I am planning your party."

"I don't know, Alex, I'm really not enjoying this party. I think I'll go home and read a good book. I'll call you tomorrow."

I went home and telephoned Brinny in Virginia.

"I just came from a horrible faculty reception. I hate those parties. At least I love my apartment. It already feels like home. When can you come visit? I have three guest rooms."

"Lili, we may need them. I have good news. We're having another baby—in March."

My sister's good news had a complicated effect on my emotions. Her first child, Louisa Grace, was one of the people in my life who still engaged my whole heart, and I knew they wanted another child. Yet their good news reminded me I was childless. Antonio was a man who should have been a father.

"Lili, can you come to Virginia for Thanksgiving?" asked Brinny. "It's hard for Tim to leave the church this time of year."

"Sure, I'd love to. I'll borrow Phil's car," I said.

"Or invite Phil to come too. I'll call and invite him. It's better for two to drive. And I'd love to see him."

"Phil and I are getting along pretty well. He's grown up a lot. I guess we've both mellowed."

The first week of classes I received a letter from Salvatore:

Ciao Lili: How is New York City? I have never been to America, but I imagine it very fast and imposing. Are there any gardens near you? Of course, you have friends and family there, so you won't be lonely. I am a little lonely. We are all brothers here in our house, but brothers are different from a woman friend. My confessor said it is good for me to be more alone. Sometimes really I wonder why. What is the harm of a human attachment?

I am teaching classical Latin this year. How do you like teaching French literature? Rome is cooling off—delightful now. I saw Professor Passacantando who sends his best regards to you.

Your faithful friend, Salvatore.

Chapter Twenty-Two

My students were the best distraction. They were young. Some were eager. Some were intelligent. After midterms, when the department evaluated new faculty, Andre Beaulieu asked me to his office for the interview. His desk was neatly arranged, but he kept moving pens and the inkwell around and dusting the leather surface with the side of his hand. He insisted on speaking French, of course. "Madame," he was careful to address me as a married woman this time, "how do you feel your classes are progressing?" He picked up a pen and opened a file.

"Assez bien. Of course, it is a survey course. Yet I think they got a sense of the classic theater before midterm break."

Andre sat back in his chair and smiled, "Ah, the classics. Which of the classic playwrights do you personally prefer?" he asked.

I laughed. "You remind me, when I was at the lycee in France, people always asked me who was my favorite French poet. It is a question few Americans teenagers would ask or could answer. Most of my American friends didn't know enough poets to have a favorite... I like Moliere of the classic dramatists, but the seventeenth century is not my favorite period of French literature, to tell the truth."

"May I ask who **is** your favorite French poet?" asked Beaulieu.

"Francois Villon will always be number one, but I also love Baudelaire, Rimbeau, and Paul Verlaine. Victor Hugo wrote some great ones. They are the most powerful for me," I answered.

Andre closed the file and practically threw it into a basket behind him, "Ah, the nineteenth century! How would you like to design a course next year of nineteenth century poetry? I find instructors teach best when the create their own courses."

It was a wonderful offer. I didn't expect such an opportunity so early, yet I wasn't sure I was ready. I said, "Could you give me a little time to think about it. I know people think that after four and a half years I should be back to normal, but I'm just slowly picking up my life. It is easy for me to teach the survey course or an elementary language course, but developing a new course would require a lot of concentration and energy. Could you give me another month to see how much energy I have?"

Beaulieu looked suddenly deflated. I guess he expected me to jump at the chance. Perhaps I should have. He looked around him for the security of my file to mark. After writing something in the file, he spoke, "All right, Madame, please let me know in a month. We have deadlines you know." I stood and left.

I called Dean Penham who encouraged me to accept the new French course. In the meantime, I asked Penham if I could also teach something in the Italian department for spring semester. I didn't want to have all my eggs in Beaulieu's basket.

Phil was pleased to drive to Brinny's for Thanksgiving. He picked me up on Wednesday in his white Lincoln Continental. I couldn't help commenting, as I eased my back into the soft grey upholstery, "What a glamorous car. We have certainly come up in the world."

"Only the best," he opened the door for me. Driving down the New Jersey Turnpike we listened to fifties music on the radio. I felt almost normal, that is, happy. I thought of Antonio with pleasure and love, but without pain for the first time. "What are you smiling about?" Phil asked.

"I think I made the right choice to come back this year. Did Brinny tell you they are expecting a baby in March?"

"Brinny and Tim are certainly doing the whole traditional thing— house in the country, two kids. They probably even have a dog— just like my brother," said Phil.

"Someday I'd like to do the traditional thing, if I'm not too old. I've lost a lot of years. But I wouldn't trade anything for Antonio."

"Are you thinking of dating?" asked Phil.

"I really can't imagine it. I mean I can't imagine a sexual relationship. I still feel attached. But I don't know how I'm ever going to have the house and kids. It's just going to take more time."

After several minutes of silence, keeping his eyes on the road, Phil said, "Lili, when you are ready to date, remember I'm here. I told you'd I'd be a good husband. And I've learned a lot since the old days."

I put my hand on Phil's shoulder. He was a very attractive man and I loved Phil. "Phil, you think we'd be happy, but we might not be. You deserve better than what I have left now. I don't really know what I want... But I don't want to hurt you."

Louisa Grace was sitting on the front steps of their white clapboard colonial house watching the brown leaves fall to the grass and waiting for us. She jumped up and down when she saw the New York car pull in. "Aunt Lili, Uncle Phil." She was excited as a cricket. I enjoyed bringing her gifts—usually art books or art supplies when I came to visit from Italy. This time I brought her a soft stuffed bear dressed in a granny dress with a bonnet. Phil had gifts too: cheeses from New York, French brandy, and chocolates. We ate the Thanksgiving eve dinner of tomato soup and sandwiches in their country dining room and caught up on all the news around the dining table. I asked Brinny if I could help with anything.

"Yeah, you can stuff and cook the turkey. Raw meat gives me morning sickness," she laughed.

"That's great. Louisa and I will make the stuffing. I'll give you roast turkey a la Romana. You'll love it."

We had a wonderful Thanksgiving—my first in eight years. Brinny, Tim, Louisa, Phil and I felt like one happy family. I thought of Antonio again and missed him, but again without pain. I knew he would want me to be happy.

I began attending the Episcopal Church again in Advent at the Cathedral of St. John the Divine near Columbia. The lovely Advent hymns and scriptures with the message of waiting expressed my own state of mind. They incorporated hope without denying sadness:

O come, O come, Emmanuel
And ransom captive Israel
Who mourns in lonely exile here
Until the son of God appear.

Rejoice, Rejoice, Emmanuel shall come to thee, O Israel.

Disperse the gloomy clouds of night
And death's dark shadow, put to flight

Rejoice, Rejoice, Emmanuel shall come to thee O Israel.

The spring semester started the end of January. I was teaching the continuation of the two sections of French 201, and a section in the School of General Studies, the night school, of Intermediate Italian. The class list for Italian 103 contained an Italian name, Franco Domenico. The first night I wrote my name on the blackboard and asked the students to introduce themselves in Italian. "Lei, come si chiama?" Franco introduced himself as Frank Domenico, a Vietnam veteran from Long Island. He looked in his late twenties— tall, big-boned, and dark, with powerful shoulders, arms and back. I figured his ancestors came from Calabria, Compania, or even Sicilia. He did not look aristocratic like Antonio. But Frank had an intelligent broad forehead, strong jaw and dark eyes that watched me all evening. When the students were leaving, I nodded good-bye and noticed that Frank managed to walk with a macho swagger in spite of a pronounced limp in his left leg.

Language classes met three times a week from 7 to 8:30 p.m. The twelve older students in the night class worked hard and seemed motivated to learn. Frank had the best facility for speaking, in his low slightly gravel voice, although he needed help in his written work, in both Italian and English. His family spoke Italian at home, but he had refused to learn as a youngster.

It was frigid and dreary in New York on March 18, which would have been Antonio's forty-second birthday. I remembered his thirtieth birthday party in New York when we danced together for the first time. I must have looked depressed, because after class Frank came to my desk to ask, "Can I talk... I mean, May I talk with you, Professor?"

"Sure, sit down, Franco. I'm in no hurry to go home," I said.

He seemed both confident and shy, "I've been wondering something about you. Your name sounds Italian. You speak Italian the best I ever heard, but you don't look Italian."

I smiled, "My husband was Italian. I lived in Italy for eight years. I speak Italian well only because I studied—like you."

"I hope you don't mind me speaking to you like this, but I've been noticing you—especially tonight—how sad you sometimes are—and worried—and I wondered if you want to go out with me for coffee or a drink."

I thought a minute. I didn't know of any rule against it. I said, "Why not. This is a special day for me. It might do me good. I didn't realize my feelings were so apparent in class."

Frank said, "Maybe the others don't notice, but I recognize these things. I am wounded too. You probably noticed my leg."

"Yes. Were you wounded in Vietnam?"

"I lost my leg—amputated above the knee. But I gained a lot too. Do you wanna go talk—down to Marty's?"

I was touched, and interested in hearing his story. I packed my books, put on my coat and hat. Walking down the stairs, he apologized for taking two steps on every stair. We walked around the corner in the cold pouring rain to Marty's Tavern, where we found a quiet booth in the back. Frank seemed to know the bartender and the regulars. He ordered two draft beers from the bar, brought them to our table, sat down and lit up a cigarette. Frank's voice was low— a baritone, not a bass. "Do I have to call you Professor or do you have another name?" he asked looking pleased.

"I'm not a professor, you know, just an instructor," I said. "Tonight you can call me Lili."

"Good, I like that...Lili." Our eyes made contact, then Frank asked, " You said it's a special day for you, Lili. What makes it special?" He sat still as a statue and focused on me like an eagle over prey. But I didn't feel threatened or invaded.

I took a drink of beer and returned his gaze, "Today is my husband's birthday. Antonio died when he was thirty-seven years old. He would be forty-two today..."

Frank silently nodded and took a drag on the cigarette. "How did he die?"

"A car crash. He loved to drive fast. He was hit by a truck and killed instantly... As you noticed, I am still recovering. We were... It's hard to explain how we were." Words seemed inadequate to convey my love for Antonio, but Frank seemed like a good listener.

"Life can change very suddenly," said Frank and inhaled deeply on his Lucky Strike.

"I guess you've seen a lot."

"It's also hard to explain, so I don't..." He extinguished the butt in an ashtray. "But I'm a different person—attracted to different things than I was...Like you...Your sadness for your husband... I wouldn't have seen that before—or been drawn to it."

"He was a wonderful man, a doctor. We were very happy."

"Any kids?" he asked.

"Sadly no. That would have helped, I think."

We both allowed a silence to rest between us, then I looked up and smiled, "I am much better since I came back here actually. I do feel alive again. For a long time I was barely living."

"He died in '68?" asked Frank.

"Yes, May 15, 1968. We almost made our third anniversary. Now the anniversary of his crash is the hardest day for me to get through."

Frank said, "I was hit the spring of '68. Maybe the universe is working something out here. I keep my mind open to any possibility now."

I didn't have the faintest idea what he was talking about, but I went back to my own question, "Did you grieve a long time too?"

"Did I grieve a long time?" He was finishing the beer and adjusting himself in the booth. "Every time I stand to walk or want to dance or go to the beach I grieve. I sometimes grieve when I see myself walk. That can't be me. But it is. As you saw." Frank shook his head in what could have been disgust or only regret. "I'm frustrated when I go up and down stairs—so much slower than I want. I hate showing this to a pretty woman. I'm probably going to grieve until I die, but not all the time. I saw guys get worse than me. I have friends who are living their lives in VA hospitals." He looked pained to remember them, then he lifted his big open hands as if to announce a blessing, "But I'm alive. I can walk." He touched his head, " My head is clear. I learned how to focus my mind in meditation. I came out a lot stronger mentally. The saddest casualties are the head cases. I had to change, but the change made me better. That's why I said, 'I have gained a lot.' I can deal with my grief," he put his hand on his left leg, " my stump, my prosthesis. Sometimes other people have trouble dealing with me, like my Dad and my brothers. Dad still tears up around me. But that's his need to grieve."

"You have brothers?"

"I have two younger brothers, 24 and 17…Rocco and Gino. They are both hotshots like I was. Full of piss and sh… I won't say it… Excuse my language. I lift weights so they still can't beat me up. We were all tough guys."

"You still look pretty tough to me." I teased. "Even if you **are** in college. How did you decide to come to Columbia?

"I worked with a shrink at the rehab hospital, who helped me a lot. He suggested I go back to college. I did well on the tests, so they told me to come here. If I knew the professors were so pretty, I would've studied in high school." Frank cracked a smile and seemed to be trying to read me. His voice dropped very low and he said quietly, "Lili…I don't dare take your hand with your beautiful wedding ring. I might be accused of trying to influence the professor—or, I mean the instructor. Maybe when the semester is over…in May…when you have that anniversary to face, I'll take your hand."

He put his big hands under the table. "One thing I learned in rehab is patience."

I stood up and looked at Frank, "Thank you, Franco. Grazie. I'm so grateful you asked me to talk tonight. I sometimes forget that other people have losses too."

"May I take you home? I have a car down the road," he asked.

"Thanks. If it's not out of your way. It'll be hard to get a cab in the rain."

On the way home I asked Frank about his academic major. "Psych," he said. "I have two semesters after summer school to finish with undergraduate. Professor Kleinberg, my advisor, thinks I could get into a graduate school—clinical psych they call it. I think I'd be a good shrink. I have these intuitions about people."

CHAPTER TWENTY-THREE

Spring came in late March. Already there were green things pushing through the mud and fat buds on trees and shrubs, leafing out in pale green promises. Brinny gave birth to a son, Anton Timothy. First I cried because my sister named her boy after Antonio, then called Phil to see if he wanted to go to Virginia with me. Phil managed to break away the next day, so we arrived two days after Anton was born.

Brinny looked radiant, if tired, holding little Anton. He was tiny and perfect. I enjoyed helping Brinny and Tim with meals, laundry and giving attention to seven-year-old Louisa. Phil and Louisa worked under my direction in the kitchen. We made Brinny's favorites: home-made minestrone, chicken pot pie, roast leg of lamb and baked rice pudding with raisins. It was fun to feel like a family again.

The last night after the tired new parents had gone to bed, Phil and I sat by the fire. I said to Phil, "Hasn't this been a wonderful week?"

"You and I make a mean pair in the kitchen, Lili."

Watching the flame move and reform itself I thought out loud, "Phil, would you give up the fast track in New York and stay down here to live a simple life…if you could?"

Phil didn't hesitate, "No, I honestly don't think I could. I love my work. I've gone too far. I like the pace and power. That isn't to say that I wouldn't like a family—but in the city with private schools and a summer home. How about you?"

"I don't really know what my future holds. I'll go back to Rome this summer for the sake of the Francescos. Sometimes I feel I've been too self-absorbed… One of my students lost his leg in Vietnam. He doesn't seem to pity himself. How did you manage to escape being drafted?"

"I was just a little too old," said Phil. "I was lucky. I've been lucky in everything but one thing."

"You mean me?"

He nodded. I said, "Phil, you could have so many women. You're intelligent, successful, and good-looking. You overestimate me, which is flattering. But haven't I always encouraged you to find a girl? Especially now. Whoever loves me has to cope with Antonio too."

"You don't have to tell me that. You underestimate me. I've been coping with Antonio since I met you."

The next morning as Brinny was contentedly nursing Anton, I told her about Frank Domenico. She said, "I don't know where you find such dramatic men. If you really want a normal life, you have to choose a normal man like Tim or Phil."

"I like Phil as much as you do, Brinny. He's one of my best friends. But it's never been romantic. I love Phil, but not that way."

Brinny said, "I worry about you. I don't think you're a great judge of stability."

"It isn't going to be easy for me to fall for anyone, Brinny. Antonio is a hard act to follow, especially because he died."

Once I accepted his offer to teach the poetry class, Andre Beaulieu acted as though we were best friends when I saw him on campus. He often greeted me in Italian, "Buon giorno, Professoressa."

I still answered, "Hi Andre," but I had to give him credit for giving me the opportunity to design a course and for renewing my contract for the next year. I enjoyed teaching both literature and language and realized I was more a teacher than a scholar. Towards the end of the semester, he stopped me in front of the book store to ask me what I was doing over the summer.

"I'm going back to Rome to spend time with my Italian family.

I'll also be working on my course," I said.

Andre said, "I"ll be working on a book in Paris, but I intend to go to Rome to visit friends. May I call you there?"

"I'll give you my number. It is the home of my husband's family."

"I understand they are high society in Rome," said Andre.

"Antonio wouldn't put it that way. They are lovely traditional people."

Andre was about to say something more and thought better of it. I was glad that he hurried off. His pretentiousness irritated me, but I wanted to be diplomatic as he was technically my boss.

Since our meeting over coffee, Frank had not made any effort to speak to me privately, but he smiled each night after class as he nodded good-bye and occasionally even winked at me, as if we shared a secret. I found myself enjoying this unobtrusive, if presumptuous, intimacy.

At the final exam of Italian 103, Frank gave me a note: "May I invite you to dinner this Friday. It is May 15. I haven't forgotten." F.D.

I wrote on the note and passed it back to him: "Grazie, Franco. Yes, you are kind to remember." G.L.F.

Phil remembered the date too. He called me on Wednesday to ask me out Friday. I thanked him for remembering but told him I was going out with a student. He was upset, "A guy? Who is he? Since when did you start dating? On **that** day?"

"Calm down, Phil. What's got into you? I am a grown woman and I know what day it is, believe me."

He slammed down the phone. I felt guilty. Not about going out with Frank, but about Phil. I leaned on him a lot. I knew he carried a torch for me, but I had never made him any promises. I decided to wait for him to cool down.

Frank and I met in the Village at a neighborhood Italian restaurant owned by friends of his family. He held a black leather jacket on one shoulder over a white open-necked shirt. His dark wavy hair curled over his handsome neck under the starched collar. With his confident-shy smile Frank asked, "May I call you Lili again tonight?"

I touched his arm and said, "Please, no more Professor. It makes me feel so old. How old are you?"

"Twenty-eight in years, but very old in wisdom," he was relaxing. I sensed that we had shifted gears out of the teacher-student relationship.

I said, "I'm thirty—almost thirty-one. I wish I were older in wisdom."

"You have a Ph.D. You must know a lot," said Frank.

"Frank, the Ph.D. doesn't mean that much, but yes, I have learned a lot about Romance languages. But you know that is not the same as wisdom. I'd like to have what you said you have: intuition about people."

Frank introduced me to Al and Marie Lombardi, the owners of the restaurant. They embraced him and kept patting him on the back, calling him a 'hero.' Frank told them it was a special evening, ordered wine, and indicated a table outside in the back garden, where potted azaleas were blooming on the patio, hurricane lamps flickered on the tables, and strings of white Christmas lights draped overhead on an acacia tree. We could hear the accordion playing Neapolitan songs inside the restaurant. I was a sucker for Neapolitan songs. After decanting the wine and lighting up, Frank took his glass and hesitantly offered a toast, "To Antonio."

I appreciated his priority and touched his glass in agreement. "To Antonio." Then I heard myself add, "And to the future."

Frank picked up my cue, "Lili, do you want me to tell you your future?"

"Can you do that?" I took his bait, enjoying the idea that we were beginning to flirt. But he was not exactly flirting. Frank's powerful body and focused presence made him seem rooted like an old oak—much older than his years—and unsettlingly serious.

I felt the intense focus of his dark eyes, as he said, "I told you I have strong intuitions about people." He was speaking very slowly and deliberately. "I see a strength in you, Lili, that you haven't developed yet. You could be happy again. I think you can be healed. And I think you'll be a wonderful mother to your children."

I reached over to touch his hand. "Frank, please don't do this yet. Give me a little more time."

"Lili, you can have all the time you want. I know you'll need to bring your husband with you when you come to me."

Annoyed at his overconfidence, I raised my eyes to look at this man who was speaking to me so impertinently of my husband. I met Frank's eyes, as deep and dark as a river at night, and felt his big hand lift my hand gently to his cheek, which felt rough and stubbly. He turned his face to kiss the palm of my hand. I felt my anger melting away, and my heart beginning to hurt, but my throat tightened when I tried to speak. I almost choked. "Frank, I can't talk like this. Can we take a walk."

"I didn't mean to upset you..."

"I'm fine. I just need to walk around."

As we left the restaurant, Frank signaled the Lombardis that we'd be back, and then we walked side by side in the narrow old streets for many blocks. My heart felt as if had contracted, trying to protect itself from feeling. My mind was confused. My whole body was responding after so many years of drought. Finally, I started to cry and took Frank's hand, "Frank...you are opening me up again, and I am afraid. I am scared to death. I was eighteen when I fell in love with Antonio. I am...I need time... But I don't want you to go." I started to laugh through my tears. "I'm afraid of you, Frank. I'm afraid of my way of loving...I don't know."

He said, "Lili, you are afraid of getting hurt again... I don't want to upset you. Can I hold you?" he asked.

"Yes, yes, for pity's sake," I was laughing and crying.

Frank stepped closer and put his arms around me and held me in the curve of his massive torso. I felt his artificial leg for the first time and cried and cried—for myself because I was coming alive, and for Antonio because he was dead, and for Frank because he was brave and hurt, and for all human losses: for Phil and Salvatore, Uncle Ed, Wendy, my father and mother and the Francescos. When I finally stopped sobbing and wiping the tears on his shirt and my hands, I said, "You must think I'm a mess."

He said gently, "I knew all those tears were in you, Lili. I don't call that a mess."

He took my hand, and we walked back to the restaurant. Completely drained, I looked at him and said, "What are we going to do?"

"First let's have some supper. Then I think we ought to get to know each other better... Then I think we should get married."

"You're crazy," I said suddenly laughing. "How did you get so sure of yourself?"

"Lili, I can't explain it. I just know some things."

"But I have to go to Italy this summer," I said, remembering who I was and where I was going.

"That's good. You do need to go back. Lili, you don't have to worry so much. Remember, I told you the universe taught me patience. I'll be here when you get back. I'm going to summer school."

We had a little dinner. I told him about my family, the Francescos, and Antonio's hospitalization. He told me how he played football in high school and won an athletic scholarship to Penn State, then dropped out to join the Special Forces, the Green Berets. After supper I invited him to see my apartment.

When we walked in, Frank looked around without saying anything. I wondered if he could appreciate my taste, or if he might be put off by my silks and antiques. I said, "I'll make some tea or coffee. What would you like?"

He said, "Just sit down with me. Here next to me. I want to hold you, Lili. Are you okay now?"

I sat on the sofa next to Frank. I felt small next to his strong frame. He put his arm around me and just patted my shoulder and said softly, in an intimate voice that transformed the crudeness of his language, "I'm not gonna f...I mean, I'm not gonna try to...you know, Lili? I've got my own fears. We have to be slow and careful. I feel Antonio all around here." He picked up my photo of Antonio in the Alps from the coffee table and studied it. "Maybe you have to go back to Italy and make peace with him about this. He was a doctor, right?... Was he rich?"

I sat back and looked at Frank, discussing my life on my sofa and said, half amused and half angry, "You are the most impertinent, audacious, crazy man... You don't have to clean up your language around me. My father used all the four-letter words in the book daily, and I'm hard to shock. And, just because I invited you here, doesn't mean you can assume that I **would**....you know."

Frank was trying to suppress a knowing smile as I continued, "Yes, Antonio was a wealthy man—and very classy. His family is wealthy. He left me enough money to live pretty well. It was one of his ways of taking care of me."

Frank said, "I saw the beautiful wedding ring—and this apartment...I couldn't afford anything like this." He looked around again, then looked at me. "Of course, he would be classy.... I guess I've been, as you said, impertinent. You can teach me about class. You're pretty classy yourself."

"You, Frank Domenico, are in a class by yourself."

That night I lay awake, confused and very happy, wondering how I would explain Frank Domenico to my family and friends.

The next morning, Frank called and asked me to come to his ground floor studio on Amsterdam Avenue. The apartment was neat and clean—almost military, with a kitchen area, a double bed made up with a navy blue bedspread, a stereo, his weights and a chinning bar across the entrance door, a plaid sofa and several wooden chairs, a bookshelf filled with textbooks and a desk neatly cleared. On one wall he'd hung a poster of a snowy mountain range in the clouds. The other wall held a scroll with Chinese calligraphy. There was a pistol in a holster on a hook by the door. He saw me look at it and said, "It's legal."

A photo on the bookcase showed Frank in his special forces uniform standing with what I assumed was his family. I could almost smell the swagger of the soldier dressed in his high paratrooper boots, shoulder ribbons and beret. I picked up the photo and met Frank's dark eyes. He said, "That was before I got hurt."

I looked at the picture again and at Frank. "Classy," I said.

Frank half smiled, "I used to have a way with women. Do you want coffee, Lili?"

"Let me fix it." I headed toward kitchen area.

"No, Professor. Lesson number one in being with an amputee is don't baby me. I can make coffee. When I want help, I'll let you know, okay?"

He limped over to make coffee. I asked, "Do you use the prosthesis all the time?"

"No, baby, but without it, I can't walk except with crutches. I don't bathe or sleep with it, but I'm not ready for you to see that yet. That's lesson number nine, I think. To tell the truth I haven't let a woman see it, except the nurses and physical therapist. We have to take our time."

I sat thinking while Frank made coffee. How could I ever fit into his life? How could he fit into mine? We were so different. He was so different from Antonio. What would his disability mean in the future? I thought he was right about going slower emotionally. Maybe it was good that I had to go to Italy.

Frank interrupted my reverie, "What are you thinking, Lili?"

"I'm wondering about you. You told me my future. How do you picture your future?" I said.

Handing me my coffee, Frank sat down on the sofa. "Lili, when I was twenty-three years old, I was blown away. If I had stayed on drugs and let myself be defeated, I could be in the gutter today. Right now I have a positive outlook. I'll finish school and go to graduate school. I'm hoping for a normal life: no more big adventures. I want children and ordinary kinds of happiness, like my parents. I expect and need lots of miracles to pull my life off." He stroked my hair and continued in a softer voice, "I'm praying you are one of the miracles. There's something healing about you, angel. Maybe that's it. You're an angel the universe sent to me." He leaned over and kissed me lightly on the lips.

I felt that choking tightness again in my throat and lungs. "God, Frank, you grab me in a deep place." I took his big hand and put my cheek next to it and tried to breath more evenly. Frank's body felt peaceful and strong to me.

"Lili, angel, I have a good feeling about us."

We spent the whole morning talking. He explained why he didn't want to have sex yet. "I don't want you to have any guilt or regrets about your husband. And I guess I don't want you to be half-way with me. I want you to be in love with me first, so that any difficulties we have with my leg won't turn you away. I don't want you to compare me to that classy guy. You have to know who I am first. I don't want to worry. You need to know that about me."

At noon we went out for a donut and coffee at Chock full'o Nuts on Broadway and walked in Riverside Park. The wind was blowing up the Hudson into little whitecaps. I said, "You know I'm supposed to go to Italy in June for two months. You have summer school, but could you come when it's over—around the middle of August? You could practice your Italian."

He laughed, "No, I can't afford it, baby, and you're not going to pay for me. I can wait for you. Maybe we'll get married when you get back."

"Did I say I'd marry you, Frank?" I was still laughing at his audacity.

He smiled a cagey smile, "No, you didn't, but I know you will. Didn't I tell you I know things."

Phil called me late that afternoon and apologized for hanging up on me. "You know, I don't want to be a big brother, but I guess I was jealous. Who is he?"

"A student from my Italian class. Frank Domenico is his name."

"Don't tell me he's Italian."

"He's American, but yes, Italian-American."

"Lili, did he know what day yesterday was?" asked Phil.

"Yes, that's why he asked me out. Phil, you're going to have to meet Frank. I guess he's…"

Phil interrupted, "You're not in love with him already. How long have you known him?"

This was difficult. I didn't really know what I felt for Frank, and Phil was jumping to conclusions as well as annoying me by being so possessive. Yet I cared for Phil's feelings and opinion and didn't want to hurt him. "I told you he is a student. He was in my Italian class. I've known him since January. I'll be spending time with Frank, so you're going to have to meet him."

Phil groaned, "I can't believe this. **I have to meet him?** Like

you're introducing your old uncle to your new lover or something."
He was getting mad again.

"Phil, we are not lovers… Just cool down. You have no right to
be so jealous," I said.

His voice sounded quieter, "Right or not, I am jealous and in-
dignant too. You, a doctor of literature, widow of a distinguished
medical researcher, are flirting around with a guinea night student.
How old is he?" asked Phil.

"Phil, you are not my inquisitor. I'll tell you about Frank, but
not when you use that tone of voice. You **do** sound like my old
uncle!"

Silence on the other end. Finally Phil said, "Are you going to
Italy next month?"

"Yes, of course, I am," I said.

"Is he going?"

"No, I plan to be in Italy two months with the Francescos."

"I think I'll come in July to meet Annamaria, as you once suggested."

"That's a great idea. You can stay as our guest at the Francescos'
house—but only for a week. We can't impose," I said.

"I'll stay at the Hassler as long as I want. You can arrange some
activities."

"Thanks Phil. Now cool down. Okay?"

CHAPTER TWENTY-FOUR

One fresh spring night Frank and I were walking in Riverside Park, looking at the moon glitter on the Hudson River. The new leaves on the trees still smelled green. The sound of the breeze in the trees mingled with the traffic murmuring below on the highway. Frank noticed something in the sky, "Lili, see the stars tonight?"

I looked up and drank in the sparkling firmament. "Isn't it strange, Frank, that sometimes we look at the stars, without really seeing them. But other nights—like tonight—they surprise us—almost break your heart. Like we are seeing them for the first time."

Frank deliberately took my hand, "People too, Lili. So many men stop seeing their wives. They became part of the furniture. But it doesn't have to be like that. We can work at staying conscious of what we love."

I put my arm through his elbow, feeling the hard muscles of his upper arm, looking up at his raven black hair, walked closer to him, and said, "I know Antonio will never come back to the earth… You are helping me a lot, Frank. You are interested in hearing about it, and you don't rush me."

Frank kept looking at the dark heavens and said, "I've learned to trust the Universe." Then he looked in my eyes, as if he were about to kiss me, but he just put his hand to my cheek and looked away as if talking to himself, "I have to trust the Universe," patting my hand, as if I were his best friend.

The only thing Frank didn't talk about was Vietnam, but he explained, "When I came out of rehab to Columbia, the undergraduates were demonstrating against the war. I tried talking to them but they can't understand what it's like. No civilian can. The guys who

were there are the only people I can talk to. I've discovered I have
the choice of being completely frustrated and angry over and over,
or of giving up and becoming calmer and peaceful—and slow...
Every day I try to choose peace over anger... But some days I fail..."

I decided to introduce Frank to my family. For my thirty- first
birthday, my parents had invited Brinny, Tim, and the children up
from Virginia, and Wendy and Jessica, who arrived both dressed in
jeans and flight jackets. I didn't make a big deal about introducing
Frank, just asked them to set an extra place at the table. Frank
picked me up in his Chevy Caprice—a gift from his parents when
he came home from the war. I had given him an expensive Italian
cotton shirt and silk tie printed with stylized nasturtiums, hoping
he would wear it. He got the hint and looked gorgeous, but somehow silly in the elegant clothes—not in character. I realized how
foolish I was to try to remake him into Antonio. I loosened his tie
and told him he looked great.

Peter, my youngest brother, at first monopolized Frank to ask
him about the Green Berets. I was shocked when Peter asked Frank,
"Did you kill anybody?" I hadn't dared to ask such a question.

Frank answered Peter in a gentle voice, "Yes, I did. That's what
soldiers have to do." Mama pulled Peter aside to hush him. I thought
about the gun Frank kept in the apartment and meant to ask him
about it later.

I was so happy to see Brinny, Tim, Louisa and Anton and to introduce the children to Frank. Holding Anton, I told Frank, "He's
named after Antonio. I wish you could have known him." Then I
laughed, "Actually that could be quite inconvenient."

After dinner, as I washed the dishes and Wendy dried, she commented, "Lili, it's great to hear you laugh in the same breath as remembering Antonio. It's a good sign."

"Wendy, I'm feeling so much better." I handed her a dinner plate,
"How are you and Jessica?"

"She's starting her own printing business. My practice is growing. I learn more every day. Each client teaches me something new.
I really help some of them."

I loved Wendy since we were children. She seemed to have grown more serious in adulthood—maybe too serious. I wondered if her profession increased her sadness or helped it. "Wendy, would you answer a question as a psychologist?"

"No charge."

"How does Frank seem to you? Brinny and Phil mistrust my judgment. I am very taken by him. He awakens all my feelings, but I'm also terrified."

Wendy answered, "I can't give you an opinion about Frank. I'd have to talk to him in more depth. But your terror makes a lot of sense to me. In your experience, to love is to lose. Remember, that does not have to happen. At least not until old age."

It was easy to discuss my concerns with Wendy, who knew me so well and didn't offer opinions about how to manage my life. I continued, "He did use drugs and won't talk about Vietnam. He's so different from Antonio in almost every way. Antonio was older than me; Frank is younger. Antonio was more educated than I am; Frank is less. Antonio was wealthy; Frank is not. Antonio was such a great dancer and athlete; Frank can't dance because of his leg. Antonio and I both loved classical music; Frank likes acid rock. Antonio was a little fragile mentally. He had a tenuous hold on life really; Frank is rooted like an oak—very sure of himself—except for one thing..." I stopped washing and looked at the watery suds slip down the crystal wineglass. "Antonio and I had sex all the time. We were always falling into sex. Frank and I haven't made love— not even necking. And it's not because I don't want to. He wants to wait. "

Wendy took the wineglass from my hand and started to dry it, "That doesn't sound like a **bad** sign. Lili, it can't hurt to take it slow and trust your own judgment. You were right about Antonio in the long run. You opposed your parents and his parents, and you aren't sorry. Trust yourself. Frank looks like a real guy to me, except for the tie. Where did he find that corny tie?"

I blushed, laughed, and admitted, "Yours truly gave him the tie. What's wrong with nasturtiums?" We giggled like girls.

While we were washing the dishes, Frank was conversing with Tim and Brinny. I only heard the end of what Frank was saying when I walked over to them in the living room. " ...marry your sister."

"Frank, what are you telling them?" I couldn't believe he would talk like that to my family.

"I'm just telling Tim and Brenda how the Universe is compensating you and me for our losses by bringing us together."

I took Frank's arm and told Briny and Tim, "This man is crazy, but I can't resist him."

Brinny laughed, "Frank, you have met your match. My sister has had a dramatic life already at only thirty-one. She has a talent for it. Tim and I prefer a quiet life. You should come down and visit us—any time, with or without Lili. Maybe when she's in Italy or when Lili gets back at the end of August."

I was pleased that Frank got along well with my family. My parents respected his military service, unlike some Americans who blamed the military for our national anguish in those late Vietnam years. Everyone was relieved that I was regaining my natural energy and was obviously enjoying this new relationship. The more difficult introductions lay ahead: Phil, Professor Penham, Alexandra and the Francescos.

I saw the tough, even violent side, of Frank's nature, one night during summer session at Marty's Bar when one of the regulars, also a veteran, Joe Chavez, after drinking too much, put his hand on me and started to say how much better I'd like him than Frank. I did wish Frank was paying attention to me instead of the Mets game, so I got up and walked over to where Frank was sitting at the bar. I whispered, "Frank, Joe is bothering me. He's had too much to drink."

The energy that I felt from Frank's body was frightening as he pushed his bar chair away, walked over to Joe, grabbed his collar roughly and muttered something under his breath, then dragged him to the door and threw him out in the street. He came back and said, "Don't ever talk to him again, baby. I don't want to worry." I was surprised that I liked this toughness. Later I asked Frank why he kept the pistol in his room.

"Only for protection. I wish there were no punks in the world, but they are out there. They have guns, and I can't run as fast as I used to…" I guess I looked scared. "Don't worry, Lili. I am learning how to help, not hurt. But I'd be a fool not to be able to protect myself."

As I was digesting my interest in a man like Frank, I received a letter from Salvatore, the gentlest man I had ever known:

> Dear Lili, Spring is arriving in Rome, but I feel no peace in my heart. We have had an unsettling winter in our house. The Church is changing so fast. Until now the changes in the Church since Vatican II have seemed very positive to me: mass in the vernacular, increased freedom from superstitious rules for laity and religious orders, increased power in the people, increased dialogue with other denominations and faiths, Pope John's great encyclical of peace, *Pacem in Terris*. But now the changes are unsettling our house. Seven brothers have left the Society for secular life. Three of them are marrying. It feels like seven abandonments. You, who have suffered so recently, may understand that I am grieving myself now. It makes us all question our life.
>
> I made my final vows sixteen years ago when I was twenty years old. Now I am doubting so much and wondering how I could have been sure when I was young. You remember that I was not completely comfortable with the all male world of our order, although I so greatly admire the Society's courageous and noble history, I am even wondering whether our monastic way of living is God's will for me. It would be hard for a lay person to understand what loss this is. Perhaps it is something like a divorce, when you still love the spouse.
>
> My friend, I don't yet know what I am going to do. I would love to walk in the garden with you and discuss these matters. You have an earthy point of view which I miss. Perhaps when you return, you will help shed light

on my darkness. Keep us in your prayers.

Faithfully, Salvatore.

The weekend before I went to Rome, Frank invited me to meet his family in Forest Hills, Long Island. We parked in the driveway of a small two-story house in a predominantly Italian neighborhood. The flower beds that lined the brick walk had been cared for by a diligent and loving hand. The Domenicos opened the front door before we reached the steps, and greeted us warmly with hugs for Frank and welcome for me. When Frank told them I was his Italian professor. His father reacted, "A professor is so young? And she doesn't look Italian?" He addressed me in Italian, "Professoressa, are you from the North?"

"No, no signore, signora, I am American from Riverdale. I lived in Italy for eight years when I was studying. My husband was Italian from Rome," I answered.

Mrs. Domenico asked, "You are divorced?"

"No, I am a widow. I thought Frank would have told you."

"Frankie?" Frank's mother raised her eyes to heaven. "We never know what Frank will do. But he is a good boy. I am sorry about your husband. Forgive me for asking. Frank never brought a lady here before."

I looked at Frank who appeared slightly pained. His father called upstairs, "Gino, your brother's here. Come down and meet the professor." Gino, a younger and slighter version of his brother, bounded down the stairs and threw his arms roughly around Frank. Frank teased, "Take it easy, Gino. You're gonna knock me off my foot." They laughed and boxed each other. Frank asked, "Where's Rocco?"

"He's working. He'll be home later tonight," Mr. Dominico said, then looking at me, he explained, "He's a cop."

Mr. and Mrs. Domenico asked me about my family and work. When they brought out Frank's war decorations: campaign ribbons for two tours in Vietnam, two purple hearts, a bronze star and a silver star, Frank went into the kitchen and came out saying, "Let's put the war away and talk about something else."

Mr. Domenico said, " Okay, okay." He whispered to me, "Frank doesn't like to tell us about the war, but his friends told us he was a hero." Then raising his voice to normal volume, he said, "Frank is learning good Italian, no? Better than we speak here, no?"

"He's an excellent student. He was the best in the class," I agreed.

Suddenly Mr. Domenico began to turn red and his eyes brimmed with tears. He left the room. "Mi dispiace, signora." Mrs. Domenico excused herself and followed him. Gino, mortified, left by the front door. Frank grinned, "Well, we cleared the room. I told you, sometimes they can't cope. They'll be back in a few minutes."

"I like them, Frank. Your family loves you so much."

"They are impressed with you, Dottoressa. Who would have thought Frank Domenico would bring home such a classy chick?" he patted me in his brotherly way.

After about five minutes the parents returned apologizing. Frank called Gino back and we all sat down for soup and homemade raviolis, which were delicious. Frank asked Gino about his college applications. Gino obviously idolized his brother and was following Frank's lead to college. Frank said, " There's no reason why a tough guy can't also be a smart guy," knocking Gino in the head.

The day I was cleaning out my desk to leave for the summer, Dean Penham peered around my office door, asking if I had a minute.

"For you, Professor, always." I was happy to see him.

He sat down, making himself comfortable amidst the mess and said, "I'm glad you accepted Beaulieu's offer to teach the nineteenth century poets. He's no fool, and he can help you. He appreciates quality."

"I may see him in Rome. I gave him our phone number."

"I understand Phil Cohen is planning to visit you in Rome too. He called me and asked if I knew anything about your new man friend. He's worried about you."

I was pissed at Phil. "Phil is worried about himself. He was just as meddlesome when I was dating Antonio. He had no business calling you about me."

"He's known you a long time and claims to be looking after your interest. I know better than to interfere in such matters. It sounds as though you will have a busy summer over there. I hope you have time for your work."

"I always have. I've finished my work under much worse circumstances than this. You know that."

"I trust you, Grace. Just remember you are young, attractive, wealthy and emotionally vulnerable. Take your time," said my dear mentor rising to leave.

"Thank you. I won't do anything rash. I'll keep my head, I promise."

Although he wouldn't admit it, Frank was anxious about my leaving for Italy. In spite of his bravado and his hard won emotional strength, he wasn't sure he could hold me. And I wasn't entirely sure either. Because he didn't want to have sex, we had not even kissed passionately. I was afraid the relationship might die of starvation.

On the eve of my departure we sat on the couch at his place listening to a Bruce Springsteen tape. Frank was smoking Lucky Strikes and brooding. I gave him my address in Italy. He took it saying, "I'm not going to write you, baby. You have to do what you have to do. And I'll have to take it. If you make peace with Antonio and his family, you'll find me right here in this room when you come back. Just come knock on my door. I'm not going anywhere." He stroked my hair.

I looked at his face and saw all the sadness he was usually able to overcome. I wanted desperately to hold him and reassure him. "Frank, please kiss me properly, not like a brother. I want to know that part of you before I go."

Frank pulled me over onto his lap, a sad, wild look in his eyes, and put his open mouth on mine, kissing me with the intensity of a hungry wolf. I felt his penis like steel under me in his trousers. Then he let go, pushed me off his body, turned his face away and struggled to his feet. I was so confused. I really didn't understand why he resisted our physical involvement. He began pacing the room. "Frank, do you think I'm not coming back?"

"Lili, I don't know what's going to happen. Anything can happen, baby, believe me. Can't you feel how much I want you? It's killing me. But I don't want you just for tonight. I want you in my life. I have to play my cards right. You have to do what you have to do first. It'll drive me crazy if I kiss you again." He looked out his window into the dark street.

"Lili, there's power in our sexual feelings, and I want to conserve that power for good—to reinforce our promises to each other. We need that power to heal us, so I'm not willing to squander it. You need to be ready for it, baby. We're just gonna have to wait."

"I hate to leave you like this. I'm so unhappy," I said.

"Did you think you would enjoy going? This is life, Lili. I hope you come back. If you do, I promise you I'll kiss you right, and we'll fu…." Frank's eyes filled up, but his voice didn't crack, "God, Lili, I want to… And we'll have babies. I promise you everything… When you come back…" He sat down and held me quietly for a long time. I was frustrated physically and miserably muddled mentally. I wanted to stay and to run away. Stroking my hair gently he said, "I'll miss you, angel. You have no idea how much I'll miss you."

I sat in his arms feeling his strong chest breathing well into the night. Then, since it was late, he wouldn't let me go home alone, so we dozed until the sun rose at 5 a.m. I rushed home to pack and leave for Rome.

CHAPTER TWENTY-FIVE

I arrived in Rome the next day exhausted. Annamaria met me at the airport. Her resemblance to Antonio revived my feelings of grief, which were intensified when I saw the streets and piazzas Antonio and I had strolled together. In the Francescos' paneled library I brought out photos of my New York apartment and of Brinny's family—especially Louisa and baby Anton. Signora asked, "Perhaps you will bring your sister and her family with you next time? There is nothing like a baby to heal the heart?" She tried to wipe a tear from her cheek inconspicuously, but her pain evoked my own. When the Francescos showed me to the big bed I had often shared with Antonio, I felt myself slipping backwards into depression and decided to call Dr. Belsanti in the morning.

I told the doctor about the ten months in New York: my pleasure in teaching and in my new home, about Brinny and Tim's new baby, about Phil, Beaulieu, and my feelings for Frank. He commented, "The important part comes out last. Why don't you see me for the weeks while you are here, Signora." I gratefully scheduled a weekly appointment. In addition, I went back to Santa Maria in Trastevere to pray for guidance. I decided I had to write Frank a short letter:

> Dear Frank: I know you are not going to write to me, but I have to write you at least this once. Leaving you in New York was much harder than I had expected. So is coming back to Rome. I have decided to work with the psychiatrist who helped me through the early stages of my mourning. He was also Antonio's doctor. You were

right. I have work to do here. I haven't forgotten what you promised me. I think of you working in summer school. I wish I were there too.

Love, Lili.

Salvatore's voice on the telephone had a beneficial effect on my mood, although he sounded different. Not the cheerful, peaceful monk I had known, but another anxious human being. We met at our usual cafe in Trastevere on a pleasantly hot afternoon. The owner of the cafe recognized and greeted me, but he did not recognize Salvatore. Salvatore had changed both outwardly and inwardly in one year. Instead of his black shirt and Roman priest's collar, he was wearing a light blue shirt, striped tie and summer jacket. He still wore his large silver cross around his neck. He had grown a full black beard. Salvatore embraced me, "Lili, you look wonderful. New York agrees with you."

"You look so different," I said. I was shocked actually. "What have you done?"

"Yes, I'm a civilian now. I left the Society of Jesus six weeks ago. It probably seems sudden to you, but it is not really. I didn't burden you with my thoughts when I was your pastor. It has been a long struggle and a long time coming. I lost my job. The post is for a priest, so I am working at the Santa Clara Hospital as a social worker. The Society gave me good preparation for earning a living. I am adjusting now, but the decision was difficult."

I didn't know what to ask him next. I had to reorient my whole relationship to him. "Well, what is it like for you?" I asked.

"Strange, really. It is strange for me to feel freer… Good too. More whole. Less like a eunuch."

"I feel that in you too Salvatore. It may complicate our friendship," I said, teasing; but he was serious.

"Such a complication would be my fantasy come true, of course," said Salvatore.

I couldn't believe it. After five years of loneliness and emptiness, my life was becoming as entangled as a soap opera. I had to simplify. I took a deep breath and said, "Please, my dear friend, I am very happy for you. And you know I care for you and am grateful for all your care for me... But I don't need another suitor. I am all twisted up now. Can't we remain friends? I'll try to be as good a listener as you are. And I won't tease you. I am sorry about that."

Salvatore looked only slightly crestfallen. "Sure, Lili, I knew you would say that. My fantasy was presumptuous. I'm new at this. Forgive me?" he asked.

"There is nothing to forgive. Actually it's refreshing to be with you. You are so kind and easy. The other male relationships in my life are raw and painful right now."

He asked me to tell him about the relationships, and he listened to me once again like a pastor. His only comment was, "Love is complicated, no?" I invited Salvatore to come to the Francescos' for Sunday dinner, and he gladly accepted.

For the next three weeks I tried not to think, except at Belsanti's office. Dr. Belsanti thought that my awakened sexual interest in Frank was a good thing. I had trouble explaining to him and to myself the intensity of Frank's effect on me. "Frank is a good-looking man, very macho, but that was never my type. Big athletic men like my father used to scare me. Antonio was my ideal man: elegant, intellectual and sophisticated. Could it be because of five years of deprivation and Frank's playing hard-to-get sexually that I feel like this?"

"I don't think it's simply sexual hunger, there have been other men around you. From what you have told me, his withholding the full sexual relationship has not been particularly positive for you." The doctor was pensive. "Tell me more about his injury."

"He lost his left leg five years ago in a booby trap in Vietnam. It is amputated above the knee, so he walks with a prosthesis. He lives with his loss every day...like me. But he achieved what seems to me a pretty heroic adjustment. He works at keeping his spirits up. He doesn't let it defeat him. I admire his courage and strength of mind. I think part of me needs his strength."

"What part of you?"

"You know, the sad part. I admire his come-back ability. I need it."

"His handicap became a strength?"

"Mental strength, of course, is what I mean... And he said he could see strength in me which I haven't developed. I'd like to start my life again as a stronger person somehow... also, I think Frank's handicap brings out my protective feelings. I have always had a soft spot for people who are lame, or blind." I began to feel tears rising. "I don't want him to hurt any more."

"You yourself probably don't want to hurt anymore either."

"I don't seem to have a choice. At least Frank understands it."

"Yes, that is important." The doctor let me sit in silence before asking, "What are you feeling?"

"It is very frightening to love again. If I hadn't met Frank—if he hadn't grabbed me so, I think I could be happy married to Phil. We're such good friends. I know Phil is reliable and competent, and we have more in common. I want to have children. I want to have the family Antonio and I planned to have."

"You can never have the family you planned with Dr. Francesco, Signora. If you remarry, it will not be his family." His voice was kind and firm.

Tears returned to my tired eyes. "I know, I know. I'm still pretty mixed up. I don't know how I'll ever forget him."

"You don't have to forget him. You know that. But you may need to feel that he releases you. I think you are doing very well. Let time do its work, Signora."

We went to the country each weekend, where I sat near Antonio's grave and wandered around the hills. When Salvatore came along, he often chatted with Annamaria. They both worked with poor families and were devout Catholics. I was happy to see him growing and changing. We went to mass on Sundays, and I prayed a lot.

In mid-July Phil arrived in Rome and phoned from the Hassler. His voice was softer when he asked how I was doing.

"Better, but I'm still upset with you, Phil. I don't like your talking to Professor Penham about me and God knows who else as if I were a retarded, naive girl. You know he's my boss as well as a friend. You make me sound like an incompetent."

"Let's have lunch," said Phil. "I have some information you need to know."

"I'm going to the doctor's office tomorrow at four. I'll meet you at the Hassler at one."

As Phil's business empire increased, his personal bearing changed. He had formed a sort of holding company to merge all his media interests. He was thinner than he'd ever been, tan, confident. I could hardly remember the awkward chubby graduate student who used to hang around my desk. When I walked into the elegant foyer of the Hassler, he was talking on a phone with a glass of wine in front of him. He motioned me to come over and sit down while he finished his business conversation. Phil looked very much in charge. As he asked the captain to seat us at the best table, he was in great spirits too. "Lili, you look fantastic. What may I order you to drink?" We sat down to a delightful bottle of champagne and toasted Rome. When he thought I was relaxed, he said, "I've come to propose something to you."

"You said you were coming to meet Annamaria."

"I know, I'm going to meet her, aren't I? But first I have to tell you my plan." He put down his champagne glass and faced me intently. "You asked me last spring if I could give up my life in New York and settle down to a family life in the country. I wasn't thinking straight when I answered. And you didn't know either. I think you were sounding me out and I blew it—big time. I can't believe it. I'd been waiting thirteen years for the perfect moment, and I blew it.... Now you're looking for that house and kids in the wrong place... The entirely wrong place. So this is my proposal." I was listening but wishing he would leave me alone—give me time to sort things out.

"I'm reorganizing my business and hiring a whole management team. I'm delegating. I can do what I need to do myself anywhere and have normal business hours. I don't think I have to prove to you how much I care for you. We get along well. We enjoy each other. For thirteen years I have watched you and waited, but I've waited too long. I want to give you a beautiful house in the suburbs and…I'm not as expressive as Antonio…I propose that you marry me, Lili, and make me the happiest man in the world."

"Oh, dear Phil…" I started to talk. I wasn't ready to make any decisions, but before I could protest, he put up his hand.

"Wait, there is something else you have to know. I don't like to do this now, but it's relevant to your answer. You may need a few days to digest this. Lili, what I am going to tell you may sound like hardball to you, but it's just that I care so much. I don't want to blow it again. I investigated your student Sergeant Franco Domenico. It is true he has an honorable discharge from the Army following his amputation. He was decorated for bravery, but I wonder just what that means. Lili, you know Green Berets are professional killers. I'd worry about that, but more importantly—what I don't believe he told you is he is a recovering drug addict. His long two-year rehabilitation had to do with both his physical therapy and drug rehabilitation… Lili, a drug addict is not the man for you. No matter what you decide about my proposal. Think about it. You don't have to answer me now."

I was furious. Too angry to cry. I stood and said to Phil, "What happened to you? I told Penham I would not make rash decisions, and I won't. Not for you. Not for Frank. I am in Rome to spend time with my husband's family and sort out my…" I started to cry, "…Antonio's spirit. Please leave me alone. You are not helping me." I was sobbing as I walked out.

I went directly to Dr. Belsanti. He listened to my account of the upsetting conversation and asked, "Signora, do you know why you are so angry?"

I sobbed as I said, "I'm afraid Phil might be right. He usually is."

"And, if he is right, why are you so angry?"

"I don't want Frank to be an addict. I don't want him to have had any more troubles. I don't want to have to let him go."

"Signora, does it make a difference to you if Franco were an addict or used drugs only casually?"

"I suppose yes." I was regaining my voice. "I grew up around alcoholism. Addiction is a very frightening word to me. Frank has other problems, which I think I could handle. But if he started to drink heavily or use drugs, I couldn't bear it. I won't marry an addict."

"Marry?" he responded.

I too was surprised to hear myself say the word. How could I marry again? How would Antonio feel? How about Antonio's parents? Belsanti said, "You said you want to restart you life a stronger person. Do you think it would take more courage to marry or to wait a while?"

"I don't know... What do you think?" I asked.

"As you know, it is not for me to say. You are here to settle something with Dr. Francesco. I think you still have many questions. But I think you just answered one question."

"What?"

"You said, 'I don't want to have to let him go.'"

"I think I'd better write him today."

July 18, 1973 Dear Frank: I have to write you another letter because I have an important question to ask you. It would help me if you wrote back soon. You told me that you gave up drugs, so I was not concerned. Then someone here who supposedly is looking after my interest raised a question about your possible abuse of drugs—that you were in rehabilitation for drug abuse. Can you tell me something more that might relieve my mind and the mind of those who say they care for me.

Frank, I am suffering over this question. I am praying in the churches and in the hills every day. I never exactly knew what you meant by the Universe, but it sounds like something ultimate like God. Please write.

Love, Lili

In the middle of this turmoil Andre Beaulieu flew into Rome from Paris. I didn't want to deal with him alone, so I invited him to join a party of the Francescos, Annamaria, Salvatore and me for dinner at Roberto, a fashionable restaurant. I still wasn't speaking to Phil. Andre was thrilled. He loved what he called high society.

Andre was in magnificent form. He spoke beautiful Italian, made erudite comments and greatly appreciated the food and wines. Charm gently floated towards all three Francesco women. He managed to get the Francescos to invite him to the villa for the weekend, so I invited Salvatore to come too. I needed to spend some quiet time with Antonio, but I hated to leave Annamaria alone with Andre. On Friday before we left I received the special delivery letter from Frank:

> Lili Angel: You don't have to worry about me and drugs. They had to use a lot of narcotic—morphine—when they saved my life. Pain control is tricky, and they overdid it, so I became dependent. I had to detox and eventually changed to non-narcotic pain killers. I haven't told you much about those days. I really don't want to remember it.
>
> I don't want you to suffer. I never actually told you something very important. I love you, Lili. Frank D.

I crossed myself and thanked God and the Blessed mother. I was so happy that I forgave Phil. I called Phil right away, but didn't get through. I left a message for him to call me in the country.

The end of July is hot in Rome. The only reason we were staying in the city was my weekly visit to Dr. Belsanti. It was a relief to pack for the weekend and drive into the hills where there were cooling breezes and trees. The elder Francescos retired to their private quarters on arrival. Annamaria conferred with the cook about dinner and took Andre and Salvatore on a tour of the grounds. I excused myself and took my lunch to the cemetery where I sat down next to Antonio's grave in the shade of a beautiful old cypress tree. I caressed Antonio's name on the stone and felt peaceful for the first time since I'd left New York. I waited to feel his spirit join me. Then I said to him, "Antonio mio, I want to have children."

I felt him smiling in my imagination. "Lili mia, there is only one way." Antonio and I never had trouble communicating about sex.

"Do you think Frank would be a good father?"

The sun was brightening the yellow grasses and a playful breeze blew up the pale undersides of the olive trees nearby. A little sparrow flew over my head cheerfully. Then my in imagination I heard Antonio say, "More than that, cara mia. You love him."

Tears surged up in my eyes as I lay down on the earth over Antonio's buried body. "Antonio, I love you."

"I know. You have my blessing."

I don't know how long I lay there feeling the security and quietness of the earth, thinking gratefully of Antonio, his dashing figure on a horse; his grace as we danced; his gentlemanly, sexy way with me; his beautiful curly head and his romantic voice speaking his native language. All the hopes we had. Then my imagination turned to Frank, earnestly listening to me speaking Italian in class, his broad shoulders under a white shirt, his brave way of hiding his limp and especially his beautiful dark eyes. I wondered if it were possible to love them both. Frank said he knew I would ' bring your husband with you when you come to me.' I felt I was leaving part of Antonio here in Italy, but I would always carry another part of him in my heart. I turned over and watched clouds drift in the blue summer sky. When I stood up, I touched the gravestone once more and whispered, "Grazie."

I returned to the house and found the Francescos serving tea to the guests. They were all chatting about the heat, the liturgical changes in the church and women's liberation. I said to Salvatore, "The liberation movement can be a new chapter in your study of women."

He said, "That book is closed. It was the study of a different man."

"Don't be too different," I said. "I like the Salvatore I've always known."

He blushed. He hadn't changed that much. We had a delightful dinner. The Francescos seemed happier with more people in the house. Andre and Salvatore were solicitous, knowledgeable and witty conversationalists. The next morning we all went to the village out-door market to see the fruits of the summer farms, smell the freshly baked country breads, and taste the local cheeses. We ate lunch in a cafe and returned to the villa in a sunny mood. As we walked in the door, the phone rang. It was Phil. He asked if he could join us. I said, "I want to tell you something first. I forgive you for your be-havior last week. Your proposal was touching and kind, Phil. You have been so kind to me. I know your motivation is to help me, but I was upset by your investigating Frank and telling me what is good for me. I realize…"

Phil interrupted me, "Lili, you don't have to answer me now. Let me come see you."

"Phil, let me tell you… First I have to tell you. Frank was ad-dicted to morphine because the hospital gave him too much for pain. He's not an addict. I'm not making any definite decisions, but you were dead wrong and meddlesome about Frank."

"Lili, I'll be there in two hours," said Phil and hung up.

Three hours later we were enjoying an aperitif in the garden. The air was slightly cooler, and the light from the sun made the countryside golden. Annamaria was surrounded by men. Phil en-tered as though nothing unusual had passed between us and began paying attention to Annamaria. He said, "Signorina, we met at Lili and Antonio's wedding in 1965. I was a great admirer of your brother. Antonio helped me buy my first suit and tie—and my first pair of Italian shoes. He introduced me to the opera."

She smiled, "My brother was a gentleman who touched many lives."

Salvatore said, "And so do you, Anna. All the children you teach every year. It is like planting seeds."

Anna used her graceful hands as she spoke, touching her breast-bone as she referred to herself, and pointing to the surrounding blooming bougainvillea as she referred to her home. "The school keeps me in touch with life's realities. Then I escape here to my rarefied world of privilege. I'd be a different person without the bal-ance my work gives."

Salvatore eagerly responded, "The monastic life works in much the same way. We were removed from peoples' problems so that we could re-enter and be part of the solution." Then he looked crestfallen again, "But for me, we were too removed."

Andre added, "Teaching is truly a calling. I often think of Jesus teaching on the mountain as my model of a teacher."

I almost choked on my Cinzano. I said, "But Andre, Jesus didn't teach Balzac as you do."

"Signora, you do me an injustice and you know it. You puritanical Americans have scruples we Europeans don't understand."

I started to rise to Andre's challenge, when Anna stepped in to diffuse it by saying, "What else do you teach, Professor?"

"All of French literature from Chretian de Troyes to Francoise Sagan," said Andre.

Salvatore said to Andre, "Signora Grace wrote her dissertation on Chretian. Of course, you know that."

"You seem very familiar with Antonio Francesco's widow, Professore. Have you been acquainted a long time?" asked Andre.

I spared Salvatore Andre's sarcasm by answering the question, "Salvatore is my best friend, Andre. I've known him since I came to Rome in 1964 when he was still in Holy Orders. He was my pastor until recently."

Phil came out of his lair, "I thought I was your best friend, Signora Grace. I've known you since 1960."

I glared at Phil with eyes that said, "Shut up."

Andre gloated to Anna, "It seems your sister-in-law has quite a few male best friends, Signorina."

I couldn't quite figure out what was going on. Andre was not helping himself by attacking me. I tried to remember he was my boss. Anna in her gracious, cool way stood and walked behind me, put her two hands on my shoulders, and said with the dignity of her aristocratic upbringing, "Lili will always have many friends, Professore, *come no?*"

Salvatore was looking at Anna with a new affection. I was tickled and wondered how their story would play out.

After dinner I could see Phil was a little drunk. He led me by the arm outside to the terrace by the fountain and stung me again, "Have you told your in-laws about your one-legged, low class boy-friend?"

"Phil, please. I've tried to be conciliatory with you. You're mak-ing our relationship impossible. I'm sorry I hurt your feelings."

"You haven't told them, have you?"

"Phil, I am going to ask you to leave this house and not call me again until you can be civil. I've done nothing to deserve this cru-elty."

Phil said, "I didn't mind losing out to Antonio. But I can't stand to see you with a low life."

"Phil, dear Phil, believe me. Frank Domenico is not a low life. You haven't even met him."

"Who has met him?"

"My mother and father, Brinny, Tim, the kids, Wendy and Jes-sica. Call any of them if you're really concerned about me. You aren't losing out to anybody, Phil. You don't understand my needs. If I were you, I'd see a shrink. I see one. Antonio saw one. It might help you understand your problem with me."

Phil moved towards me, "Can I kiss you just once, Lili?"

"You're pitiful Phil. You must be drunk. Of course you can't kiss me, here of all places. Please see the best doctor in New York and then, call me. Now leave this house. " I ran back into the company.

After he left, I worried about his driving in his inebriated condi-tion. He was right about one thing: I needed to prepare the Francescos. In the morning I checked the Hassler to be sure Phil had arrived safely.

The Francescos, Salvatore, and I went to mass together at the little village church on Sunday. Kneeling next to Annamaria, I felt a clarity well up in my heart and a peace I hadn't experienced since Antonio's death. I knew that I loved Frank. I knew that I wanted to have a family. I knew that I had Antonio's blessing. I prayed for the grace to speak to the family at lunch about my intentions to remarry.

After the Sunday dinner was served and digested, I announced to the Francescos and Annamaria that I had something to tell them. I thought they knew what was coming. Hadn't they been encouraging me for five years to meet people and saying I would remarry. I said, "You all know how I love Antonio. And I shall always love him… I went to the grave Friday to spend time with his spirit and ask his blessing on a new relationship. I want to have children."

Signora Francesco began to cry. I continued, "I have met a man who is kind to me. His name is Franco Domenico. His parents are Italian. He is American—a decorated veteran. He wants to marry me. We would live in America, but I hope we would come here often. You are my family and Antonio is my first husband forever. I will have a second husband who honors my attachments here. I hope you can give me your blessing."

I felt Annamaria wanted to jump up and kiss me, but she watched the Francescos' reaction first. Signora dried her tears and looked at Signor. He said, "My child, it is good. If you feel Antonio would bless you, so do we. Please don't leave us forever. Bring your children to us, as we have no grandchildren."

He embraced me kindly. I hugged Signora and said "Thank you, Thank you." Anna felt free then to express her enthusiasm, and she kissed me and congratulated me.

It was a bittersweet afternoon. We all felt the sadness as well as the hope in my remarrying. I could go on with a new life, but Antonio could not. The Francescos were allowing life to go on. I felt Annamaria would lean on Salvatore, as I had done myself for five years. I decided to return a week early and wrote a short note to Frank to tell him to expect me.

CHAPTER TWENTY-SIX

Landing in a humid August haze in New York, I called Frank from the airport, then grabbed a cab up to his flat. He appeared before I could knock, standing in the doorway in a black T-shirt with his hands clutching the chinning bar above his head, looking at me with happy eyes. "You came back, baby. Let me touch you." He moved his big hands from the chinning bar to my waist, slowly up my ribs to my breasts, around my back and kissed me long and strong as he promised. "Do you know how much I wanted to touch you like this? How I held myself back? Are you okay now. angel? Can we do it?"

I laughed, "You promised." We walked into his room, arms around each other, laughing and kissing.

Sitting down on his bed, Frank said, "I'm gonna remove the hardware first, baby. Be patient with me." I watched Frank take off one shoe, pull up his shirt, showing me his muscular chest and arms, take down his loosely fitting pants and pull his good leg out. Leaving the pants hanging on the artificial one, he unstrapped the laces of the leather cuff that held the prosthesis to his thigh, removed a strap from around his waist, and dropped the false leg to the floor, showing me his stump. It was scarred, but not unsightly to me. Frank looked like a broken statue of a Roman god, sitting on his navy blue bedspread in his jockey shorts. His eyes had a questioning look as if to say, "Well, that's it. Can you love me?" I knelt down to touch the amputated leg, to make love to every part of this beautiful man I was enclosing into my life and my body.

The power he had been reining in erupted as we held each other. I felt my eyes flood with tears as our bodies finally met. Frank had grabbed me deeply months ago with a simple kiss. Our making love sealed the bond that was profound and permanent. We think we conceived the baby that first time, or as Frank would say, the Universe conceived new life.

Breathing the humid city air that was cooling down, we listened to late afternoon street sounds and thunder approaching across the river. Frank said, "This old stump doesn't scare you, Lili?"

I said, "No, Frank, what scares me is that you might have died over there, and I wouldn't know you. I don't ever want to leave you again. Why do I love you so much so fast?"

Running his finger along my collar bones and down between my breasts, he said, "Let's get married before classes start. Let's go to Virginia and see your sister and ask Tim to marry us there."

"There's one more thing I need you to promise," I said. "I know it's ridiculous to ask, but...you can't die, Frank. You have to drive carefully and stop smoking and don't do anything dangerous and grow old with me."

Frank smiled, "I'll do my best. I'm pretty hard to kill. I don't want you to worry so much, baby."

We called Tim and Brinny to arrange to spend a week with them. We called our respective parents. Everybody cried.

We decided to move to my apartment and turn one bedroom into a study/exercise room for Frank. My money was obviously helpful, but an emotional hurdle for Frank. He had been living on student loans, a partial disability pension and V.A. scholarship for tuition and didn't want to use my income other than for rent, which he rationalized was acceptable because he didn't want me to be deprived. He said he had already given up a lot of his pride but wasn't willing to take money from Antonio. Somehow, we would have to live more simply than I had come to expect, so that he could feel he was living within his means or at least within the income he could project when he finished graduate school.

As we drove up in Frank's Chevy, Brinny greeted us with her arms outstretched to hug us, but shaking her head. "I don't believe you guys. What's your hurry?"

Frank was buoyant, "Heh, little sister. I never had a sister before." He lifted Brinny as he hugged her, then greeted Tim, " Or a priest in the family either."

Brinny put her arm around me, "Are you sure you know what you are doing?"

"No, I suppose I don't. Except I'm madly in love. I'm very happy. I can't resist Frank. He's like a force of nature," I said.

Frank and Tim were carrying our bags into the house. Brinny and Tim had told Louisa that we were coming to be married, so they felt comfortable putting Frank and me in the same room. Brinny pressed me, "But Lili, you don't know each other all that well. Why did you decide so quickly?"

"Brinny, Frank told me he wanted to marry me last May 15 on our first date, and I told him he was crazy. When I left for Italy, he told me we'd get married if I came back to him. I talked with the psychiatrist in Rome. And Phil sort of brought things to a head. I prayed. I even talked to Antonio. I can't describe it… I didn't see a reason against it. Brinny, he grabs me. I love him a la folie. That's the only way I can describe it. He'll win every argument we ever have. The women's movement would disown me. I guess I'm not very good at loving halfway."

"Sister, you are a goner. It sounds settled. But what about the wedding? What are you going to wear? What kind of party do you want?"

"Oh, Brinny, that's not important. We don't need a party. Let's keep it simple. It's as if we are eloping except you and your children are with us. I'm beyond wanting a big wedding. But I should buy a dress. Let's go shopping tomorrow. We have to wait a few days for the blood test and license anyway."

Tim felt a responsibility to offer some premarital counseling before Frank and I made our vows. As we sat in the Rector's office in big old wooden chairs, Tim said, "As Lili's brother-in-law, I'm not the best one to give you premarital counseling, but since you seem to be in a hurry, and I know both of you had the benefit of some psychotherapy, I'll do my best… What is the hurry about?"

Frank answered, "It doesn't feel like a hurry to me. I'm a disciplined guy, and I've learned patience when there is a good reason to wait. I want to be Lili's husband. I want her to be my wife, not a girlfriend."

I added, "We've been lonely long enough."

Tim said to Frank, "Why Lili?"

Frank smiled, "What an easy question." He looked at me. "The first time I saw you in class—so pretty, smart, young and sad—I thought, 'She could be the miracle I'd been expecting.' I just had to reach you and convince you. But I felt the power of the Universe was on my side."

Tim asked, "What do you mean 'power of the Universe'?"

Frank said, "You know, the power we feel all around us but can't pin down." He hesitated, then continued, "I had a kind of vision when I was being transported back to the States in poor condition. I guess I was doped up. I knew my leg was gone and I didn't really know what was left of me. I'd been a very physical guy—football—quarterback—ladies man—fast on my feet—and a green beret. I was a cool guy." He smiled at himself. "I didn't know how to be anyone else. Being disabled didn't fit me. And I was grieving bad. I'm a tough SOB, but I was caving. Then it fell on me like a curtain of light. I could feel, but couldn't understand, that I was going to be okay—great—better than before. The Light, which I call the Universe,—maybe you call it God— told me that one day down the line, after a lot of shit, pain and work, I was going to be...golden. That momentary intuition or vision or whatever you name it kept me fighting the two and a half years I spent in the hospital learning to be a different kind of man, rebuilding. Then I came to Columbia and found I have a good mind and some talent with people. Then I met Lili." He reached over for my hand.

"I saw she was hurting, and I had an intuition about her. I could see her strong and healed. I told her that I knew she was going to be happy again. She believed me. I wanted her to be my wife and mother of my children, so I didn't take advantage of her... You know what I mean... I think I could have, but I waited." Frank looked at Tim, and back at me. "The hard part was letting her go to Italy, but she came back to me. She is a big part of my miracle, Tim. I didn't just find her by luck. The whole Universe gave us to each other."

Tim turned to me, "Lili, how did you find this man?"

I smiled at Frank, "He calls it the Universe. I think we have been slipped a love potion."

When Tim asked if we knew of any marital differences we might face, Frank answered again, "Yes, musical taste and money. Lili has Antonio's income, and I have a lot of pride."

"How do you feel about the money issue, Lili?" asked Tim.

"Why can't we call it **our** money and look at it as a gift from the Universe? Pretend you won the lottery, Frank."

Frank laughed, "I have won the lottery, in more ways than I ever suspected. What's important to me is to live simply enough that I am not reaching over my head. I'm not going to try to keep up with Antonio. I'm just a normal guy who wants a normal life."

Our wedding day was one of those breezy late August days that teases with the promise of cooler weather. I had bought a knee length short sleeve cotton dress, white with a tiny flower pattern and a scalloped eyelet collar. We picked phlox and daisies from the garden for bouquets for Brinny, Louisa and me, and we pinned a yellow rose on Frank's lapel.

The church was cool, though not air-conditioned. Tim's organist played 'Jesu, Joy of Man's Desiring' which always gave me a sense of an intelligent and loving order in the Universe.

"I Franco take you Grace to be my wife…until we are parted by death."

"I Grace take you Franco to be my husband…"

I moved Antonio's ring to my right hand and wore Frank's gold band on my left hand. I changed my name to Grace Domenico.

We soon realized I was pregnant and decided to quickly send wedding announcements to our friends and families:

Mr. Frank Domenico and Mrs. Grace Long Francesco Domenico
are happy to announce their marriage on
August 27, 1973, Christ Church
Charlottesville, Virginia.

Chapter Twenty-Seven

"**I** guess I have to meet him eventually. I'm working with my shrink on my feelings about you and Frank. It'll give me fodder for therapy," was Phil's response to my invitation to dinner to meet Frank.

"Phil, you'll like him. I've invited Alexandra too." I was honestly a little anxious that Phil and Alexandra might snobbishly judge Frank because of his clothes, accent, or his lack of education. I had told Frank the drama of Phil in Rome, and warned him about my cousin's cafe society life. They arrived together—more than fashionably late as usual. Phil was wearing a great pin striped suit. Alexandra wore a colorful Pucci silk print. This time I had enough sense to leave Frank's wardrobe alone and let his clothing express himself. When they rang the bell, Frank greeted them at the door.

"Come on in Alexandra, Phil. I'm Frank Domenico. I guess this is all pretty sudden for Lili's friends."

I kissed my cousin and Phil and brought them into the living room, where I had arranged gold chrysanthemums with small pumpkins on the coffee table. Frank and I had compromised on what music to play. I didn't want his loud hard rock music or even Bruce Springsteen. He didn't want Wagner, Beethoven or even Brahms. We played Aaron Copeland and the Beatles. We served drinks, and I sat down next to my husband in a big chair. Alex said, "Wasn't it just a year ago we met you at the plane, Lili, and were worried you'd never come out of mourning."

I laughed hugging my hunky husband, "Frank gave me a good push."

Phil seemed to have regained his sense of humor. "Frank, I have to toast you and Lili, you bastard. Did she tell you how I tried to beat you out?"

Frank answered, "Yes, she did. I've always hated war stories."

I watched Phil sizing Frank up. He said, "I guess I don't understand women. You look like an ordinary guy to me. What does she see in you that's so special?"

Frank surprised me by sounding almost Italian, "Che mistero, eh?," and he kissed me on the cheek. I could see his good Italian accent put him up a notch in Alexandra's estimation.

Phil grimaced, "Don't remind me that you're Italian. Did Lili tell you how she threw me out of her house in Italy and told me to see a shrink?"

"It's the best thing I ever did for you, Philip," I told him. "You're acting civilized again. But all that is past. Alexandra, did I hear you went out with Andre?"

"It's platonic, I assure you. He told me all about visiting the Francesco's villa, and the scuttlebutt about your priest— or should I say ex-priest?— friend and Annamaria."

"What about Annamaria and Salvatore?" I asked.

"You must have had your radar down, Lili. They are practically engaged," said Alex.

"I guess I was preoccupied," I said, "but how perfect. I couldn't be happier. I'm actually not surprised. Salvatore is a gem. I'll write to them both tomorrow." I turned to Frank, "My sister-in-law and one of my best friends. This is wonderful news. Maybe we should go to Rome for Christmas."

Frank stroked my back, "Slow down, baby. I'm not going to Rome for Christmas. You're gonna have to slow down a little for me. Maybe next summer after I finish school."

Phil said, "You'd better not slow her down too much, Frank. She's used to the good life."

"Lili and I are trying to live quietly and enjoy the simple things," said Frank.

Phil and Alex looked at each other. I realized Frank was right, but so was Phil. Without noticing it, I had gradually become accustomed to traveling in Europe without counting the cost. Frank seemed to expect me to forego all that, even though I could afford it. I hoped he would get over his pride and prudishness about using my Francesco money.

Alexandra asked Frank where he intended to pursue his Ph.D. He said, "I'd like to end up in some rural place like the University of Vermont for five years. Or maybe the University of Virginia. They have a good psych department, and I've heard Charlottesville is beautiful farm country. And it's near Brinny so the sisters could raise kids together."

"Lili, you could probably teach wherever Frank goes," Alexandra said.

"I'd like to keep my hand in teaching. I've just started teaching my course on the late nineteenth century French poets. It's such great material. Like abstract painting." As Alexandra and I began comparing the common elements of Beaudelaire, Rimbeau and Les Fauves, Phil and Frank started to talk football. I was grateful to Phil and remembered again what a good friend he had been to me.

Over my potato leek soup, Phil said, "Frank, I can't figure out why I don't hate you. I thought I would. But I don't. Maybe I feel sympathy for a war hero."

"I'm no hero," objected Frank, who had apparently been making his own evaluations. "You probably don't hate me 'cause you're a nice guy." He grinned, "Or...you are falling under my spell. Why do you figure I don't hate you—seeing as you covet my wife?"

"You have no reason to hate me. I'm just an old family friend, getting older every day." Phil winked at me. In his best humor, Phil always made me smile.

After dinner Alexandra remarked, "Lili, I think marriage agrees with you. You are putting on a little weight."

My body was changing. The waistline was going. My breasts were fuller. I tired more easily. Frank liked my blossoming body. He became less self-conscious about his stump, which is what he always called it. He explained the phantom pains and itches he felt from nerve ends in the stump, which gave him the sensation of still having his left leg and foot. Around the house he occasionally allowed himself to forego the prosthesis and use crutches.

Frank's missing limb was a constant and real factor in our daily life, which was much easier for me to accept than for him, but the nightmares were frightening to both of us. Frank's usual serenity, or his peaceful sleep, could be brutally shattered by a sudden noise, or by a dream of the past. He bolted up, eyes wild, body trembling and sweating, reaching for his gun. The first time, I was terrified and was little help. I cried out, "Frank, what's wrong?"

He looked crazed, lost, confused in the dark of our room. Then, he seemed to realize it was a dream. "I'm okay, baby." His breathing quieted down a little, but he was still out of breath. "I'm sorry. It's a flashback... I don't know when they're gonna come. Don't worry. I won't hurt you. I just have to calm myself down now."

We were both unable to get back to sleep, so he taught me his meditation exercises as we sat facing each other in the moonlit room on the bed: "Just close your eyes and let your mind notice your breathing. Let the breathing slow down and deepen naturally. Feel the air come in the nostrils, and down into the lungs, without any effort or rushing. Just breath quietly and effortlessly. On the 'in' breath I say 'Trust,' and on the 'out' breath I say 'the Universe.' That's what I say, but you can pick your own mantra. Something to remind you not to try too hard, or not to worry."

"That's like the Jesus prayer I learned on retreat."

"It doesn't matter what you call it. It's the power to overcome fear."

Before the sun came up, we had fallen back onto the pillows and the healing of a peaceful sleep.

Frank came to the fall President's faculty reception with me and met Andre, who spoke to us in Italian, "Piacere, Dottore."

Frank insisted in English, "Thanks, Professor, but I'm not a doctor. That was Lili's late husband, Antonio Francesco."

Andre looked flustered and annoyed and said under his breath in English, "Of course, I know that. I know the family rather well. It is merely a form of courtesy, Mr. Domenico."

Frank answered in a normally loud voice, "Dr. Franscesco earned the title. My wife earned the title. You earned the title. When I earn it, I'll welcome it. But for now I'm satisfied with Mr. Domenico—or please call me Frank. Lili calls you Andre."

I suggested, "You could legitimately call Frank 'Commendatore.' He is a decorated veteran."

Annamaria soon wrote me her good news:

Lili Carissima,   November 2, 1973

Felicitazione to you and your husband, Franco Domenico. As you have told us your husband is a kind gentleman, so we are happy that you are building your new life. I know that you will be pleased to hear our news from Roma that I am going to be married also. Our dear friend, Salvatore di Palma, has asked Papa for my hand in marriage. You of all people know how good is Salvatore's heart. I am so happy to have waited these many years for the best possible husband. Mama and Papa are proud to call him 'son.'

We plan to marry next June. Since you brought Salvatore into our family circle, we especially hope you and your husband will be able to join us then. Lili, many prayers are being answered. Perhaps my brother in heaven is interceding for us all.

Love, Your sister Annamaria

Note from Salvatore: Your humble student in the heart of women is happy to graduate in such a blessed announcement. God is good. Annamaria and I hope you and Franco will be with us next June, if not before. S.

To me, this wedding was a miracle. New life for Anna, new life for Salvatore, and new life for the Francescos. The only prayer remaining to be answered would be Francesco-di Palma grandchildren.

We spent Christmas at the Domenico's on Long Island, where

my obviously pregnant condition was a cause for pride and happy speculation about the baby's gender and names. I favored beautiful Italian names like Michelangelo for a boy and Caterina for a girl. Frank laughed. "He'd change it."

"How do you know?" I asked.

"I promise. He should have a good American name like Mark."

"How do you know it's a boy?"

"I know. That's all."

I never mentioned Frank's New York way of speaking to him, but he listened to me speak English the way he listened to me speak Italian and gradually changed his Long Island accent.

I watched from the window as Frank threw a football around with Rocco and Gino in the front yard. When Gino made a good catch, Frank and Rocco hugged him and hit him on the fanny. When Frank missed a catch, usually one of the brothers ran to get the ball for him. In the evening I asked Frank, "Do you remember today when you fell in the grass trying to get that throw?"

He reddened, "You saw that?"

"Yes, I could see you weren't hurt, but Rocco looked funny when he helped you up. Sort of superior. Does he suffer a need to compete with you?"

"Rocco wanted a football scholarship, like I won, but he didn't get it. So he didn't go to college. I think he should have enlisted in the marines, but our folks wouldn't allow it because of my close call. In a way Rocco suffered because of my injury too."

Gino idolized Frank and began to idealize me too. He was curious about college and about Italy. I told him, "You could study in Italy in an undergraduate college program. That's the best way to learn the language. Do you have family still living there?" I asked looking at the parents.

Mrs. Domenico answered, "Sure, all my aunts, uncles and sisters are in Napoli, and the Domenico family in Sorrento are constantly writing to invite the boys. But they didn't want to go yet." She lifted her arms in exasperation. "Who knows? Maybe Gino, the baby, will go."

Gino winced, "Ma, don't call me the baby."

Frank and Rocco laughed and patted Gino on the head. Gino raised his fists, but they laughed him out of his anger.

Frank won a fellowship to continue his studies in clinical psychology at the University of Virginia from OVET, Overseas Veterans Education Trust, which supported research in the psychology of combat and of healing traumatic experiences. We bought a red brick colonial house near Brinny and Tim, surrounded and dwarfed by towering oaks, tulip trees, and magnolias, which were covered with vines and filled with birds in the spring. A giant elder oak in the back yard provided a branch for a swing, and Frank and I began to learn about gardening.

When the honeysuckle and boxwood drenched the air with sweet and pungent fragrance, I gave birth to Mark Angelo. The nurse handed me the tiny bundle, and I saw the dark shock of hair on his head, the pink face and the wide open dark eyes, and I fell in love again. I couldn't stop smiling. He was a robust, healthy boy. Finding the rhythm of breast feeding, I felt I belonged to the earth, and that I might be learning to trust the Universe.

As we gazed at Mark's chubby arms, legs, fingers and toes, I wondered out loud, "Maybe he has the hands of a pianist?"

Frank looked at me as if I were a Martian, "My son? Lili, he'll probably play football... I only pray there won't be any damn war when he's eighteen."

CHAPTER TWENTY-EIGHT

I did begin to trust the Universe through small moments of shared understanding, in shared rest and tiredness, in shared disagreements, and in the garden.

Our first Christmas in Charlottesville, I offered to prepare the Christmas feast for our two families, because Tim and Brinny were occupied with church activities. I wanted everything to be perfect. I envisioned a sparkling, decorated living room with a warm blaze in the fireplace; gifts wrapped in silver and blue ribbons; my kitchen filled with the smells of turkey roasting, biscuits baking, and spiced cider brewing. Like Martha of Bethany, I was anxious about many things, and, as the feast time neared, I became increasingly cranky and miserable.

On December 21, the winter solstice, Frank came home from his last exam and collapsed in the den in what was becoming his favorite corduroy chair. He opened a green bottle of Heineken, and sat down to gaze at our first Christmas tree, decorated with popcorn and cranberry ropes.

I was feeding Mark Angelo with my teeth clenched, angry that I hadn't had time to polish the silver, write the last of our Christmas card/new address announcements, and bake some sugar cookies, in the shapes of Santa, bells and reindeer. The baby was spitting out his pureed chicken and vegetables and trying to wriggle out of the highchair, where I had strapped him down. Frank called to me from the den, "Hey, baby, what 'cha doin'?"

I was annoyed that he seemed so relaxed, while I was freaking out, but I called back civilly through my tightened jaw, "I'm trying to feed the baby, but he won't sit still."

Frank paid attention to my every clue. I heard his footsteps coming behind me and felt his hands between my neck and shoulders, which bothered me for a moment, as I tensed self-protectively even more.

Then his calming slow touch felt good, and I turned to look him in the face—our eyes meeting—he wondering what was disturbing me.

"I'm so frustrated. I can't accomplish anything because Mark didn't take his nap today, and I didn't even get a good night's sleep.... There're only four days to Christmas, and I don't see how I can do it all."

Frank quietly put the Judy Collins Christmas album on the stereo and helped me clean up Mark Angelo's dirty face and messy fingers. He said, "Dinner can wait, baby. Let's sit in the den by the tree."

I unclenched my teeth and unstrapped the baby, and we went to Frank's big comfortable chair and all three sat in a pile by the popcorn tree. With Frank underneath me and Mark on my lap, my mind slowed down. I heard the words Judy was singing:

O Holy Night, the stars are brightly shining.
This is the night of the dear savior's birth.
Long lay the world in sin and sorrow pining,
'Til he appeared and the soul felt its worth.

I started to feel deeply sad and to cry.

"What's sad, baby?" asked Frank, stroking my back again.

I felt ridiculous as I said, "I guess it's Christmas. It should be so beautiful. Our first Christmas in our new home with Mark Angelo. But I've been in such a bad mood."

Frank just kept stroking me as we sat glued together and listened to the music. Gradually Mark Angelo's chubby arms and legs became limp, his eyelids slid over his serious brown eyes, and his head tilted over to my chest, heavy and warm. Frank and I looked at each other, and smiled a joint love of the innocent and easy relaxation of our child. Frank mimed me a kiss in the short space between us, and I returned his gesture from the depth of my gratitude, as Judy sang:

O hear the angel voices.

O night divine, O night when Christ was born.

Frank and I learned together about common love. Love is being present. Love is touching. Love is wordless understanding.

As a psychologist, Frank soon realized that part of my sadness predated Antonio's death. He asked me why my father always sat in front of the TV when we visited them, and why my father and mother never visited us or Brinny in Virginia. I tried to explain it. "Rex is…limited, Frank. He likes to be near his supply of liquor, so he doesn't like to visit. I think he has paralyzed his emotional life. He wasn't always this way—not when I was a little girl. I've already grieved my relationship with him. I lost him a long time ago. He doesn't have the faintest idea of who I am. The only person he really knows is Mama."

When Rex actually died ten years later of cirrhosis of the liver, Mama was devastated as I could well understand. Three months later, she made her first visit to our house in Charlottesville in remorse. She said, "Lili, I'm so sorry I didn't come to you in Rome when Antonio was killed. I feel terrible that you didn't have your family around you. I should have come—at least to the funeral. I realize that now. Can you forgive me, please."

"Of course, Mama. You did what you had to do. God provided for me—but it was lonely."

At Rex's funeral my cousins and surviving uncles and aunts told many stories of Rex's wild days in his youth. Ricky remembered with glee, "the time he kept taking the clean dishes and putting them in the dirty pile, so the aunts kept washing and washing and washing. And then Aunt Augusta got so mad, she broke a dish on his head." Julius reveled, "Remember when he put us children in the trunk of his car and snuck us through a police roadblock that was searching for an escaped convict. And how mad Uncle Ed was?" Although my cousins thought the stories were amusing—even hilarious—I did not. Frank held me close that night and stroked my back. "Baby you say you admire my courage… You and Brinny grew up in a war zone."

"It seemed normal to us."

When Mark Angelo was almost two years old, Annamaria and Salvatore asked me to be godmother to their first son, named inevitably Antonio. It seemed a good time to go to Italy for the Baptism, but Frank did not want to travel. Sitting in our kitchen after classes as I prepared green beans for dinner, his forehead wrinkled and his hand went to his stump. "You can go, Lili, but I'm staying here. You probably can't understand what I feel, but it takes a long time after a war to settle the mind. I don't want the stress of going to Europe with the baby. It's irrational, but I don't even want to get on an airplane. I really like the earth under me."

"But, Frank, you'd enjoy Italy. It's beautiful and very romantic. You'll love Salvatore and the Francescos, and they would love you too. And I don't want to leave you."

"Lili baby, I know I'm stubborn, but I know myself. I'd like to make you happy, but not at the expense of my peace of mind. Then neither of us would be happy. Stress makes me more prone to nightmares... It makes sense for you to go. It's probably important to your friends and to you. I'll stay here and take care of Mark. You won't be gone too long... Maybe we need to practice more independence."

I felt anxious about leaving Frank, yet I had to say, "I promised the Francescos I wouldn't totally abandon them. Salvatore was so good to me. And Anna is like a sister. I hate to go alone, but I have to go."

"I know, Lili. You have to go. It will be good for you. And I'll have to take it. Mark and I will do some male bonding. It'll be good for us too." He joked, "And think how sweet it will be to come together again."

"But Frank, do you think you'll ever want to travel by plane again?"

"I hope so because you want it. For me, I don't know. I am satisfied with a very simple life, but I don't want you to be bored."

I went to Italy that June, without Frank or Mark. The first two days I worried about everything at home. Then I let go. Little Antonio Francesco di Palma was baptized in the country church near the villa on a rare June morning. It was wonderful to see the grandparents so proud and happy. The baby looked exactly like Salvatore.

After the luncheon I wandered toward Antonio's grave. The familiar plot felt gentle to me. I could feel how much I had grown in just three years. I had a new sense of myself as an adult separate person. I had a new and peculiar feeling of strength and security, even a sense of power: the power to satisfy myself and my family.

Salvatore eventually followed me. He asked, "How does it feel to come back?"

"I miss Frank and Mark, but I'm so glad I came—to see the Francescos hold their own grandchild—to see you married and a father. And you have taken the edge off Anna. She seems to me less reserved, more natural."

As we approached the familiar stone, the site of so many tears, I realized how vulnerable Antonio and I had been— passionate and capable in professional ways, but not strong. Like two canaries in a storm. If I still retained some of my canary qualities, I felt now like a canary in a sturdy oak tree. I said to Salvatore, "Frank probably knew it would be good for me to come here without him. It gives me time to reflect rather than having to explain everything to him. He has good intuitions."

"Are you happy with him, Lili?" asked my friend.

I wondered if Salvatore hoped that I still needed him. I had no trouble answering, "Yes, I am happy. I didn't think it would be possible, but I am." I looked at the stone. "It's all right with Antonio. He wasn't a jealous man. I had to move on."

Salvatore mused, "I am happy too. I deeply love Anna. Yet I sometimes wonder...if you hadn't gone back to New York and met Frank...if you might have married me."

"Of course, I might have." I avoided looking Salvatore in the eyes. "But God arranged it differently. You and Anna are made for each other. Frank says the Universe brought me and him together. You would love Frank, Salvatore. Everybody does— even Phil. Especially Phil. Frank and Phil are buddies. Frank is sort of charismatic—very talented as a therapist too."

Salvatore nodded his head and said in a soft voice, "You are once again a woman in love."

"Yes, I am in love with Frank, but there is more to it. I hope I am growing stronger. After all, I am a mother now."

Salvatore said, "And I am a natural father, but being a father makes me feel more vulnerable, not less."

Frank completed his Ph.D. in five years and went to work for OVET in research, in what came to be called post-traumatic stress syndrome. We had our daughter, Caterina, when Mark was four years old, a delicate, dark-haired child with the face of an angel and her mother's flirtatiousness.

When Caterina was born, we asked Phil Cohen to be her godfather. Wendy and Jessica agreed to be Caterina's godmothers, but Phil wasn't sure he should do it. He asked over the telephone, "Isn't it a little unusual to have two Lesbians for godmothers and a Jewish godfather for a Christian Baptism? Is it kosher, so to speak?"

I said, "Tim says it's not exactly kosher, but Tim breaks some of the rules because, 'the Sabbath was made for us, not the reverse.' All you have to promise is that you will see that she is educated in the Church and to care for her if Frank and I aren't here."

"Don't I have to remember her birthday and give her Christmas gifts or something?" asked Phil.

"You can do that if you want, Phil. If you need help finding something for a girl, I'd help," I offered.

"You underestimate me, Lili. I just might know more about girls than you think. I'd love to be her godfather."

Frank's parents moved to Virginia to be near us after Caterina was born. His father didn't cry any more and helped us transform part of our backyard forest into a flower and vegetable garden. The experience of gardening played a part in my transformation as well. I had previously lived and survived using primarily my intellect—constantly reasoning to survive. I began to use other faculties—listening to owls and crickets; smelling the boxwood, tomato plants, and honeysuckle; feeling the weather change; and lingering on the texture of the onionskin I was peeling or the holly I was pruning. I enjoyed putting my hands in the soil, getting muddy, then cleaning up; and serving fresh vegetables, canning, and pickling.

Wendy and Jessica visited at least yearly. We and the Thompsons talked about how and when to explain their relationship to the children. In 1982 Wendy and Jessica asked Tim to bless their relationship in a religious ceremony. As the marriage of two women was not sanctioned by the Church, Tim had to search his conscience. He finally agreed to break the rules once again. "I can't honestly see any reason not to bless your commitment to each other. Here in Virginia, for God's sake, the church blesses the hounds in a fox hunt! I'm sure our Lord would have bent the rules to affirm human love."

Wendy said, "Tim, you'll never know how much this means to us."

Jessica said, "We need to limit the guest list to people who would guard our confidentiality: just family and a few Lesbian and gay friends."

Wendy added, "One more thing. We'd like to write our own vows—and to include the reading from Judy Chicago."

Wendy and Jessica's wedding was a celebration of love that stretched us all—especially Frank and Phil. Wendy, who was already prematurely gray, wore a beige summer antique dress which she had saved from the attic at the farm and delicate high-button leather shoes. Jessica wore a long sheer cotton print dress and wide brimmed straw hat. Caterina was their flower girl. Tim began to preach sermons in which he introduced to the congregation the probability that Christ, who lifted up people on the margins of his society— Samaritans and Gentiles— would be in strong solidarity in our time with the gay community, as it sought recognition and dignity.

And then all that has divided us will merge
And then compassion will be wedded to power
And then softness will come to a world that is harsh and unkind
And then both men and women will be gentle
And then both women and men will be strong
And then no person will be subject to another's will
And then all will be rich and free and varied

And then the greed of some will give way to the needs of many
And then all will share equally in the Earth's abundance
And then all will care for the sick and the weak and the old
And then all will nourish the young
And then all will cherish life's creatures
And then all will live in harmony with each other and the Earth
And then everywhere will be called Eden once again.

Judy Chicago

The National Vietnam Veterans Memorial in Washington, D. C. was dedicated in November, 1982. I'll never forget that first visit to the wall. The park was filled with Vietnam veterans in uniforms with special patches, hats, ribbons and medals indicating their different experiences and locations. They were, of course, by then in their thirties and early forties, some balding and out of shape. Some still had a hairy hippie look. Many seemed to be of working class backgrounds. Frank didn't wear his uniform. As we walked over the grass to the wall, we saw veterans and their families searching the names, telling stories, embracing each other, and placing memorial items on the wall. Some stood quietly crying. That silent black wall, studded with names, stretched over our heads and farther in each direction than my mind could or wanted to encompass.

We walked through the crowd. Frank was uncharacteristically quiet, holding my hand very tightly with one hand and Mark's hand in the other. Caterina held on to me. Frank greeted a man in a wheelchair who had no legs, and told us he had met him at the amputee center outside D.C. "Some people can't get used to walking with prostheses—or there is too much damage to fit one."

He found the names he was seeking fairly close to each other listed chronologically by death: Albert Martinez, Ed Williams, Gerald Swoboda. He put his hand on each one. Frank explained to the children, "These men were my best friends, and they were killed, before they had a chance to have children like you. You wouldn't be here either, if I didn't survive. So I'm so grateful I did... Even though I have this broken leg, it's nothing compared to missing your whole life." As he hugged them with tears in his eyes, Mark looked serious and bewildered. Caterina hugged her Daddy. Frank continued and looked at me, "This is the only way I can begin to share that time with you—in this holy place where the living meet the dead."

An army officer in uniform came up to us and slapped Frank on the back, "Hey, Domenico, you look like a damn civilian."

Frank smiled not very enthusiastically, "Yeah, Captain, I am. This is my wife, Lili; my son, Mark; my daughter, Cat. This is Captain Forester. He was my commanding officer the last tour."

"Mrs. Domenico, your husband was quite a soldier. I don't know how much he has told you."

I said, "Nothing, really. Frank doesn't like to talk about it."

Frank spoke up, "I don't want you talking to my family about that time, Captain, okay?"

"Sure, Domenico, as you like it. Let me just tell you this, Mrs. Domenico, Mark; (He ignored Caterina.) he was as tough and as fast as they come. Smart too. But I hear you're still on our side, Domenico, working for OVET."

"You got it, Captain. We have to go." Frank turned away and shook his head. He was holding his emotions until we found his friends, Tommy Sullivan and Lou Russo. The three men hugged and laughed and cried at the sight of each other. Lou's wife and I introduced ourselves and children, as the men carried on exchanging news and hooks and jabs. We sat with Tommy and the Russos during the ceremony. The wall is humble, sad, and courageous, quiet. That day brought me closer to Frank in a way, but also told me how much of his experience I would never know or understand. I saw him with the people he might have died to protect: men who were once as close to him as I was. Men who saw him run and leap over walls. Men who saw Frank kill. I couldn't begin to imagine it.

That night we partied at a bar in Georgetown. Normally at parties Frank drank a few beers and didn't show it. That night he got a high on beer and vodka. I began to feel hot and sweaty and found myself ripping my paper napkin into shreds. When he got up to relieve himself, he lost his balance and fell on the floor. I burst into tears and cried as Tom and Lou helped him back to his seat. "Frank. You're drunk. Get up and come back to the hotel with me."

He was laughing, which infuriated me more. "It's okay, baby. I'm just a little skunked."

I cried louder, "Frank, I'm leaving and I'm taking the car keys. If you don't come with me, you can walk back to the hotel."

Still sitting in the booth with a kindly but serious expression, he reached for my hand and pulled me next to him where he gently said, "Baby, it's me, Frank. I'm not going to scare you or hurt anyone. I'm just a little drunk with my friends. You don't have to worry any more. I love you, Baby, even when you're mad at me."

Frank was a good psychologist.

When the Vietnam veterans groups sued the government to compensate for the effects of Agent Orange and other toxic chemicals of war, we all struggled again with the ethics of war. Tim and Brinny were pacifists, believing in non-retaliation in all aspects of life. We talked sometimes late into the night in the Thompson's living room.

"It isn't really a question of ethics," said Frank, "so much as nature. If a maniac with a gun threatens any member of this family, I'm gonna have to kill him. Whether I'm right or wrong, I'll do it, so it's useless to decide about right and wrong. I don't say killing is right. It just has to be done."

Tim answered, "Maybe I would tackle the maniac and try to knock him out. Obviously I'd try to stop him, but I'm not prepared to kill before I try every alternative."

Frank said, "By that time you might be dead. Where would that leave your family?"

Brinny asked Frank, "Would you let Mark or Caterina fight in a war?" Frank answered, "Believe me, I don't want that. There is so much stupidity and waste. I'd tell them that. But if Mark wants to serve in the military, I probably couldn't stop him. Do you think my parents wanted me to enlist? I was in college, playing football. My coach wasn't too happy either. I went on my own." He smiled at himself, "I was a stubborn SOB then," looking at me, "not easy going like I am now."

I giggled at Frank's mistaken self-image, "Frank, my love, you are easy like a tank."

He continued, " Anyway, I went and I lost a lot. Some people lost a lot more too. But that was the path we chose."

I said, "I couldn't bear to lose a child in a war. It would seem even worse than a disease or an accident, because it is preventable. I don't see how those parents ever accept it."

"They have no choice," said Frank. "You know it, Lili. After the death of a spouse or a child, the survivors have to decide to live or die. Some people are aware of the very moment they decide to live. Do you remember when you decided to live after Antonio died?"

I reflected a moment, then said, "Intellectually, I decided I was a survivor before Antonio died. I had thought about it, because of our fear of Antonio's suicidal thoughts. But I learned that surviving and living are quite different. I was in emotional limbo before something caused me to accept the job in New York. I didn't want to leave our former life..." I looked at my Frank, "Thank God I did."

Frank said, "I see it every day. People who find a way to go on living, as well as people who can't bear to live. I saw a burn victim whose face was practically inhuman. The pain she went through is unimaginable. Yet she wanted to live. Others want to die rather than readjust to a relatively minor disability. Sometimes, when I see a person who is resisting readjustment, I remove my prosthesis and tuck my pants leg in my belt and greet the patient on crutches. It gives me credibility. I'll pull any trick I can think of. I love to find the key to that positive choice. But I can't do it for them. They have to decide."

By the time I was forty-five, my hair was entirely gray and I needed eyeglasses to see. Frank had put on a few pounds working the sedentary job, and he was graying at the temples. Brinny fought aging by dying her hair and wearing contact lenses. She said, "How come we are all getting old, and Phil keeps getting better looking." Phil lifted his hands and smiled, "Clean living, you guys. Clean living."

Chapter Twenty-Nine

When we celebrated Frank's forty-sixth birthday, his back was bothering him. He thought he might be getting arthritis, so he was checking it out in D. C. I saw Frank and Tim in deep conversation a couple of afternoons. Then he came home early from D.C. in late October to talk to Tim. It was a beautiful fall day. Mark was at football practice and Caterina was playing soccer. I asked Frank to tell me what was going on between him and Tim. He said, "Let's take a walk."

We walked around the block over the falling yellow tulip leaves and brown oak leaves, smelling the musty decay of summer. "I need Tim's ear about a spiritual matter, Lili...it concerns us all. I guess I have to tell you now."

I turned blank and worried.

He began, "When Antonio died, you were only twenty-five. He died suddenly, which is the hardest way for the surviving family. And you sort of shut down for four or five years until I came along."

I was struck dumb, just waiting. Frank looked at me carefully and took me in his arms. "I hate to tell you this, Lili, but you're a grown woman now. The docs tell me these pains are cancer. I don't smoke any more, but I have lung cancer. I checked it out with three specialists. I'm not going anywhere for a long time, but I'm gonna need you, baby, to be peaceful with me and strong." He was still holding me in his arms. I was in shock. I didn't dare look at Frank's face. I was staring at his cotton sweater and the back of his neck where his dark hair always tempted my fingers. Frank kept talking.

"You are my angel, remember. I'm not afraid of cancer, but there's gonna be a lot of people hurting. I need you to be with me, Lili. I

185

mean emotionally fully present and strong. I can help the others like my parents and brothers and the children. Tim will be a great help with the children."

My heart was beginning to hammer, my head going fuzzy. I was trying to be a grown woman, to find my strength, but panic was rising from a dark place inside me. I managed to ask, "What do you mean 'a l-long t-time? What treatment do they recommend?"

Frank looked at me with regret in his eyes, "Lili, baby, they can radiate it for pain, but...I have to tell you straight. The cancer is very aggressive—large oat cell it is called. It has spread already... that's the pain in my back. It's in the bones and lymph nodes. Only a miracle...."

"But we believe in m-miracles, Frank. We could have another one."

My head felt like it contained the fuse of a stick of dynamite gradually approaching the explosion.

Frank stroking my back seemed unbearably calm. "I don't know. A lot doesn't make sense to me this time. It doesn't add up right. I feel much better having told you now. That was the hard part."

We started to walk again as I held Frank's arm with both hands and felt the flame of the fuse moving. "What's going to happen?" I asked in a little weak voice, still trying to mask what was rising within me.

"We have some time, they say. Probably a year, maybe more. As a student of death from way back, I want to do it right. If it has to be."

Suddenly I stopped. The flame had reached the end of the fuse. I felt like a slow motion explosion. I cried, "This isn't true. It can't be true. It's a n-nightmare. Frank...not you...not you...Please not you." The word 'you' was filled with eighteen years of healing, companionship, commitment and passion. *You, My Frank, My Husband, The father of my children. No...This cannot happen. We had our share of hurt already.*

I ran blindly back to the house sobbing. When Frank got back to the house, he came into the bedroom where I was staring into space and sat down on the bed. "Lili, you need to cry a lot. I do too.

I know you're in shock now. But we have a lot of time yet. I want some of the time to be about life. Enjoying the children. Putting closure to my work. Just having some normal days."

I shook my head. My heart was hurting now—like I might die. I sobbed, "I can't accept it. Not you.... You're the one in touch with the Universe. You're the one who always tells me not to worry...to trust...Not you. I'm older than you. I'd rather d-die myself this time." I saw Frank's pistol hanging in the holster. My hand went for the pistol. Frank sprang over me like a cat, grabbed the gun and held me in a hammer lock until I let go.

His voice was commanding, "That is precisely what you must not do." He threw the gun up into the closet. "Don't scare me like that, baby. I might have hurt you. Are you okay?"

"N-no, I'm not okay. You just told me you have c-cancer, Frank." I looked him right in the eyes and put my hand on his face. "You are my anchor, Frank. I need you, Frank. Frank, I can't bear it." I turned my face from him and buried it in the pillow to sob.

His body and voice turned soft again, as he put both arms in shelter around me, from behind, "Listen to me, baby...Lili, baby... you will bear it... You have to." he gently turned me around to look at him, and said, "You and I are going to do this dance together, okay? Tim's been through this before. He'll help us. The enlightened part of me knows it's another part of life. We don't get only the happy times. Things change."

Only Frank could have compared dying with dancing. I knew he hadn't danced in over twenty years. He knew I loved to dance. I stopped sobbing and said, "We never d-danced together in our lives. I thought you couldn't dance."

Frank smiled, "I found the right image for you, didn't I? Damn I'm good." Then he laughed, " I love you, Lili... I don't want to leave you. We will pray for a miracle—that the cancer will recede or take a long time... I want to stay mentally strong, even if I get physically weak. My personal prayer is that I can remain whole—in one piece mentally and spiritually. I want to help Mark and Caterina take the least damage possible."

I turned around and feasted my eyes on my one and only Frank.

Tears began to choke his voice, "Lili, baby, you were so sad when I met you, and we've done so well together. I know that you want me to take care of you. I've done my best. But I'm telling you now, you can trust the Universe. It's very important to me that you don't collapse... Especially after...You're gonna have to stand on your own. You have to raise the children for me. You hear me. I want you to be strong for me."

I put my arms around Frank's shaking body. "This is the hardest thing you could ask of me."

"I know that. I didn't choose this." Frank looked momentarily defeated, then his face filled with life again, "I'm still alive, baby. That's what counts right now." He kissed me and we held each other as if we could make time stop, and we made love as if we had heard the world was about to end.

We lay on the bed in silence until Frank said, "We'll talk to get used to the idea. Then we have to tell the others. I want to have time with the children, my brothers and parents. A few friends too. It's going to be okay. I promise. You have to believe it's going to be good. Haven't you ever heard of a good death?"

"Not of someone forty-six years old, Frank. Not the father of two teenagers. Not you."

"Well, this will be a first," he said.

"Why do you have to be so special? It only makes it harder for me. I should know by now you're going to be a hero." I looked at my husband's dark eyes which held so much sadness. I said—my voice sounding more in control—"Frank, this is the end of the world—a total eclipse. I'll need a miracle to do what you want."

Frank tried to control the process in the following weeks by planning and talking. We talked to each other and to Tim and Brinny. The familiar fist of sorrow gradually closed me in its tightening grip. The difference was I had Frank and the children with me every day. I tried to concentrate on each day and realize how rare each breakfast, lunch, hug and touch was. " What do you want for breakfast, Frank?" was a wonderful sentence. "Let's take a walk, baby," was better than music.

Frank underwent radiation treatments, which tired him. He told OVET that he was going on disability after the first of the year. A week after Christmas Frank decided we needed to tell the children. Not that they could really understand what losing their Dad would mean, but he wanted them to have time to get used to it. He wanted to be emotionally connected to them. On Sunday after church, he lit a fire in the brick fireplace with logs and newspaper, and we sat around the Christmas tree. Frank had it all planned. I was dubious. Mark had already changed his church clothes and was running out the door when Frank called him in.

"Mark, we need you and your sister for a while. Come here and relax." Caterina and I were already on the sofa together. Mark looked annoyed. He was just beginning to exhibit a defiant attitude, but he was still in awe of his father. He sat on the edge of the chair nearest the door, as if he were already half out the door. Frank muscled in, "Our family has had a lot of happy times, and we're going to have more." He looked at Caterina, "Remember, Cat, the time we got lost in the woods up at the Blue Ridge, and it got dark?" Caterina moved over to sit with Frank as he motioned her to come. Mark looked bored and restless as Frank continued. "Well we don't get only happy times in the Universe. So we're also going to have some sad ones. I've got a problem…" His voice began to shake. He took a breath and looked at Mark and looked at me, "This is harder than I anticipated. You tell them, Lili."

Now Mark was paying attention as I tried to co-operate with Frank's program. I said, "Dad has cancer. It's a serious disease, as you know. He has been the strongest person in the family until now, probably the strongest person I've ever known, but when…" I had to take to breathing slowly now, "…when he gets weaker, we have to get stronger to help him and to help each other. We all have to help him when he gets s-sick."

Caterina was listening and hugging Frank, nestling her head in his neck. He was kissing her hair with tears falling on top of her head.

Mark and I looked at each other. I think as I spoke, Mark was growing up in a matter of seconds. He said, "John O'Mally's dad had cancer, but he's okay now. He got chemo and went bald. Dad's gonna be okay, isn't he…after he's sick, I mean."

Frank smiled obliviously, "Yes, son, that's the whole point. I'm okay most of the time. Even if I die, I'll be okay. What's more important is I want to give you as much as I can before I die because I don't have as much time as I thought I did."

Mark stood up and looked down at Frank, "You're so full of bullshit. You mean you're **not** going to be okay." Mark turned to me, "Mom, is Dad going to die?"

I just nodded and cried. Then Caterina started to cry and Mark ran upstairs. "Frank, go talk with him," I said.

Frank went upstairs and brought Mark down for the rest of his presentation. "Maybe you're right that I'm full of bullshit. Bullshit is one of my ways of overcoming what I've overcome. I'm not changing now. It's bullshit to the end. I've arranged for you two children to talk with a psychologist, starting this week. You may not think you need it, but it helps me to think you aren't suffering or hiding anything to save your Mom or me."

The bomb had been dropped and we sat in the silent wreckage. The fire in the fireplace had turned to smoldering coals, the newspaper, just ashes on the blackened brick floor. Frank spoke again, "Bullshit aside, I want the time we have together to be about life. I want your lives to go on as normally as possible under whatever circumstances occur." He looked at Caterina, her eyes red and her hair straggling over her face as she blew her nose in a tissue. "I love you, Caterina. I'm gonna tell you every day. I don't want you ever to forget how I love you." Then he looked at Mark who was really just a tall boy, just beginning to shave, " I love you, Mark. I'm proud of you. This is a hell of a time of life to go through a problem with your parents, but I can't help it, son."

Then he looked at me with those dark eyes and said, "And I love your mother." He couldn't look at me too long; the tears filled his eyes, and he looked away. "Mark, remind me to tell you about women." He looked back at me, "My Dad told me that women need loving like a mushroom needs humidity."

Mark just shook his head, "Dad, you are a piece of work."

CHAPTER THIRTY

What we choose to fight is so tiny!
What fights with us is so great!
If only we would let ourselves be dominated
as things do by some immense storm,
we would become strong too, and not need names.
      When we win it's with small things,
      And the triumph itself makes us small.
      What is extraordinary and eternal
      does not want to be bent by us.
      I mean the Angel who appeared
      to the wrestlers of the Old Testament.
Whoever was beaten by this Angel
(who often simply declined the fight)
went away proud and strengthened
and great from that harsh hand,
that kneaded him as if to change his shape.
Winning does not tempt that man.
This is how he grows; by being defeated, decisively,
by constantly greater beings.

                    "The Man Watching" by Rainier Maria
                    Rilke, trans. Robert Bly in *The Rag and Bone*
                    Shop of the Heart

Frank and I, who originally connected through painful losses, now were dancing the macabre reprise, but this time we were together which doubled our griefs. He had moments of anger and defeat as his body unrelentingly declined. He struggled to discipline his mind as his body went down the steps to new levels of loss. I tried to follow his lead, so that my own defeated times did not coincide with his.

A major crash came in March, earlier than expected. He had been getting weaker and tired. He stopped lifting weights with only momentary resistance to this loss. Then he got up in the night, using crutches, stumbled and fell, breaking his good leg. Frank had fallen many times over the years, but never had broken a bone. At the hospital they told us the bone weakened by cancer would heal slowly if at all. They put a hard plastic brace on it to allow it to mend and confined Frank to bed or a wheelchair. Being in the wheelchair was an enormous psychological defeat for Frank, who had overcome his original injury with determined courage and success. Frank hated asking for everything. The doctor recommended the services of Hospice, which sent nurses every day to help him bathe and dress, and eventually to manage medications, oxygen, bedpans and catheters.

The supervisor from OVET, Mike McCurdy, came to visit Frank privately one day, all the way from Washington. As he left the house Mike said, "Mrs. Domenico, I told Frank he is entitled to a military funeral. He'll tell you about it. I'm sorry."

I went to the study where Frank was arranged in the wheelchair. I said, "Frank, what is McCurdy talking about?"

"Sit down, Lili, I've been doing a lot of thinking."

"That sounds dangerous." I was trying to be humorous, but Frank was in a bad mood.

He said, "It wasn't supposed to turn out like this. I didn't know how I would hate this helplessness. I've been helpless before but with hope. I was younger too—without responsibilities. I don't like living like this. I considered asking McCurdy for a pill. Intelligence has painless escape drugs, but don't worry...I don't want to do that to you and the children. I'm just going to have to take it. Maybe it's good I'll never be old."

I was grateful he decided against shortening the time. I wanted every minute. But hearing Frank's anguish was excruciating. I felt like a crab who had wondered out of its protective shell and couldn't find my way back. I realized my dependence on Frank's strength was not going to work any more. I was praying as Frank continued, "They're giving you a pension, which you don't need, but use it for the kids' education. They are giving me a military funeral because I've been working indirectly for the Army all these years. You can give the gun back to McCurdy after... I think they are also nervous about claims being made about Agent Orange. Some vets say it causes some kinds of cancer. It really gets me down to think this isn't the work of the Universe, but the fucking carelessness of the Army."

After that day he seemed to have surrendered to a new level of loss. Gino came to visit, having spent the night with his parents. Frank's father had taken over tending the yard for us, diligently planting my salad and beans and fertilizing the holly and azaleas. Gino at thirty-four still hadn't married. He worked for a New York bank as a junior officer. The children loved to see Uncle Gino. He always tossed the football with Mark and listened to Caterina's tales. When Gino walked in the door and saw Frank, I could see his face drop. I hadn't noticed the change in Frank's appearance until then. He did look older, a lot thinner and pale from lack of exercise and being indoors all winter. Frank always looked good to me. The Hospice people had tucked his trouser leg neatly around the short stump, and he had his broken right leg in the brace on the sofa. Gino said, "What hit you, big brother. You look like hell."

Frank liked that, "Yeah, I hope heaven is closer. You're a sight for sore eyes. Come here and hit me."

Gino punched Frank in the chest. Frank came alive, stopped only by the leg brace that prevented his rising to wrestle his brother. As the two brothers embraced, I left them alone smiling. It was hard to keep my mind on the children when Frank was hurting, which was getting to be more and more of the time. Brinny helped a lot with keeping track of schedules and meals.

After lunch that same day, Phil came to visit. He gave me a friendly kiss and hug and asked how I was doing. "I'm tired, Phil, but I promised Frank I'm not going to fall apart like before. We have the children. I just hate to see Frank go through this.

"How is he?"

"Go see him, Phil. He's a hero."

I listened at the door when Phil went to the study, "She says you're a hero, and all you did was get sick. You still have to tell me your secret with women."

"Yeah, I do, 'cause you're clueless and I have a job for you."

"What can I do for you, Frank?" Phil sat down giving Frank a pat on the back.

Frank saw me standing in the doorway. "I hope you still care for my wife because I need someone smart to look after her. Tim and Brinny are here. I've assigned them the kids. Lili will be vulnerable for a while. I want you to respect her and come down here and keep her company while she recovers. Maybe take her to a nice dinner, I don't know. I don't want to think of her all alone or getting abused by someone. I'm probably overprotective and a male chauvinist. She's smarter than you and me, but she's vulnerable."

"Are you saying she'll be safe with old Phil?"

"Will you ever stop putting yourself down, Phil?" said Frank. "I'm saying...a dying man is asking you in her presence," he nodded to me, "to respect her until she's recovered. She'd have to give you the clues. That's the secret with women. Pay attention to their clues. Hell, with anyone."

Phil turned around and looked at me, "How does Lili feel about this?"

I said, "Frank and I both know you'll be there for me, Phil. Frank likes to have everything planned."

By May Frank was in pain and coughing. He wanted to postpone using morphine because he didn't want to waste consciousness. He was using self-hypnosis and massage, as well as non-narcotic pain killers.

We celebrated Mark's seventeenth birthday, inviting the family: Frank's parents, the Thompsons, Gino came down from New York, Rocco and his wife Kathy with their daughters, and Louisa Grace came home from law school. It was a sunny day. We barbecued outdoors under the oak and pine trees. In spite of Mr. Domenico's efforts, the ivy was overgrown, protruding into the peonies and over the edges of the patio. Mark and Gino helped Frank come outside to sit on a lawn chair. His mother baked Mark's favorite chocolate cake. Tim grilled steak and sausages on the grill. Brinny and I made salads. Rocco and Kathy brought good Italian bread from New York. We tried to stay focused on Mark's birthday, not Frank for a change.

Mark reminded Frank he had promised to teach him to shoot a gun when he was seventeen. Frank said, "The first lesson is: don't use a gun when you're in poor health, which I am. Uncle Rocco will teach you. Rocco, that's your job."

Rocco got Frank's pistol out of the closet and took Mark and Anton into a field to teach them to shoot. Tim didn't look pleased, but Frank got his way. Louisa Grace who was a pacifist like her parents, said, "I wouldn't have a gun in my house, Uncle Frank. I don't want to live in that kind of world."

Frank loved Louisa. He said, "I respect your ideals, Louisa...You know...someone had to kill this steak we're eating. And that robin over there kills worms. Death is part of life. We don't only get the pleasant part."

Frank's father started to cry and walked out of the yard. We could hear the gun going off in the field down the street. I decided to play some music to block out the sound of the pistol. Vivaldi revived the celebratory mood, such as it was.

When dinner was ready, Frank's father came back along with Rocco and the boys. We stood in a circle as Tim said a birthday thanksgiving prayer. Frank toasted the birthday in a hearty voice with a strength which belied what we all knew, " Mark, I want you to remember this good day. You are the best son a man could imagine. I'm proud of you. Happy Birthday." Frank's father almost collapsed. Frank motioned his father to come over to embrace him on the lawn chair. Frank put his arms around his Dad, as they both wept and kept patting each other on the back. Gino and Rocco had their arms around their mother. Mark announced that he had a toast too, which helped everyone stop crying. Mark said, "I toast my parents and thank them for everything. Especially Dad, for teaching me about discipline, courage and especially for the bullshit." Mark started to laugh, "Dad told me that women are like mushrooms. I figure that's his secret formula. Mushrooms thrive in manure." Mark was sparkling his seventeen year old smile at Frank. Frank was a happy man. The rest of us were laughing— even Frank's parents. Frank's mother went to light the eighteen candles on Mark's cake.

After the others had gone home, the children were in the house finishing homework, Frank and I sat outside enjoying the first warm evening of spring in the dappled evening light under high branches. I pulled a lawn chair next to Frank's and put my arm through his, my head on his shoulder. Frank said, "Lili, do you want me to tell you your future?" He smiled peacefully at me.

"No. I don't want one. I only want this day with you, Frank. Mark's birthday is such a good memory. This evening is so benign. Let's not think of any future."

"But I want you to know your future," insisted Frank.

"You always get your way, Frank Domenico."

"Lili, after...you know...I'm gone, you're going to be okay eventually. I promise. It'll be a long time—maybe longer than after Antonio died, but you'll go through it. I promise. And you'll be stronger than you've ever been. Didn't my first promises come true?"

"Frank, I'm happy now with you. Even in this terrible time. I'm happy with you...I don't understand why the Universe gives me so much and then takes it away."

"I can't explain anything any more, baby." Frank used his arms to shift his weight to face me and say, "I've never asked you to compare me to Antonio." He laughed, "But here's the problem. They wrote about it in the Bible. When I get to heaven, I'll see my buddies: Gerry, Al and Eddy. Then I'll see this cool handsome well-dressed Italian, and it'll be Antonio. I'm older than Antonio now too. What do I say to him?"

"Frank, Antonio released me a long time ago. You know that."

"Yeah, but when you come to heaven, who will **you** look for first? Me or Antonio?" Frank's dark eyes looked at me like a child.

I felt peaceful, strong, and sure as I answered, "Frank, you are the love of my life. I can't resist you—I never could." I put both arms around my Frank. He was smiling.

I said, "Probably when I come to heaven, I'll be an old lady, and you two studly Italians won't even notice me," I smiled at the thought. "Frank, if you can, when you're over there, keep talking to us—me, Mark and Cat."

"Did you ever know me not to talk if I could?" asked Frank.

"No, Frank, I didn't."

We all knew that most people who came to visit us that spring came to say good-bye. Wendy came for that, but also for me. Wendy still looked youthful in jeans and a blue denim shirt, despite her graying hair. When I looked in the mirror, I didn't linger on my tired reflection.

"Lili, you look thin. How are you holding up?" she asked.

"Some days are better than others. Today I'm glad you're here. I could use some Wendy hugs. How do people get through these things?"

Wendy gave me one of her best hugs. She knew how to hold a person, not letting go too soon, nice and long without rushing. She said, "All different ways. Whatever works for you."

"You lost your father and mother when you were so young. I never realized what you might be feeling," I said.

"How could you? Anyway, each grief is different. The important thing is to be easy on yourself and take care of yourself. I mean, eat enough and try to sleep. Can you talk to Frank about it? I mean about his dying?"

"Wendy, Frank can talk about anything and everything. Yes, we do. It would be lonely not to... But I'm lonely anyway sometimes. We haven't had sex since March. I guess we never will again." I started to cry and said, "Another loss. Sometimes life feels like nothing but loss."

Wendy put her arms around me and cried with me.

Salvatore also came to visit all the way from Italy. He remembered the darkest years of my youth and was worried about me. I met Salvatore at Dulles Airport. His hair and beard were gray which emphasized his kind eyes as he greeted me. We went directly back to Charlottesville because I didn't want to leave Frank too long. On the way home I prepared Salvatore for Frank's condition. We spoke Italian because Salvatore's English was minimal.

"But he is willing to talk about dying?" asked Salvatore.

"Oh God, yes. Frank has worked with death and dying for years."

"You seem very open too, Lili."

" Salvatore, I have pulled up every ounce of strength to be open for Frank. I didn't think I had it in me."

Frank was eager to see Salvatore again. They had met seven years before, when the Francesco parents died within four months of each other, and we had gone to Italy to pay our respects. Frank and Salvatore had been immediately drawn to each other, but they could not communicate very well, because Frank's Italian was only slightly better than Salvatore's non-existent English.

He waited for us in the wheelchair in the living room in remarkably good spirits. "Come in, Salvatore. Welcome. Excuse my condition here. I broke my good leg in March."

Salvatore tried haltingly to speak English as he extended his hand to Frank, "I am happy to see you again, Franco…and sorry for your leg. It is difficult time for you both, no?"

"I'm sorry I've forgotten most of my Italian. Remember how we tried to talk in Italy? "

"Yes, yes. I remember well. Please to speak very slowly, so I can understand."

"Or Lili may have to translate. I know you've come to see Lili, but there is something important I think you could do for me. Then I'll leave you two to talk Italian while I rest a little."

Salvatore looked confused, so I translated.

Frank continued, "Lili, tell Salvatore I am an ex-Catholic, and he is an ex-Catholic priest, so he seems a good person to hear what I need to tell—even if he can't understand everything. I want to make a confession—maybe after dinner or tomorrow before he goes.

I have a burden to turn over, and Tim and I are too close."

I translated. Salvatore nodded and said to Frank in English, "I will hear your confession—when you want."

Frank reached his hand to Salvatore, "Thank you, father. I'll go rest. We can talk after dinner."

Frank wheeled himself back to our room, and I helped him to the bed. I said half-seriously, "You don't have to confess any woman sins do you?"

Frank shook his head, "No baby, it's the war. We did—had to do things that aren't resting easy in my soul. There's a part of me you don't know, and I don't want you to know. The old Catholic in me wants a priest's absolution."

"He's a good man. I'm glad you trust him."

"I haven't told you or Tim and Brinny because you couldn't understand how it is in war. It's a different world, baby. And I was a different person."

"You don't have to explain anything to me, Frank."

He lay back on the pillow and connected his oxygen. "Come get me for dinner, okay?"

Salvatore and I had a glass of wine and looked at each other. I remembered how he brought me through the years following Antonio's crash. It seemed providential he should come to us when Frank needed him. I was tired and subdued. I said, "I wish we could entertain you under happier circumstances."

"I haven't stopped being a priest in my heart, Lili. Maybe God sent me here for Frank's confession."

"I'm so grateful."

When Caterina came home, I introduced her to Salvatore. "Caterina doesn't speak Italian, but she's studying French." While Salvatore and Caterina practiced their French with each other, I fixed a simple supper. I was too tired to worry about impressing anyone with the food. When Mark came home, I asked him to get Frank for dinner.

We all spoke English extremely slowly and loudly at dinner so Salvatore could catch at least some of it. We asked about their four sons and Annamaria. Young Antonio was studying pre-medicine. The poor kid probably never had another choice. Cristoforo was thinking about the priesthood, but Salvatore discouraged him, saying he was too young to decide. The twins were adventurous and sports minded, especially soccer and skiing. Salvatore still worked at the hospital, but Annamaria had retired from teaching devoting her energy to raising the boys and managing the properties.

After dinner Frank and Salvatore went into the study together. Mark helped me with the dishes and Caterina practiced the piano. I waited in the living room well over an hour and finally sent Caterina to do her homework. When the door to the den opened, Frank wheeled himself out. I could see he had been crying. I looked up to see Salvatore had been crying too. I walked to Frank and put my arms around him. He held me and buried his face in my hair. He said, "I am so lucky, baby. I've had a full life."

I smiled and looked up at Salvatore. "Yes we are very lucky."

Frank finally allowed morphine to give him some pain relief. Breathing became a struggle. He needed full time oxygen. He was too weak to sit up in the chair, and he was catheterized. I didn't like leaving his side. At night I slept next to him in the Hospice hospital bed. Every day the children came in to see him before school. When they came home, the first stop was to see Frank. Sometimes just a kiss, sometimes they told a story from their day. He listened but talked less and less. He said to me in a raspy whisper, "I never thought I could be like this, but my pride is gone. I still want to live now just to wake up and see you and the kids each day." He moved his arm over to my arm. "All I have left, baby, is love."

"That's all I need, Frank."

Frank Domenico died peacefully in my arms in the night of June 21, 1991. Though my heart went into a total eclipse, I didn't cry for a change. I thanked God for taking him out of pain into the Universe and for the eighteen years I had as his wife, and for our children. I felt gravely wounded. I also felt gravely blessed.

We had the military burial service at Tim's church. An American flag draped the casket. A color guard carried his body. We sang "For all the saints who from their labors rest." I sat in the front pew with Mark, Caterina, Brinny, Louisa and Anton. Phil, Wendy and Jessica sat behind me with my mother and brothers. Frank's parents and brothers wept in the row across the aisle. I felt Frank close to me and knew he was there in the curtain of light which gave him his center and his courage. We buried his body in the cemetery near the church.

Tim read the blessing falteringly between his tears:

"In sure and certain hope of the resurrection to eternal life through our Lord Jesus Christ, we commend to Almighty God our brother Frank; and we commit his body to the ground; earth to earth, ashes to ashes, dust to dust. The Lord bless him and keep him, the Lord make his face to shine upon him and be gracious unto him, the Lord lift up his countenance upon him and give him peace. Amen."

Chapter Thirty-One

I have been one acquainted with the night
I have walked out in the rain—and back in rain
I have outwalked the furthest city light.

I have looked down the saddest city lane
I have passed by the watchman on his beat
And dropped my eyes, unwilling to explain

I have stood still and stopped the sound of feet
When far away an interrupted cry
Came over houses from another street

But not to call me back or say good-bye;
And further still at an unearthly height
One luminary clock against the sky

Proclaimed the time was neither wrong nor right
I have been one acquainted with the night.

From the Poems of Robert Frost
The Modern Library, 1946

A great silence fell over our lives after we buried Frank. It wasn't a terrible or painfully lonely silence. More of a foggy white silence in which we walked around and went to school, cooked for holidays, but there was a cavern carved out of my heart. The weeds grew promiscuously in the yard, and the ivy began to take over the patio. When I tried to talk to Frank, I felt only his peacefulness, no words. At times I had a strange urge to limp like Frank. I even listened to Jimi Hendrix.

In the first year I often went to the Vietnam Veterans Memorial because Frank had described it as a holy place where the living meet the dead. I hoped to see him there again, maybe smiling at me from the black stone. But everything was changed. Even the memorial wall was emptier without Frank with me. As I looked at the engraved names, I felt the sorrow of the world as well as my own losses, and I felt somehow more human—more connected to all people.

Brinny, Tim, and their children helped us immeasurably by being our family and sharing our sadness. I asked Mark, a high school senior, to apply to the University of Virginia, so that he could stay in a dormitory on campus, yet stay close to home. I couldn't stand any more changes.

Frank's father never recovered. He died of a heart attack four months after Frank. Frank's father's funeral was terrible. We all felt he had died of sorrow, and we grieved for both of them. I remembered that Frank had said mourners make a decision about whether to live or die. I had promised Frank I would live, but could well understand his father's temptation too. His mother finally moved back to New York near Rocco's family and Gino.

My Caterina was the irrepressible spirit of those years. She cried and grieved, but there was many times she was a normal teenage girl, running around with friends, experimenting with make-up and flirting with boys.

Phil kept his word to Frank. He visited often, took me out, invited us all to New York to the theater, and waited for my grief to unfold and run its course. He seemed to back away from me in a way, in honor of Frank. But I was glad he was there.

Mark and Caterina continued to see the psychologist Frank arranged for several years. Mark was at an age, when he was reserved about confiding in me. I hoped that he shared his feelings and worries with Tim and Anton as well as the counselor. Caterina, on the other hand talked to me every day and shared her hopes and worries. She was only thirteen when Frank died. When she was fourteen, she asked me who would walk her down the aisle when she got married. I said, "Who do you want to walk you down the aisle?"

"I wish Daddy could come back just that one day."

"So do I, Cat, " I agreed. I felt sorrow for her and ached for Frank that he was missing so much and would miss that happy day. I suggested, "How about Uncle Tim?"

"No, he'll be the priest. I was thinking about Uncle Phil. He's my godfather. When is he coming down again? I love to talk to him about plays. He knows all the actors and actresses. He said he'll take us to see *CATS* next time we're in New York."

I agreed, "Phil would be a good choice. He's known you since you were a baby, and he's known me even longer."

At Tim's suggestion, around the first anniversary, I decided to apply for a teaching job at a private Episcopal secondary school. Teaching French to high school students was exhausting, but helpful in keeping in touch with Caterina's age group and in focusing my mind on the larger community. I occasionally went out to dinner with colleagues and friends, but social occasions were the loneliest times—the times I longed for Frank next to me and his smiling eyes when I closed the door at the end of the evenings.

I had more time than I wanted to think about my own future, realizing only too well that in a few years Caterina would go to college, and I would be completely alone again. Of course, I hoped to stand on my own, but I wasn't sure how to do it. I thought that I needed a dream, vision, or cause to inspire my energy and passion, a good intersection between the world's needs and my time and talent, but I couldn't seem to find it.

Following a visit to see Mama, I called Phil to ask if I could stop in New York to see him. We sat in the library of Phil's duplex apartment on Park Avenue, on a brown leather couch by the fireplace, drinking a dry red wine with the German Shepherds at our feet. I said, "When Caterina goes to college, I'm going to be alone again. Honestly, Phil, I'm scared. I'm afraid I'll get depressed. I've been racking my brain to think of what to do with my life. Do you have any ideas?"

Phil's face filled with a mischievous grin, "We could go to Paris or Hawaii. Where do you want to go?"

"I'd like to visit Salvatore and Annamaria. But there's time for that. I would love to take a trip. Do you think we could travel together, or would people get the wrong idea?"

"Do you really care what people think, Lili?"

"I mean the children and…"

Phil interrupted me, "We can talk straight to the children. My problem is how do **you** feel. I don't want to get my hopes up again and have you fall for some young gigolo."

"Phil, why do you mistrust me so? Have I ever had a gigolo?"

"No, but my ego has been wounded enough. I don't want to be a fool at my age, Lili."

"Everything is different now…" The wine was making me feel a little romantic, and I began to smile inside. We were both leaning against sheep skin cushions. I moved my hand from the soft sheep skin to Phil's hand.

Phil looked confused. "I guess what I need to know—very straight— is whether you want me to keep my 'friendly' distance, or could I kiss you…make love to you? I promised Frank I would wait for your cue."

I looked Phil in the eyes. He was as steady as ever, but he had no gift for romance. And, in spite of myself, I still felt married to Frank. Softly I said, "Phil, you are a precious friend to me. That's why I'm here confiding in you." I took a breath and was surprised to feel tears filling my eyes, "But, Phil, I can't kiss you. I'm sorry."

He stood up abruptly and turned his back to me. I felt terrible. I was hurting him again. I realized that I shouldn't have touched his hand. Loneliness is not the same thing as love. I wanted to love Phil, but we always seemed to disconnect just as we were about to connect. We were out of step again.

I said, " I really don't know why you didn't drop me long ago."

"Damn it, Lili, you know why. Do you want me to humiliate myself again? Just go back to Virginia and think about **me** for a change."

I went back to Virginia, recognizing again that I needed some new stimulation, a passion, but not a romance. At the age of fifty, I probably had another thirty years to live. At home I tried to immerse myself in the children's lives, but the timing was wrong. Mark Angelo had his own world at college. At fifteen years old Caterina was trying to define herself and make decisions on her own. She needed less mother, not more.

In the early fall I went alone to the beach, the Outer Banks of North Carolina, to walk the dunes and to breathe in the ocean's power. That was when I conceived the idea of writing the story of my two marriages in the hope that the future would become clear to me. I became obsessed with writing and escaped the present grief every day by evoking memories as I wrote. I listened to Verdi, Brahms, and Puccini which Antonio and I had enjoyed together. I listened to Bruce Springsteen's recordings. I looked at photographs, and felt pangs in my heart. Then I read through my French and Italian papers, hoping a new academic interest might excite me. I talked to Brinny and Tim, who were also in need of renewal, but their dreams were not my dream. A new dream or vision did not appear.

CHAPTER THIRTY-TWO

Perhaps I needed something gray and brown
And did not know it,—something spent and bare,
That morning on the back-road, in November.
I may have stood in need of something bedded
Like the ledge beside me barnacled with lichen,
With a great wave of juniper breaking on it;
Or darkly needed something straight like cedars,
Black on the raveling cloud-fringe—something steady,
Like slate-gray mountains in behind bare birches.

Perhaps I needed something bright and scarlet,
Like winter berries on the stone-gray bush
Beside the rock-pile,—something sweet and singing,
Like water in the gutter running down
From springs up in the pasture out of sight.

But if I needed these, I did not know it.
If you had told me that I wanted fullness,
Or life, or God, I should have nodded "Yes";
But not a bush of berries,—not a mountain!
—Yet so it was: fantastic needs like these,
Blind bottom hungers like the urge in roots,
Elbowed their way out, jostling me aside;
A need of steadiness, that caught at mountains,
A need of straightness, satisfied with cedars,
A need of brightness, cozened with a bush...

Abbie Huston Evans (1881-1983)

At the winter break, Phil invited me to go to Jackson Hole in the Northern Rockies with him. "But what about Caterina? She'll be on her break too… She has lacrosse camp every day."

"She could do camp from Brinny's. Honestly, I think you need to give her some space… I'm the one who needs company… But separate rooms, okay?"

I agreed, "You're right, as usual. I need a change too. Thanks, Phil."

Phil had rented a spectacular log house at the ski area complete with fireplace, hot tub and magnificent views of the Gros Ventre Mountains. I brought my writing and a lot of books to read. I didn't plan to ski, but planned to cook, so we wouldn't have to go out to eat.

The weather was so beautiful that, when Phil went off to attack the mountain, I couldn't stay inside. I rented cross- country skis and drove to the the trail described as the Moose-Wilson Road, which was actually a traveled road in the summer, but unplowed in winter.

The snow was sparkling, and the sky was blue. As I left the parking area on my skis, I found a track laid by a lone skier earlier in the day which seemed to lead east towards the Snake River. I had forgotten how quiet the mountains can be in the snow. The only sound I could hear was the swish of my skis and poles. The sun was so warm that I shed my hat and gloves.

As I moved through the fresh, clean air, I began to feel a loving connection to all the benign and beautiful surroundings: pine trees, clouds, the mouse tracks in the snow, a raven overhead. I felt grateful to the bright and glistening snow, for covering the world and for filling in our prints and tracks and making the world look new.

I realized that I had needed to see snow. Snow is so temporary. It would melt in a few short months, yet it filled the present in this moment gloriously. The self-forgetting snow. "Mais ou sont les neiges d'antan." "But where are the snows of yesteryear?" That is surely my favorite refrain in all poetry. The passage of time is mysterious. Where are my loves of yesteryear?

When I reached the Snake River, my eyes hungrily drank from its slate-blue depths—as a starving deer—as a thirsty magpie—as a person in pain. I felt the Spirit of life and beauty everywhere around me and running through my veins. Tears of love began to constrict my throat, as I stopped to catch my breath. I had read the Psalm of the day, number 87: "And the singers and dancers shall say, All my fresh springs are in you."

I wanted to share the power I felt with all the people I loved: Mark and Caterina, Brinny, Tim, their children, Wendy and Jessica, Mama, my brothers, Phil, Frank's family, Salvatore and Anna and their children, my French students, all the people at church. My passion, my love does not need an object, a project, or a cause. It doesn't even need a particular person. My eyes filled with tears of joy. I can love everything in the Universe!

Immediately, I felt Frank's presence close beside me, very clear and strong. He was smiling with his beautiful dark eyes. I heard him speak to me for the first time in over two and a half years. "Angel, I was right about your strength, wasn't I? You'll fly on your own soon. Don't forget the vets. Baby. I love you."

Then I saw Antonio come and tap Frank on the shoulder in his cool, reserved, elegant way, and Frank turn around and recognize him, and with his leather jacket over one shoulder, put his arm around Antonio's shoulder as they turned and walked away together.